.EXE

.EXE

A Cadence Turing Mystery

ROBIN JEFFREY

To Sarah — Happy Reading!
R Jeffrey

ROBIN JEFFREY

Robin Jeffrey

To my father, Richard Jeffrey.
I always keep my promises.

Contents

I

Chapter 1

To be human is to know that one day you will die; there will come a time when you stop, like a ball hitting a bank of snow. Until we acquire this knowledge, we're some half-things, fairy-like in our innocence, powerful, but not altogether human. This is why many adults find children so disquieting.

I didn't become human until the night my mother died. I was seven. I snuck into her room, the adults downstairs talking in the hushed voices death always brings in its wake. I crawled up onto her bed and touched her arm. She was pale and cold; eyes still open, but empty of anything that I recognized as my mother.

That was not my mother. I wondered if it had ever been, or if it had ever been anything other than a shell; I began to wonder what I was. Every morning I woke, wondering, and today was no different. The hotel room reeked of smoke, sweat, and mold, a tangy, sweet mixture that choked me when I gulped down the rancid air.

Why couldn't I remember to stay away from Petrarchan whiskey after midnight? It always gave me nightmares. Shaking, I kicked off the stain-covered sheets and twisted my face into the pillows, my damp forehead sticking to the threadbare cotton. Minutes passed, and the sounds of the bustling city below penetrated the thin walls of the room.

I flung out my arm and picked through the stubs and stimulant packets on the bedside table, grabbing for my nix case. I turned onto my side with care, wincing as blood sloshed around my swollen brain. I took a black cylinder out of the case and twisted off the tip, the chemicals sparking and the nix smoldering.

Always the same nightmare. Twenty years gone now, and my subconscious could still recall the waxy texture of her skin, the metallic stench of the air around her red, clenched mouth. The fear in her dead eyes, looking past me, as if whatever had taken her was standing right behind me.

I shook the thoughts away with a vehemence that made me dizzy. Once I could focus again, I risked a glance at the clock. Almost half past eleven. My mobile sat a finger's length away, its thin, clear edge pulsing blue, indicating the half-dozen messages I had received while passed out. Sliding out of bed and forcing my bare feet against the scratchy carpet, I scanned the hotel room.

A self-lacing corset and a pair of torn stockings sat in one corner, confirming my hungover suspicion that I had indeed spent the night with some woman or other, though when she had made her escape god only knew. My dress clothes squatted at the end of the bed in a morose pile, like a large, wrinkled toad. Already the air was growing hot and humid – it was going to be another blistering summer day and I was in no shape to meet it.

I threw myself into the shower and let the scalding water perform its healing miracles. All in all, the week had been a success – I remembered almost none of it. I had hoped to debauch my way right through this ridiculous Hale Family Weekend, but I'd fallen just short.

Performing my morning ablutions took the better part of an hour, but I eventually gathered up my things and myself and stepped out onto the busy streets of Römer. The clean, outside air beat against my senses as I strode down the gleaming public walkways that ran through the city like veins of precious metal.

I got out a fresh nix with one hand and searched for my mobile in my coat's pockets with the other, extracting the bud from the tangled folds. My finger slid over the off switch, but it was too late; the phone was buzzing, flashing red. My mood plummeted further as my alcohol stiffened fingers accepted the call instead of rejecting it. Jaw clenching, I gave in to fate; I took a deep breath and fitted the tiny appliance into my ear, forcing my voice into its most cheerful register.

"Good afternoon, Father!"

"Chance. I trust you haven't forgotten about the party this evening."

My shoulders fell. There was a rustle of paper on the other end of the line, and I could imagine him sitting in his study, the curtains shut against sunlight so there was no glare on his trading screens. He would have just finished the day's account authorization forms, which meant he'd be more cross than usual, irritated by all that money leaving the company.

"You are going to be there."

It wasn't a question.

I brought the still smoking nix up to my mouth, squeezing the end flat between my lips. "I said I would be, didn't I?"

"An honest man always makes good on his promises. You do not."

I sighed, pushing my blond hair out of my eyes. "Thanks."

"When you are the head of this family, Chance, you'll understand the importance of keeping your word."

I began turning around and around in a tight circle on the sidewalk. "Yes, well, lucky for both of us, that's still a long way off."

"Everyone's going to be here tonight, Chance." I heard a door open and close and the squeak of my father shifting in his seat as he spoke. "I don't want any of your usual slovenly behavior. You're a Hale and you're going to act like it. And for god's sake, don't bring another one of your whores back here, do you hear me? I will not stand for it!"

He slammed his fist against the desk to punctuate this final thought. There was a hushed gasp, high pitched and ethereal, in response.

Unbuttoning my shirt at the collar, I gnawed the inside of my cheek. "Is, uh, Desdemona going to be there?"

"Of course."

I drew my hand down my face. "Wonderful."

"I'll expect you at the manor no later than quarter past three."

I glanced at my watch. "Fine. Goodb–"

The call went dead. Chewing the other side of my mouth, I ripped the bud out of my ear and shoved it and my hands into my pockets. I strode down the block and up the next without thinking about where I was going, eyes fixed on the ground, shoulders tensed until they began to ache.

Oblivious to the curious glances my ruffled black-tie ensemble garnered as I made my way through the city at midday, I rushed to the nearest cross-town AN-GRAV station and squeezed onto the next train headed for Mawson Docks. With humanity poised at the pinnacle of the 18th Great Venture, there were now hundreds of different planets colonized as our species spread itself across the galaxy. Still, it was an accepted fact that if the citizens of the Archerusia System were going to spend their hard-earned credits to go anywhere, it would be to my home planet, Arrhidaeus. This left the docks brimming with all manner of peoples, their allure matched only by their uncertainty about the new world that they had come to inhabit. Strangers in a strange land; a sensation with which I empathized and coveted in almost equal measure.

Today, however, I found no pleasure in people watching. Tasked with the ever-solemn duty of going home, the dread welled up within me thick and black like so much fetid mud. The AN-GRAV staggered up to the first of the Mawson Dock stops like a drunk man tripping his way towards the end of a bar. To the right of where I sat, the doors slid open with a whoosh of compressed air. Travelers filtered onto the train, shoes shuffling against the ribbed metal floors, suitcases bumping together like hollow drums.

Those boarding were the usual mix of interplanetary businessmen (tickets paid for by the government), female moguls (surrounded by a field of assistants and screens), and of course, families (drooping parents with dark circles under their eyes and three or four little ones underfoot). The car filled to bursting, and in a matter of minutes, it was standing room only.

The air began to spoil with body odor and perspiration, and I frowned, slouching down in my seat and stretching my legs as far out into the crowd as they would go. I had several more stops to wait until we reached a place where I could hire transportation home, a home which had felt less and less like my own over the passing years. I began to brood, fixating on my father and the demands he made of me, when, amid these musings, I looked up to find that someone had slid into the empty spot in front of me.

She straddled my legs as if they weren't even there, her back to me. Her figure was slender, but not slim. The white pants she wore stretched pleasantly over her hips and bottom. Through the thin white fabric of her long-sleeved top, a thicker cotton shirt was clear, wrapped around her chest. Even so, the curious tattoo that covered her lower back remained entirely visible through the backless garment.

All thoughts of my father vanished. My heart stuttered. I stared at her without shame. Her tattoo, an intricate line drawing full of curved parabolas and geometric shapes, was a simplistic black, standing out against her flesh like a thundercloud against a clear sky.

Sensing the weight of my gaze, the woman twisted slightly, glancing back at me through strands of hair blacker than a starless night.

I smiled. She looked away, shaking her wayward locks back towards the loose bun from whence they had escaped.

With its customary jolt, the AN-GRAV lurched forward. All those standing rushed to grab the steel grips above their heads in a desperate bid for balance.

All except her.

Our fair metropolis was the only place in the surrounding five systems to have trains as advanced as AN-GRAVs, and the unexpected movement bothered everyone who rode, first-timers and veterans alike. This woman couldn't have ridden one before, and yet she seemed to anticipate the movement of the snake-like contrivance, shifting her body to absorb the stuttering motion of the train.

I let my head fall to one side as I examined her. My smile widened as an idea occurred to me. How far could I take my curiosity and her lack of worldliness? Could I use it to transform my future, at present holding nothing but unpleasant tedium, to something far more enticing?

I stood, careful to keep a polite distance, and tapped the woman's shoulder. With nothing more than the breadth of my two fingertips connecting us, the intense heat of her radiated up my arm. I pulled back with a muffled yelp, but the bizarre sensation vanished from my mind when she turned around to face me, her midnight blue eyes carrying an indefinable expression.

I cleared my throat and leaned forward; hands jammed into my trouser pockets. "I'm sorry for asking such a personal question, but what –"

"No, you're not."

My words stumbled to a halt, her bluntness silencing me.

The woman, misreading the shock in my face as confusion, sighed, shoulders falling as she shoved her hands into the front pouch of her shirt. "If you were experiencing remorse or regret, you wouldn't ask me anything in the first place. Your preamble is clearly untrue and, therefore, clearly unnecessary; syntactically correct, but semantically irrelevant."

Her syllable-heavy soliloquy afforded me the time I needed to recover.

Throwing my hand through the metal circlet above me, I flashed my most rakish smile. "Oh, really?"

I waited for the customary blush to rosy-up the girl's cheeks, waited for the shy turn of her head, or a coy glance up at me through her long eyelashes.

Instead, she continued to stare at me, meeting my eyes with unfamiliar brashness. Her brow furrowed slowly, her stare turning into a perplexed squint. I leaned back, unsettled by her examinatory gaze.

The stranger rocked back onto her heels and blinked at last. "It's a phoenix."

"Excuse me?"

"My tattoo," she jerked a thumb over her shoulder. "You were going to ask what it was; it's a phoenix." Her eyes fell onto the seat I had vacated. She gestured to it with her pale hand. "May I have this seat? I've been on my feet for hours."

I nodded, teeth clamped down on the inside of my cheek.

"Thank you." The woman slipped around me and settled into my chair. She placed her elbow on the armrest and stared out the window, chin cupped in her hand.

Pursing my lips, I examined my potential paramour with

more care. Slumped in her seat, legs splayed out in front of her in an unladylike fashion, her dark blue eyes were half-hidden behind drooping lids. Now that I was bothering to look at her clothes instead of through them, I noticed that her garments were wrinkled and dusty.

The girl had been traveling for a long while, tired, in need of solace. She required a friend in this brave new world, someone who was only interested in her safety and comfort.

I could play at that for a while.

"I hope I didn't offend you," I said.

"You didn't." The woman lowered her gaze to the hem of her long sleeves, shaking out the material. "If you were curious, you could've just asked. You didn't have to stare."

I pressed my hand to my chest, leaning over in a bow. "I assure you I had no choice in the matter. You're quite a vision."

She looked up at me, her eyes slivers of color.

I amended my former statement with haste. "What I mean is, I can tell you're not from around here."

Her head snapped up faster than my eyes could follow. She crossed her legs, eyes widening as she thrust her upper body towards me. "You can?"

I grinned and leaned against the plastic barrier that separated the seats from the entrance to the car, shrugging. I could feel the heat radiating off her now. A shiver ran down my spine, a sensation like stepping into a hot bath after a walk out in the cold. Crossing my legs at the ankles, I smiled. "Now, don't tell me where you're from – let me guess."

She sat back in her seat with a thud. "I sincerely wish you wouldn't."

"Trust me, little one; I have a knack for this kind of thing."
My eyes roamed over every inch of her in slow, serious study. The
woman didn't move, allowing me to examine her at my leisure.

"Let's see: you're a little too pale to be from one of the inner
planets...and your Common Tongue is exceptional, but not flaw-
less –"

At this, her head fell to one side, a brow raised in question.

"–your intonation's a bit off," I explained.

A stretch of tense silence unfolded. I snapped my fingers. The
woman jumped.

"Paraesepe!" I said. "Am I right?"

"Yes." The woman squeezed her hands together in her lap and
nodded. "Yes, you are."

"See?" I laughed, flashing a wolfish grin. "I told you I'm good!"

She slid down farther in her seat, glancing at me with narrowed eyes before returning her gaze to the window.

My smile dissolved under the weight of her disinterest, but I
cleared my throat and pressed on. "So, that's where you're from;
where are you headed?"

"Into the city."

"Yes, but where specifically? A hotel? Staying with a friend?"

"I have no one here that I would call a friend," her eyes fell to
her lap, and she rolled her shoulders back against the hard, plastic seat, "and I'm not sure what hotel I could afford. But I have
a little bit of money and was planning on trying my luck with
accommodations."

The AN-GRAV slid into the second dock station, and I was
quick to snatch up the seat vacated beside my fair traveler as

people shifted out onto the platform. "You mean you don't know where you're going to sleep tonight?"

"Not specifically, no–"

"Well then, you're just going to have to come and stay with me," I said, patting her knee. "At my house, I mean. It's just a little place up north in Zahia, only a couple hours away by Professional Transport. Nothing fancy, but," I shrugged, "it's home."

The woman stared at me, mouth gaping. After a moment, she shook herself, clearing her throat. "Oh, I don't think that would be a good idea." She swallowed hard and leaned back in her seat, running her hands down her thighs. "I mean, to open your house to a stranger seems very dangerous. Unwise even. Kind though it is, I have to refuse."

I tugged at my lapels, sniffing. "You're new to this world, Miss; it's not surprising that you're unfamiliar with our traditions. We have a custom here called *tishos*; it means hospitality. We Arrhidaeans take pride in offering the best hospitality to friends and strangers alike; most especially to travelers."

The woman smirked. "This is a custom? Bringing strangers into your home?"

I nodded. Her hands fell into her lap. She pursed her lips. I could practically see the credits accounting for themselves as she turned the idea over in her mind. She was tired. She was broke. She was alone. She cast a glance in my direction from the corner of her eyes. "I assume it would be unforgivably rude to refuse?"

"Unforgiveable, yes," I said. "Rude, certainly."

"Hmm." She drew in a deep breath through her nose, straightening as she did so. "It appears I have no choice." She laid her hand flat against her chest and inclined her head in an archaic show of respect that would have been sweet if it hadn't been so ridiculous. "Under the pressures of societal convention, I accept. Thank you."

"You're more than welcome." I proffered my hand. "I'm Chance Hale, at your service."

She shook with surprising firmness. "Cadence Turing, taking full advantage of you."

My brows danced over my eyes. "Not yet."

2

Chapter 2

The hired Professional Transport, or PT, jolted out of the transport bay and soared up into the skyways, merging with the growing afternoon traffic heading north. Cadence had worked her way to the far side of the PT's dim interior and now sat mute on the other side of the cab, eyes fixed on the sky and clouds passing outside.

I watched her for a few minutes, crossing my legs and squirming against the plush seats. I had hoped to be good acquaintances by now, chatting about the mundane details of our personal lives. I made it a rule to avoid taking complete strangers to bed if I could help it, but the more I observed my new acquaintance, the more I wanted her. Cadence hadn't spoken a word since she accepted my offer, seeming to prefer to stare up into the heavens rather than get to know me one iota better.

I anchored my wandering hands over my knees and leaned

towards her. "Are you familiar with Arrhidaeus at all, Miss Turing?"

"Call me Cadence."

I smiled at this abandonment of formality. Cadence was too engrossed in the scenery to notice, continuing: "I am familiar in the sense that I have read much about the planet. The city Römer stretches across the middle section and is bordered by countryside at the poles, correct?"

"Cayeux, to the south of us, is the main agricultural hub, yes. Zahia, where I live, is where Arrhidaeus' most prominent citizens make their home."

She pressed her cheek against the window, squinting as she attempted to look at something just above the PT. When she pulled back, frowning, she noticed the skylight in the center of the cab. Crab walking her way under the window, she squeezed my thigh as she twisted around to stare up into the atmosphere. Her hand made my skin thrum as it shifted up my leg but not to where I wanted her touch the most. I licked my lips and brushed the tips of my fingers against the back of her hand.

"You know, Zahia's very different from the city; country manors, forests, and fields as far as the eye can see."

"Your sky is absolutely beautiful." Her lips parted, and her eyes were hungry and bright. She lifted her hand to point out of the skylight. "The clouds; there are so many! And all different! I didn't realize they'd all be different." Cadence smiled down at me. "That one looks like a loaf of bread, don't you think?"

"Quite!" I laughed. "Are clouds so boring on Paraesepe?"

"Hmm?" She thumped back into her seat, blinking wildly. "Oh. No. No, I suppose they aren't."

"I haven't asked, what brought you from off-planet anyway?"

"Change of situation." An adequate and polite response, in that it answered the question while offering no actual information. "Why do you live here?"

I laughed. "Well, I suppose it's because my family has lived here for generations, longer than I can count, honestly. You've heard of Halcyon Enterprises, of course."

Cadence's eyes met mine with the speed of a lightning strike; her frame stiffened, her lips firmed into a thin line. "I've heard quite a lot about them. Halcyon Enterprises is the leader in so called 'smart' tech and most AI derivatives thereof. They're at the forefront of the tech market on more than half of the planets in the system. They used to manufacture animanecrons, until such androids were unilaterally banned a few centuries ago." She edged closer to me, tucking a strand of hair behind her sculpted ear. "I have strong interests in such technology."

"How charming!" I scooted closer to her, smile widening, my arm stretched over the back of the seats. "You see, Halcyon Enterprises is what you might call the family business. Over the four hundred years it's been in operation, there's always been a Hale at the head of it."

"My goodness. What's it like to run such a prestigious corporation?"

"Oh god, no, I'm not running it! Not yet, anyway. No, I leave all that to the old man; my father, Felix Hale, he's the current head of the company. You'll get to meet him at the house."

"How wonderful." Cadence mimicked my stance to a tee, her arm falling over mine, her hand resting snug on top of my shoulder. "Does your father know a lot about computers and machines and things like that?"

"Not a bit of it. He's dreadfully old fashioned actually." I chuckled. "He has people to do the real innovating; he's mostly a paper-pusher, a businessman."

"Hmm." Cadence pulled away and relaxed back into her seat, taking in a deep breath as she focused her sight somewhere on the horizon. "That sounds like a very important job."

"If you like that sort of thing I suppose." I looked her over once again, my tongue prodding the side of my mouth. "I prefer the life of leisure. Fewer deadlines and more opportunities to meet fascinating people like you."

Cadence's face brightened and she tapped out a quick trill on the back of her hand, the beat arrhythmic and foreign.

The rest of the trip passed in silence, my companion too entranced by the scenery passing by outside to make much conversation. I found her silence oddly comforting, and the upturned tilt of her chin combined with the sunlight coming through the window served to display the curve of her neck and chest to a most astounding effect. But all good things must end and, sooner than I had expected, the PT coasted to a stop in front of Hale Manor.

Hale Manor commanded magnificence by its sheer sprawl. The house was hard to take in in one glance; even staring at it for several minutes, people often felt there were pieces of it they couldn't quite see. The windows dotting the front and back stretched from ceiling to floor and the brash white plaster that surrounded them clashed with the brown and red stones of the structure itself. To me it had always been more of a mausoleum than a home. Though it had sheltered generations of Hales, I took little pride in the whole several hundred-acre mess except in moments like these, when it could impress potential admirers.

I hopped out of the PT and held the door for Cadence. She slid across the seat, dragging her bag along behind her, and shuffled out into the sun.

"Well? What do you think?"

Cadence dropped her knapsack and stared at the great edifice. Her head fell to one side. "What do you use it for?"

"It's a house, my dear," I walked past her, scooping her bag up into my arms. "I live in it. Well, the family does."

"Oh!" She strolled behind me, her head craning ever upward as we drew nearer to the expansive front steps. "You must have a very large family."

"Not really." I mounted the stairs two at a time, throwing her sack over my shoulder. "It's just me and Father now; and the servants of course." I dragged my hand over the corrugated handle and the door popped open.

Turning, I found Cadence standing frozen several steps below me, looking first to me and then back at the house, and then to me again in a never-ending loop of confusion. I swept my hand through the open doorway. "Would you like to come inside?"

She shook her head and climbed the last few steps. "Your world is very strange."

I couldn't help but laugh as she strode into the house. "Strange and wonderful, dearest."

Stepping into the entryway was like stepping back in time. Tall bushes in decorated ceramic pots flanked either side of the large front doors. The ceiling was high and vaulted, made up of burnished cherry wood and oak. The main staircase stretched out before us, a dramatic affair with gleaming wood banisters and red-carpeted steps. Many of the main rooms of the house, and some of the guest suites, branched off on two long hallways that curled behind the steps.

For all the entryway's archaic touches, it was here that the first modern comforts became apparent. Pausing inside the threshold gave a chance for the caterpillar-like FASCs to crawl from their wall hutch to do their work. I ignored them, shrugging off my suit jacket and placing it over the waiting claw of the automatic coat cleaner jutting out next to me, the weight signaling the machine to take the jacket back to its place behind the wall.

Cadence, on the other hand, watched the FASCs with childlike fascination, holding her bangs up out of her eyes to get a better view of them. The little creatures purred over her feet and, when they at last released her, her shoes were left sparkling clean and scented with oils. The FASCs went whirring back to their home at the base of the door. Cadence followed their progress with her alert gaze and, just before they disappeared entirely, made a strange symbol with her hands, shook them at the FASCs, and clicked in a sharp language I did not recognize.

"What was that all about?"

She looked back up at me as the wooden door snapped shut, a vacuous expression replacing her intense focus. "Huh?"

"All the..." I mimicked her movement with my hands, botching it enough to make her laugh. Even when edged in exhaustion, it was a pleasant laugh.

"Oh, I was just saying thank you."

I snorted, shaking my head as I forced cufflinks free from my sleeves. "I didn't know it was a custom on Paraesepe to thank inanimate objects."

Cadence stepped back, brows high on her wrinkled forehead. "You find it strange?"

"A little, yes, but in a perfectly charming way."

"They performed a service for you." She lifted her bag from the floor, massaging her shoulder as she stared at me. "I believe it is customary in most societies to show thankfulness and respect to someone who has done that."

"FASCs aren't exactly a 'someone' though," I shoved the cufflinks into my trouser pocket, shrugging. "It's not as though they have feelings to hurt."

Her nose crinkled, frown deepening. "FASCs? That's their names?"

"Feet and Shoe Cleaners; it's an acronym."

Her gaze dropped to the floor, moving along the path that the machines had taken to return to their little home inside the wall. Chin falling to her chest, she began shifting her weight from foot to foot. "Well, I've always found it safest to assume that everything is intelligent until proven otherwise. It's only polite after all."

I shot her a crooked smile. "You are exceedingly and delightfully queer. Has anyone ever told you that?"

She thought a moment before shaking her head. "You would be the first."

Taking a step closer to her, I brushed the corner of her mouth with the tips of my fingers. "How about how incredibly beautiful you are? Has anyone ever–"

"Chance!"

I flinched and turned to meet the oncoming storm. As my father descended the stairs, I was struck by how imposing the old bat could be when he wanted. He was a barrel-chested man, as fit as ever even at the age of sixty-eight. The grey wisps of hair that fell across his temple accentuated the piercing nature of his dark auburn eyes, and with hands like uncooked hams and the bearing of a king, he had never struggled to impose his will on all those within his domain.

I, on the other hand, took after my mother; my messy crop of blond hair was hers, as were my grass-colored eyes. Tall for her sex, I was short for mine, and no matter how much time I devoted to sport, my frame remained lean, rather than bulging with muscles.

"Hello, father!" I embraced him with filial affection; the falseness of which I knew would pluck at his nerves. "You're looking well!"

His eyes bulged at my companion, color rising into his cheeks. I brought my new amour forward with a flourish. "Do forgive me; let me introduce Miss Cadence Turing. I met her on the train in Römer. She's just arrived from Paraesepe and, naturally, I had to offer her some of our Arrhidaean hospitality."

"It's very kind of you to open your home to me, sir." Cadence stretched out her hand, eyes lowered in deference. "We don't have any such customs on Paraesepe. That I know of. It's quite unique."

There was a moment when I thought the man's anger might

finally get the better of him. He looked down at Cadence's hand as if considering how quickly he could devour it, jaw clenched so tight I could hear his teeth grinding from where I stood. But the moment passed, and he wrenched his gaze up to her face, a perfunctory "Yes", falling from his lips. My father's Adam's apple bobbed up and down as he swallowed with all the desperation of a half-drowned man gulping down air. He shook her hand, inclining his head towards her. "Felix Hale, good to meet you, Miss Turing." His lip curled back into something not very much like a smile when he spied the dusty bag slung over her shoulder. "Are these your things? I'll have them brought up to Chance's room. I'm sure he doesn't mind moving into his mother's room for a night; do you, son?"

I forced a wide smile over my lips. "Of course not, why should I?" I wrapped my arm around Cadence's waist, my eyes never leaving my father's face. "Why don't you head up as well, Cadence? I'm sure you'd like to clean up a bit; unpack?"

Cadence looked between us and, after a moment's consideration, nodded. My father pressed the call button on his ring and a servant appeared to take Cadence's bag. She glanced once more at my father before following the male servant upstairs without a word.

The two of us stood there at the foot of the stairs, teeth bared, until the door to my room clicked shut above us. My father's façade vanished like a smoke screen in a strong breeze, and I saw a firm frown under his graying beard. "Chance."

I granted him a bored glance.

His hand curled into a fist. "What do you think you are doing? Bringing strange women into our house – and a foreigner!"

He huffed, crossing his arms over his chest and demanding, "How long is she staying?"

"As long as it takes her to get adjusted, that's all."

"And how long might that be? Does she know anyone here? Have any kind of marketable skill? Is she looking for service work?"

"Father," I flicked a piece of dirt off my trousers, "I didn't interrogate her."

"Well by god you should have!" My father's thick-soled shoe smacked against the wood, making the floor vibrate under us. "Chance, she could be anyone! A con artist or a fugitive! Have you forgotten about the party tonight?"

"As if I could." I started searching for my nix case, knowing that smoking was the only thing I could do to annoy him further.

"Do you really expect me to introduce this girl to all of our oldest friends? Think of our reputation; think of your reputation! When you are the head of Halcyon Enterprises, you will be constantly in the public eye." My father pinched the bridge of his nose, hissing as if I was causing him mortal pain. "You have to learn to control yourself, you—"

"Felix?" The sound of tiptoed footsteps echoed around the far corner. "The maids don't seem to – oh." Desdemona froze by the edge of the staircase, crouching over as if she were afraid she would offend someone by existing.

If you breathed too hard on Desdemona Eydis she would burst into ashes and scatter like a charred piece of paper. Her baby-blue eyes were large compared to the rest of her features, overshadowing her petite nose and mouth with ease, leaving her whole head looking unbalanced. However, Father was blind to the woman's less flattering qualities, and there seemed little to be done about his embarrassing infatuation with her except to ride it out until it came to its inevitable end.

The servant returned downstairs, startled Desdemona from her mooring, and forced her into the entryway. She scurried to my father, her frail hands clasped together. "The guests haven't started arriving already, have they?"

"Don't worry yourself, my dear." My father wrapped his arm around her shoulders, enveloping her tiny frame under his own. "They won't be arriving for another few hours at least."

"Oh, good." Her pale eyes darted across my face like a frightened animal. "It's nice to have you home again, Chance. How was the city?"

"Very dull." Leaning up against the opposite banister, I tried not to sneer as I inclined my head towards her, digging my nix case out of my pocket. "And how did you spend your week, Miss Eydis?"

Desdemona's gaze fell away from my face like a dead leaf from a tree, drifting to the floor. "Preparing for the party mostly. There are so many things to arrange."

"I'm sure you're doing a fine job." I twisted my nix to life and took a long drag, letting the smoke out slowly. "Really acting like the lady of the house now, aren't we?"

"Desdemona."

Her head jerked up as if on a string. My father, the puppet master, smiled down at her with more tenderness than his sharp tone had suggested. "Dear, why don't you go down to the kitchen and see how the cooking is coming along? I'm sure they'd value your input."

She nodded, giving me a last glance before crossing to the hallway behind me.

"Oh, and tell them to make sure they're making enough for nine people rather than seven," said my father.

Desdemona skittered to a halt, wobbling around with hands at her mouth. "More guests?"

"Yes, my sweet, but I'm taking care of it. Chance," my name squeezed its way through his clenched teeth, "has brought a friend for the evening. And Dr. Merton just called to say he'll be able to make it tonight after all."

Desdemona started back down the hall with a wave. "Yes, I'll make sure they know."

When the door to the kitchen clicked shut, my father returned to me, fury etched into the lines of his face. "Chance Tobias Hale, you will treat Desdemona with respect, do you understand me?"

He didn't even wait for my response, too eager to stomp down the hallway after his precious mistress. I bit into my cheek, silently fuming as my mind whirled with all the things I wished I could say to him, but never would.

The whole situation galled me so that I had quite forgotten about the beauty I had tucked away upstairs until the roaring sound of water and the weak whining of pipes reached my ears. I straightened, closed my eyes, and evoked the image of the soft curve of her neck, the paleness of her skin; how she must look now, with gentle pulses of water running down her body. I fell back against the railing with a groan. I should be up there right now. Breaking through her reserve had been more difficult than I had predicted, and I doubted things would get much easier once the party was in full swing. What was I going to do?

The solution broke upon me like a ray of heaven's light. I opened my eyes and managed a smile. Of course – a kindred spirit was just the thing to draw her out into the open. Besides, it was as good a time as any to get a second opinion on my lady of the evening.

The antique house phone rested on its charger outside the dining room. I picked it up, said his name aloud, and waited impatiently as it dialed, smoking my nix one handed.

"Hello?"

"Henry!" I pressed the phone to my ear with my shoulder, leaning against the wall. "Love of my life, how are you?"

"Just fine, Chance." The clacking on the other end of the line was a sure sign that I had interrupted him during one of his little pieces. "You?"

"Positively glowing, dear boy. Come up to the house, I have a surprise for you."

The clacking ceased. "A surprise?" Henry's beat up desk chair creaked as he leaned back from his keyboard, matching pitch with his quiet groan. "I hate surprises."

"No, you don't, you just say that because you're a wet blanket." I strolled into the dining room, heading for the wide double doors at the far end that opened out onto the patio. "Deep down, you love them."

He gave a derisive snort and the typing resumed. "We'll all be over later for the party. Why do you want me to come over now?"

"I said it's a surprise." I pushed the doors open, looking towards the faraway clump of trees that marked the boundary between our land and the Davers'.

"Yours is a capricious nature, isn't it?"

My smirk widened. "Keeps your life exciting, doesn't it?"

"I'll be round soon as I can. Thirty minutes?"

"Make it ten."

3

Chapter 3

Disinclined to sit within the stuffy confines of the manor, I had the servants assemble a table for afternoon tea out on the veranda and waited there for Henry to arrive. Henry Davers and I had been friends since our school days and though Henry was my absolute opposite in body and soul, my reliance on him was complete. The moment my father's manservant showed him out onto the patio, I jumped to my feet and pulled the man into a warm embrace, which he returned without a moment's hesitation.

"Henry!" I slung my arm around his shoulders, leading him over to the impromptu table. "Did I tear you away from some terribly important studies?"

"Of course you did." He grinned, settling his tall, thin body down into a plush lawn chair as one of the kitchen girls wheeled out a cart with our repast upon it.

"Good!"

He peered at me from behind the maid, frowning. "I have never known you to be so cheerful on the eve of one of your family's dreary parties, Chance. What's going on?"

I could never keep Henry in the dark for long. Highly intelligent, my dear friend was lauded as one of the great philosophers of our time, his scholarly papers published in the top academic journals on the sphere before he'd finished school. His real talent was kept a fiercely guarded secret of course, by him and me alone; his soaring poetical verses appeared in various avant-garde pamphlets under a pseudonym known only to me.

My greatest, and in fact, only confidant, his opinion of Cadence was of the utmost importance to me. If Henry implored me to do so, I would cast her out without a second thought.

I waited until the serving girl had finished placing the tea things on the table before answering, with a twinkle in my eye, "I have found a most pleasurable way to pass the evening," I leaned over to my friend and squeezed his knee, "and I desperately want you to meet her."

"Chance," Henry sat back, wide eyes fixed on my face, "you didn't."

A raise of my brows was my answer.

He shook his head, lifting his cup of tea to his lips. "Your father will kill you."

"We've had our customary fight for the day, and I have emerged relatively unscathed." I accepted my tea with a soft 'thank you'.

The maid trundled back inside with the cart. Henry sipped at his tea, well aware that it was still too hot to drink. "Where did you find this one?"

"The Mawson Docks."

His hand froze halfway across the table from where his favorite chocolate covered cookie sat. He closed his eyes and took in a deep breath. "Does she even speak Common Tongue?"

"Quite well, actually; she's from Paraesepe."

Henry completed his motion and popped the cookie into his mouth, brow furrowing as he chewed. "What compelled her to make the trip all the way out here?"

"I did ask, but she didn't say."

Henry stopped chewing and stared at me, jaw clenching.

I waved away his concern. "What does it matter? She's here, she'll warm my bed for a while, and then she'll be elsewhere."

Brushing some crumbs off his lapel, Henry sighed. "I have never understood your cavalier attitude towards the opposite sex, Chance."

"You just need to get out with them more." I slid down in my seat, grinning as I ran my finger around the lip of my cup. "Or into them more, as the case may be."

"Charming."

I watched my old friend as he reached for another sugary pastry, noting his tired eyes and tense shoulders. "You alright, Henry?"

"Father's in a mood." He grimaced, stirring his tea with the cookie. "Seems that your father has vetoed yet another one of his proposals."

"Well, you can't expect Felix Hale to know a good idea when he hears one."

"Yes, but..." Henry glanced around the veranda as he set down his cup. "Mother thinks Felix is going to fire him." He wrung his hands as if they were a sodden towel. "You know how much she cares about his career, his reputation. Our reputation."

I reached across the table and clasped his shoulder, shaking him. "Come now, I wouldn't waste energy worrying about it. Your father's been with the company almost as long as mine's been running it. I doubt he'd fire him on a whim."

"Tell that to my mother, would you? She's been obsessing over it for weeks now. It can't be good for her, not in her condition."

"Yes, I'd heard that the doctor had been round to your place. What is it now?"

"It was hepatic flu, but the medicine Dr. Merton prescribed seems to be working." Henry munched at his cookie. "It's a liquid and powder solution, the absolute devil to mix up. It's been giving me no end of trouble."

"You should ask Aunt Be for some tips while she's here." I slid my empty cup onto the table. "She handled all my mother's medications for months. I'm sure she could help."

Henry murmured a half-hearted assent.

I nibbled the side of my mouth, resting my fingers against my temple. "Of course, it didn't help–"

The patio door swung open behind me, and I shot up from my seat, grabbing at the doorknob. "Ah, there you are, darling!"

Hovering in the doorway, Cadence looked just as she had before she went upstairs, except her black hair was now damper and loose around her shoulders. I proffered my hand around the portal and led her onto the porch, the scent of my soap on her skin an intimate touch that made me shiver.

"Feeling better?"

"Yes, thank you." She stared at Henry with the intensity of a deer watching a hunter.

Henry rose and extended a hand while I made the introductions.

"This is my oldest friend, Henry Davers." I smiled and stepped back so that the two could have an unobstructed view of each other. "Henry, this is the delightful creature I've been telling you about, Miss Cadence Turing of Paraesepe."

"It's very nice to meet you, Henry." Cadence bent forward and gave his hand a firm shake, eyes wandering over him.

Color flushed my friend's pale cheeks and he stuttered out, "Y-yes, indeed. Cadence."

"Henry will be staying over this weekend for the party," I gestured to a seat behind Cadence and took up my own, the tip of my tongue caught between my teeth as I smiled, "but he couldn't wait to come over after he heard my description of you."

Henry said nothing in response to my provoking comments, still blushing crimson, his gaze intent upon my guest.

Cadence sat on the outermost edge of the last empty chair, crossing her legs and folding her hands over her knee. "Party?"

"Yes, my father's putting on a small to-do tonight." I sighed, shifting against the lumpy cushions behind me. "Just friends of the family in attendance, but he's a stickler for formality. I'm sure you have some charming little dress or something you can wear, yes?"

Cadence blinked as if I'd flicked water into her eyes. "I'm afraid not." Bands of red formed around the places her fingers interlaced. "Actually, these clothes are the only ones I have."

Henry's cup clattered onto the table. His fingers stuttered around the edges of the porcelain and his tongue flicked out to wet his bottom lip.

Cadence pushed out her chin, meeting our eyes boldly. "I like to travel light."

We both heard the lie and we both let it pass without comment, neither of us willing to confront her with our understanding. Could that small sack she had been carrying represent the totality of her possessions in this life?

Henry squirmed in his seat. "I...I think some of my mother's old dresses might fit you." He cleared his throat, blush spreading down his neck as he met Cadence's stare. "I'd be happy to have one brought over for you, if–if that sounds alright."

Cadence jerked back, mouth falling open. I was quite certain that Henry had once again overplayed the kind, considerate card and offended my guest when Cadence did something that cleared all other thoughts from my mind.

She smiled.

It was the first time I had ever seen her smile and it undid me. The edges of her pink lips skyrocketed upward in an energetic movement of unadulterated joy. She let out a hushed gasp, and her dark eyes sparkled like summer sun reflecting off still water

"Oh, yes! Yes, thank you!" She held her clasped hands to her chest. "That's so very kind of you. I promise to return it!"

"It never occurred to me that you wouldn't," Henry laughed, drawing his hand down his jaw and looking at me, the beginning of a grin quirking his lips. "We do have some time before the party; if it suits you, I could have a PT drive us back to the house and you could pick out the dress you liked best."

"I wouldn't want to inconvenience you—"

"It's no inconvenience at all," Henry stood. "My house is only a few minutes away."

Things had gotten away from me here. I had expected Henry to be taken with my creature. She was his usual type: tall, brunette, reserved to the point of coldness. But I had no reason to think that she would react to him any differently than she had to me: standoffish at worse, courteous at best. Her obvious enjoyment of him was troubling and more than a little hurtful.

I stood as well, rubbing the back of my neck and avoiding looking her full in the face. "Why don't you go wait out front while Henry calls for the PT? It should be here in a few minutes."

Cadence nodded, saving the last glimmer of her smile for Henry, who returned it in kind. I waited until the sounds of her footsteps faded before turning on my friend.

"You bastard."

"Spoiled sport." Henry rocked back on his heels, smile widening into a full-blown smirk. "You know if you keep scowling, your face will stick that way."

I shook my shoulders as if to break from the foul mood that had shifted from Henry to me. "I suppose I can trust you with her for an hour or so, yes? During which time, you will extol all my good qualities?"

"Always." Henry's smile softened and he threw his arm around me, patting my shoulder. "I do understand the attraction, Chance; she's quite striking. And I can tell she's fond of you already."

"You're not as funny as you think you are, chum." I dragged him into a parting embrace, slapping him hard on the back.

"Don't do anything that I would do. Remember, you're the gentleman."

I lingered outside for the next hour after they left, contemplating the course of the evening, and thinking about Cadence's smile; the inhuman brightness of it, its vivacity, the way the memory of it alone left me breathless, a pleasurable ache low in my belly. I lit a nix and sucked at it, the argument with my father throbbing at the back of my mind like a persistent headache.

I didn't take notice of the various servants and staff working around me, transforming the veranda with stringed lights and streamers for the party to come. Tables and chairs encroached on the lawn, looking like large white mushrooms in a sea of green, their lace tablecloths flapping in the breeze.

Henry and Cadence returned to find me right where they had left me, reclined in a chair, smoking my third nix down to the filter. The pair cut through the bustle of bodies with ease. Cadence had a long black bag draped over her arm, the opaqueness of it making it impossible for me to see what kind of outfit she had chosen for the evening.

Henry mounted the veranda steps with a spring in his step. "Still here?"

"I think I'll always be here." I exhaled a last mouthful of smoke before snuffing out my nix in the ashtray some thoughtful soul had put beside me. "I'll be here till I rot."

"Well, at least I'll know where to find you when I want to bother someone."

I gave a tense smile despite myself. "Happy to help." I pushed myself on to my feet. "Did Henry get you fixed up with something suitable, love?"

"Yes, he was very helpful." Cadence examined her bundle with a furrowed brow. "I think I might have some trouble getting into it though. I'm used to wearing simpler things."

"I'm sure we can find someone to help you with that." I glared over the top of her head. "Unless Henry has already graciously volunteered."

"Envy doesn't suit you, Chance." Henry adjusted his bow tie, smiling. "Green has never been your color."

"Sir," I turned to see the head manservant bowing at me from inside the patio doors. "Miss Gad has just arrived."

"Oh good!" I rubbed my hands together, leaning over to Cadence. "Here's someone who might be able to help with that dress."

We weaved through the dining room, ignoring and being ignored by the servants, who were arranging the antique plates, crystal goblets, and burnished silverware around the table. Victoria stood waiting in the entryway, looking as radiant as ever, her blonde hair glowing like a warm halo as it caught the light of the setting sun.

She had chosen an emerald frock for the party tonight, all too aware of the way the sharp cut of the dress showed off her sculpted ankles and calves. There were many things Victoria knew nothing about: politics, finance, literature; but if there was one thing she did know, it was how to present herself to her best advantage.

I walked towards her with open arms. "Darling, you look positively ravishing."

"I know." She leaned forward and we exchanged polite kisses on the cheek. "I worked particularly hard at it tonight, too."

"Not that you needed to."

"Not that I needed to." Victoria pulled away with a suppressed smirk.

I turned to stand beside her, revealing the rest of my entourage. At the sight of our mutual childhood friend, her lips pulled back over her teeth, but she managed to wrestle the sneer into a smile. "Hello, Henry. You're looking as brooding and pedantic as ever, I see."

Henry gave a bow. "I can't say that I've ever worked particularly hard at that, Victoria; especially not for you."

"Would someone care to introduce me to our guest?" Victoria's gaze fell onto Cadence with the same coolness she reserved for all my female friends.

Victoria would make a fine wife someday. She was the kind of woman who was certain that men would always come back to her, no matter how far they strayed; the more adventurous they were, the more liberties she could allow herself.

I walked over to Cadence and wrapped an arm around her shoulders, leading her forward. "Cadence, I'd like you to meet Victoria Gad. Victoria, darling, this is Miss Cadence Turing, recently on-planet from Paraesepe." I smiled down at my dark-eyed dove, squeezing her to my side. "We met on the AN-GRAV, and I just had to invite her to the party tonight. I'm sure you'll be fast friends."

"Oh, I'm sure." Victoria offered her dainty hand, a smile stretched over her heart-shaped face. "It's a pleasure to meet you, Miss Turing. I've always envied women who can stay so pale. Or have you been ill?"

I cleared my throat and crossed back to Victoria while looking Cadence up and down. "Cadence needs some help with her ensemble tonight, Vicky. It seems she doesn't have much experience dressing for formal occasions."

"You know, I could tell that straight off." Victoria nodded and began circling my prize, appraising her like a farmer with livestock that needed slaughtering. "Where did you say you were from?"

"Paraesepe," I answered for her.

"Hmm. This is the fashion on Paraesepe, is it?" She giggled, picking at Cadence's sheer white shirt with her long fingernails. "Are they suffering from a textile shortage?"

"Vicky," I came up behind Victoria, slinging my arms around her hips and kissing the top of her shoulder, "be nice."

"Oh, Chance!" Victoria threw her head back in a laugh, batting away my hands. "You really know nothing about women, do you?" She stood next to Cadence, wrapping an arm around her waist. "I was just teasing; it's how us girls bond. Isn't it, dear?"

Cadence blinked at her, saying nothing.

Victoria reached up and gave her nose an affectionate tap. "Aw, she's a shy one, is she?"

I tilted my head to one side, wrinkling my nose. "Not particularly."

But Victoria was too engrossed in her new project to listen to me. "I'll have her looking almost as pretty as me, don't you worry."

Henry and I stepped back to allow the pair a clear path up the stairs, Victoria dragging Cadence along by the hand. Victoria blew me a kiss from the landing before they both disappeared into my rooms, closing the door with a snap.

"When are you going to give it up and marry her already?"

"Henry," I scoffed, pushing his shoulder with my own. "I just met her!"

Quick to regain his balance, Henry grimaced at me, and returned my push with a smack to the back of my head. "Not Miss Turing, idiot – Victoria!"

"Oh." I shuffled over to the banister, leaning against it as I rubbed my scalp. "One of these days I expect. Does it matter?"

Henry shrugged, slipping his hands into his tuxedo trouser pockets. "You seem distracted, Chance. Everything alright?"

"It's just father." I stepped closer to the stairs to allow a harried looking maid to hurry by with some canapés. "He's just so damn melodramatic about everything." The maid returned, this time carrying a large ladle. My eyes followed her as she passed. "I swear, if he keeps on threatening to die, he might find himself in the grave prematurely."

Henry sighed, head lolling low between his shoulders. He looked up at me from under his brow. "You do go out of your way to antagonize him, you know."

I glared, pulling my arms tight across my chest. "Just whose side are you on, chum?"

Henry rolled his eyes and shook his head, adopting a soft smile. I swallowed, shifting where I stood, staring at the floor with all the petulance of a child.

He walked over and stood next to me, his voice low. "It wasn't over that lady friend of his again, was it? Deirdre or something?"

"Desdemona." The name dropped from my scowling mouth like a slug, making my lips feel dirtied with the mention of it. "She's moved into the house you know."

"What? After three months?"

"Why do you think I've been in town all week? You think I could stand being cooped up with that blithering ninny?"

"Well." Henry shook his head after a moment, a queer twist to his lips. "I can't believe it; it actually sounds like things are getting pretty serious. Who would have thought?"

"Thought what?"

"That your father could fall in love."

I gave a loud bark of laughter, crossing my feet at the ankles. "Call it that if you like, but we all know a man scrambling for youth when we see one. Your mum said so herself."

"She just doesn't like Desdemona very much." He chuckled and sat down on the stairs. "She's too flighty for her or something."

We were silent for a few minutes, an island of calm amidst the general hubbub of party making. I dragged my hand down my cheek, peering at him from the corner of my eye. "So...what do you think?"

"About Desdemona?"

I nudged his foot with my own, the corners of my mouth twitching. "About my newest acquisition – Cadence."

"Ah." Henry leaned back against the stairs, resting his elbows on the step behind him. "You know, I've never been off-world, let alone to Paraesepe, but she seems to be unusually out of place here. Like a creature of different matter, a being of quintessence forced to tread on the ground with us lower forms."

"Henry," I sat down beside him with a groan, "you've gone poetic again. But I think I know what you mean."

His head fell to one side. "What do you intend to do with her?"

"As much as I can convince her to allow, dear boy, as always."

4

Chapter 4

I mounted the steps two at a time, unbuttoning my wrinkled shirt as I climbed. At this rate, I would be late, but I could dress for a party with my eyes shut. I passed my father at the top of the stairs, his rooms adjoining the ones I would be occupying for the weekend. My father was so intent on smoothing out his dinner jacket that I slipped behind him like a ghost.

I disregarded his disregard as much as I could and entered my mother's rooms without a word. Focusing my attention on the occasional twittering laugh of Victoria in the rooms on the opposite side where she was helping Cadence prepare for the night, I pulled clothes from assorted drawers and closets as quick as I could, ignorant of the care with which some well-meaning servant had just placed them there.

A quarter of an hour ticked away and, presentable at last, I jogged downstairs. The sun lay nestled in the far-off mountains, the warmth of a summer day giving way to a cool, pleasant night. I made my way through the dining room to the veranda outside, where my father and Henry stood engaged in conversation.

Smiling wide, my father turned to me, all the unpleasantness of the afternoon forgotten. "Chance, m'boy, come here! Henry was just telling me about a new paper he's been working on; political, isn't it?"

"Yes, sir," Henry reached behind him for a glass of xampany, the drink bubbling at its contact with the outside air. "I'm focusing on the success, or rather, the lack of success, the Inter-Planetary Commission has had in regulating humanitarian and environmental concerns within the system."

My father crossed his arms over his chest and began stroking his beard. "You know, my grandfather opposed the proposal for Arrhidaeus to join the IPC when it was first brought up in the Chambers, eighty, no, ninety years ago."

"Yes, sir, I did know that," said Henry with a politeness our professors had always adored. "I've been reading several of the very interesting speeches he made before the Chambers about the risks he foresaw in joining such an organization."

"And he was damned right too. Inter-Planetary Commission – bunch of damn busybodies is what they are. Can't have foreigners telling you what you can and cannot do on your own damn planet."

"Yes, Lord knows what would happen if we started listening to people who had other points of view." I took a liberal gulp of the xampany Henry had passed to me. "Where's Desdemona?"

"She's upstairs resting. All the excitement of the party; it wasn't good for her nerves. She'll be down in a little while, I'm sure."

"Mr. and Mrs. Solomon Davers, sir." Behind us, the manservant stepped aside from the dining room doors to let our long-time neighbors out onto the porch.

Henry greeted his mother with his usual burst of filial affection, striding forward and sweeping her into a warm embrace. My friend's devotion to his mother was a sentimental quirk for one so reserved, but if there was any woman alive who deserved it, it was Minerva Davers. A sweet, spirited lady, she shared Desdemona's petite frame and long blonde hair. Often ill, I could remember many times during my childhood when we feared she would die, but she persevered through every trial, and while her body had suffered, her mind remained as sharp as it had ever been.

This mental acuity must have been what first attracted Solomon Davers to his wife. A tall willow wisp of a man, with bright, deep-set eyes, his resemblance to his son was striking. Solomon was young compared to my father, but in many ways, he had always seemed much older to me. Subdued and reflective, he stood with one hand hovering behind his wife, surveying the party scene with the dispassionate concern appropriate for a scientist of his standing.

"Good evening, Felix," Solomon's narrow hand disappeared inside my father's vise-like grip. "You're looking well."

"Solomon." My father pumped his employee's hand with vigor. "Always a pleasure to see you outside of the office! Or should I say outside of the lab?"

Solomon's lips twitched up in a wan smile. "You don't pay me to sit on my hands, Felix. I can't help it if I'm passionate about providing Halcyon Enterprises with the next great innovation in biomechanics."

"And we appreciate it, we do!" My father clapped him on the back before stretching his hands out to Minerva. "My dear, you are looking lovely."

"I'm feeling much better too." Minerva leaned forward and kissed his cheek. "A little bout of Hepatic Flu can't keep Minerva Davers off her feet for long!"

She turned to me, smiling, cupping my cheek with her hands. "Chance, it's so nice to see you. You haven't been by the house in ages."

I breathed in the comforting scent of her rose perfume, patting her shoulder. "I've been busy in the city the past few weeks, Min."

"Busy! Yes, I'm sure." She gave me a wink and slapped my chest with the back of her hand. "I've always felt that strapping young men should keep busy. You'll have to tell me all about it later. I actually haven't had a chance to change just yet," she stepped back to my father, interrupting the conversation he and her husband were having. "I hope you don't mind if I head back to the room and get myself spruced up?"

"Of course not." My father nodded towards the door. "It's the usual one at the end of the hall."

She headed back, waving off the attentions of a maidservant as she went, and Solomon took the rare opportunity of my father's distraction to address me, shaking my hand. "How are you, Chance?"

"Just fine, Mr. Davers, thanks."

He patted my shoulder and looked as though he was about to say something else when my father swooped in, whisking him down the stairs and out onto the well-tended lawn, interrogating him about the quarterly sales report. I shook my head and crossed to the other side of the deck to rejoin Henry when I caught sight of Victoria making her way through the dining room.

"Down so soon?" I peered around her. "Where's Cadence?"

Victoria adjusted her sheer green shawl and pouted. "Am I not enough for you?"

I flashed a smile and planted a dry kiss on her forehead. Placated, she allowed me to take her arm and the three of us walked out onto the grass.

"She'll be down presently, I'm sure. She wouldn't let me do much to her, I'm afraid. I've always been offended by women who presume they don't need makeup; but ignorance is bliss, I suppose. You should have seen the way she was carrying on when the corset was lacing itself up."

I took a steadying sip of my drink, the thought alone making my pulse dance. "I certainly would have liked to."

Victoria stared at me with sullen eyes, taking a fruit hors d'oeuvres from the small table behind her. "Honestly, Chance, I don't know how you function with all that pent-up lust."

"I have you to focus on, don't I?" Pulling her against me, I stole a bite of the sweet treat in her hand with a growl.

"And who said anything about it being pent up?"

Victoria ignored Henry's remark, turning her back to him. "Where did you say you found this girl again?"

"On the AN-GRAV coming from the Mawson Docks." I

raised my glass. "I took one look at her and simply had to extend her *tishos*."

Henry licked his lips, tilting his head to one side. "You do know that's a tradition that's been defunct for almost five hundred years, don't you?"

"I do." I tapped my glass against his. "But she doesn't. And here you thought I never paid attention in history class."

Victoria giggled. "You are positively wicked."

"Yes," I nestled my nose against hers, nipping at her lips with my teeth, "but you like me that way."

"Excuse me; I think I'm going to be sick in those hydrangeas."

Victoria tore away from me, scowling at the straight-faced Henry. "Don't be jealous just because you haven't got a girl!"

"Growing up with you has given me ample time to learn why I don't want one." He sighed, looking into my eyes and placing his hand to his heart. "Chance is more than enough for me."

I put down my glass. "Hold me, my love."

"Anything you say, pet." Henry took me in his arms and dipped me. Victoria flailed at us, ranting about how ridiculous we both were.

The manservant's drone broke through the comedic moment with practiced skill. "Miss Belinda Tanith."

Belinda swept out onto the veranda as only she could. Her long silk wrap billowed behind her, forcing all the servants to wait several moments before following her outside, lest they be entangled in the fabric sheaf, and her personality extended several feet in front of her, pushing Victoria and Henry out of her path before she was within shouting distance.

"Chance Hale, you naughty, naughty boy!"

"Aunt Be!" I soon found myself enveloped in the crushing hug I'd known since I was a boy. Belinda laughed, a deep rumble that massaged my senses with its familiarity. A substantial woman, she had skin the color of dried mud and muscle tone that men envied. Her work as a geologist had taken her all over the system, keeping her fit and active in her advancing years.

Our customary greeting exchanged, she stepped back, squeezing my shoulders, and beaming at me with all the parental pride my father lacked. "Just look at you! Still the most handsome young man in Zahia." She released me with a peel of surprised laughter when she noticed Henry behind me. "Oh, I am sorry, Henry, dear!"

"It's quite alright, Ms. Tanith," Henry folded his hands, pretending to look somber. "I've always known that Chance was the handsome one; it's why I spend all my time studying."

"Yes, well, women like a man of letters, Henry, don't ever doubt it." She winked. "We need someone to outthink us now and again."

I jiggled the thin gold band on my wrist, the face proclaiming it to be well past seven. "What could be taking Cadence so long?"

Belinda lifted her brows. "Who?"

"She's my guest tonight. Vicky, do you–"

"Last I saw of her she was still upstairs struggling with her dress."

I gave her a pointed look, eyes narrowing. "You didn't think to stay and help her, dear?"

"I'm not a chamber maid." Victoria adjusted her wrap over her shoulders, exuding the casual condescension that was a source of constant amusement to me. "It's not my fault your foreigner's a simpleton."

Henry wasn't getting into the spirit of things at all, standing to one side of me, looking as if he'd just sucked on a lemon. "Charity isn't one of your virtues, is it, Victoria?"

"Oh, Henry!" Victoria stomped her pump-clad foot, fist resting on her hip. "You have got to get your nose out of those books every once in a while and see the world the way it really is: there's no room for charity anymore."

"That is so very true, my dear." Belinda grasped Victoria's wrist, shaking it in time with her head. "It's eat or be eaten, that's what I've always said, and I don't see any problem with that! It's the natural flow of evolution; if you're not strong enough to hack it on your own, well then, to the rubbish heap with you! Can't have everybody sponging off everybody else; the whole world would collapse on itself."

I could have used Henry's clenched jaw to hammer in nails. He slammed his glass down onto the planter behind him. "Excuse me; I'm going to go check on Cadence."

"No, no," I cut off my attentive friend, striding towards the veranda before he could take a step. "It's alright, old chap, I'll do it. She's my–" I stuttered to a halt when she stepped out onto the patio. "Oh."

The light blue silk of the gown clung to Cadence's curves like a needy child. As she moved, the breeze picked up the loose fabric of the skirt and sent it fluttering against her ankles, kissing her skin. The beaded sleeves sparkled in the waning light, and I indulged in a hazy fantasy of slipping them off her shoulders, down her smooth white skin, and onto the floor beside my bed.

I didn't even notice Minerva walking with Cadence until it was too late to hide my flushed cheeks and hungry eyes from her sharp sight.

"I believe this delightful young lady belongs to you, Chance." Her grin was as sly as it had ever been, but she handed Cadence off to me without further comment, walking the last few steps to Henry and wrapping her arm through his.

"I'm sorry I took so long coming out, Henry, but Cadence and I were both having some trouble with our ensembles. You know my hands; I just can't do up those tiny clasps like I used to." She massaged her thin wrists, glaring at them for a moment before nodding to Cadence, her face brightening. "We came to each other's aid and bonded over our mutual dislike of formal wear."

Cadence, still picking at the straps of her dress, grimaced, nodding. "It is unduly complicated." The shaky little smile returned to her lips as she looked at Henry. "Your mother was very kind."

"Yes," Henry's eyes bored into Victoria, "we're a very *charitable* sort of family."

"Cadence," I cleared my throat, leap-frogging over that chasm of social unpleasantness, and turning her away from the pair of squabblers, "this is Belinda Tanith, an old friend of the family. She and my mother went to university together." I stepped away as if displaying a trophy. "Aunt Be, this is Cadence Turing, my friend from Paraesepe."

"A pleasure to know you, my dear, an absolute pleasure!" Belinda folded Cadence's hand into her own, patting the back of it.

"I'm always so thrilled to meet people from other planets in the system."

A lopsided smile hobbled over Cadence's face. "Have you ever been to Paraesepe, Miss Tanith?"

"Several times! For the Institute, of course."

"Belinda's on the board of the Fernitate Institute of Geology and Earth Sciences." I picked up two flutes of xampany, handing one to Cadence and the other to Belinda. "She travels quite a bit for them."

"A marvelous, marvelous institution. Always giving funds to support all kinds of scientists; even to Halcyon Enterprises, though I've never been quite sure why."

"All I know is Father's more than happy to take their money," I retorted.

"Now, now, dear boy," Belinda waggled a bejeweled finger at me, "just what is your father up to tonight, hm? What's cooking in that head of his?"

"What makes you think he's up to anything, Aunt Be?"

"Oh, suddenly he has to round us all up for a weekend at the manor? With so little warning?" Sipping her drink, she remembered something mid-swallow, flapping her hand at me until she could speak again. "And what queer little invitations to send out!"

"Yes, they were strange, weren't they?" Victoria shivered in the cool night air.

I glanced between them. "What? What was strange about them?"

"Chance, Chance, Chance!" Belinda wiggled her head, diamond earrings reflecting in the lights from the manor. "You didn't even look at them, did you?"

"Well, I do live here, Aunt Be," I downed the last of my drink, "and contrary to popular belief, my father does speak to me enough to invite me to a party at my own house."

"Here, I brought mine." Victoria unburied a small square of heavy white paper from her tiny handbag and passed it to me.

I examined the stiff paper with deepening confusion. "He sent out invitations on this?"

"Positively primeval, isn't it?" Victoria sucked her tongue away from her teeth, smirking. "I just about had a fit when the footman delivered it. Your father's becoming very quaint in his old age, Chance - paper invitations!"

"I'm surprised he didn't seal it with wax or the blood of his first born or something." I turned the invitation over and read the curling, embossed script:

Miss Victoria Gad

You are cordially invited to

a weekend retreat at Hale Manor.

Matters of the

utmost importance

to the Hale Family

will be discussed.

Please attend

"He's lost it." I turned the card over in my hand. "Henry, why didn't you tell me about this?"

"I thought you knew. It does say 'matters of the utmost importance to the Hale Family'. I just assumed your father had mentioned something to you. Whatever was I thinking?"

"So, you really have no idea what this is all about then?" Belinda's short fingers toyed with the necklace of bright yellow stones she always wore, her eyes wide.

"I'm afraid I'm as much in the dark as everyone else." My frown deepened. He may have been a blowhard through and through with an upsetting habit of placing great importance on trivial things, but I still thought that if there was some significant event my father wished to discuss with us all, he would have told me about it first. I looked around for him, chewing the inside of my mouth as my mind raced from one potential disaster to the next. Was it the company? His health?

A chime rang out from the house behind us, and the group turned as one body. My father strode up the stairs, beckoning us forward with a wide smile as he said, "It appears that dinner is served. Everyone, please, come inside."

5

Chapter 5

We all shuffled about for a moment, putting down drinks, picking up skirts, and finishing the last morsels of hors d'oeuvres before moving towards the house. My father waved to one of the servants standing just inside the dining room. "Could you have a maid fetch Miss Eydis from her rooms, please?"

Solomon kept pace with my father's long strides, pushing his glasses up the bridge of his nose. "Is Desdemona joining us this weekend?"

"Yes, of course! She wasn't feeling well, so I told her to have a lie down before supper. I'm sure she's feeling much better by now."

"How delightful!" Belinda clapped her hands together as she started up the stairs in front of me. "Such a pretty little thing, so lovely to have around; like a beautiful vase of flowers."

"Yes," Victoria threaded her arm through mine, leaning her

head towards my shoulder, "with the mental capacity of one to match."

My father stood at the open veranda doors as we filed inside. I ushered Victoria and Cadence in ahead of me, nodding to Henry as he passed, his eyebrows crooked at my obvious delay.

Not as observant as my friend, my father turned to head in, despite my presence at his elbow. I grabbed his arm, keeping my voice low. "Father."

He allowed me to pull him back, his jaw clenched, eyes darting down to the hand I had laid on him.

"Father," I glanced into the dining room where everyone was still distracted trying to find their assigned seats. "What's going on?"

He smiled and patted my shoulder. "I'll explain everything after dinner, Chance."

"Explain it to me now! For god's sake –" I gave the inside of my mouth a few good chews before my words burst out like the insides of a squashed grape. "I know we haven't always seen eye to eye on things, Dad, but I am your son. And if something's wrong, then I–"

"Nothing is wrong, Chance, I promise you." He smiled again. It was a sickly, withered smile, that wavered on his lips like a dead leaf clinging to a tree branch. "There are just going to be some changes. Changes for all of us."

He turned and walked inside. I bit down on the tip of my tongue to keep from screaming at him.

With the air of a kicked dog, I took up my seat. We never used the room when it was just the two of us, both preferring to take our meals in our rooms rather than sit together. I stared at Desdemona's vacant seat with a grimace. Running a hand through my hair, I looked away, eyes flitting around the room in search of my guest. It was with considerable disappointment and a muttered curse that I spotted Cadence reclining at the far end of the table.

Henry was beside me, but I refused his attempts to engage me in pleasant conversation or casual frivolities. Unmiffed by my coolness, he ceased once I had made it clear that the most he could do was leave me alone. My father beamed with pride when Desdemona at last made her timid entrance, standing stiff at attention. I focused on the dark red soup pouring into my bowl and pretended not to notice her sliding into the chair across the way.

Despite my morose silence, the room hummed with conversation. Belinda had received an invitation to join a soil study taking place on the moons of Pataea. Henry and Solomon spent several minutes debating the merits of a biography of the famous Yenni General Hukspurt. Even Cadence, my quiet little sparrow, found something to say, making some innocuous comment about men's fashions that earned her an eye roll from Victoria.

I was distracted from the horror of my father holding Desdemona's hand on top of the table by the entrance of our final weekend guest. Merton stumbled through the dining room doors, his large feet tripping over each other as he struggled out of his overcoat. A flustered maidservant stood behind him, trying to take hold of the flapping fabric and assist the man, but often being forced back by his violent attempts to work his arms free of the sleeves.

I hadn't seen the good doctor for many months, well before

Desdemona had swept the household into a tizzy. A bell-shaped man with drooping shoulders and thin graying brown hair cut close to the scalp, his small, nimble hands twitched and jumped across his clothes as he attempted to straighten himself out. His dull brown eyes hid behind thick, brown glasses. Besides Solomon Davers, I knew no one else who had opted for the archaic method of correction, what with transplants being so convenient. Solomon found glasses aesthetically pleasing, but an unhappy few, like the doctor, were allergic to the nerve thread used in the surgery and condemned to a less than perfect existence behind cold glass lenses.

"So sorry I'm late." Merton stuttered over the esses, gaze flickering around the room. "Urgent call came in just as I was leaving. Couldn't be helped."

"Don't give it another thought, Doctor; we're all just pleased you could make it." My father swept his arm out over the table. "For those of you who haven't had the pleasure, this is Dr. Douglas Merton, a longtime associate of the Hale family and the best damn doctor on this side of the sphere."

Merton mumbled some sort of polite response and walked to his seat, avoiding the eyes now fixed upon him. He collapsed into his chair and began fiddling with his utensils.

"Minerva," my father waved a hand towards her, "you know Dr. Merton, don't you?"

"All too well." Minerva turned to face the man beside her, sipping her drink with a sly smile. "I've always felt it must be so awkward for doctors at parties. I mean, no one's ever really happy to see you, are they?"

My father laughed at his friend's expense. Merton's jaw tightened. "Should you really be drinking alcohol, Mrs. Davers? In your condition, I–"

"Of course, I shouldn't. That's the whole point." Minerva, whose first glass had disappeared with its usual speed, downed the puddle left of her second with a pointed raise of her brow. "You should have some, too; it'll brighten you up a bit."

"Thank you, but I'm fine with water." He picked up his glass and gulped down a mouthful, regaining some composure at last; a composure which vanished when he noticed Cadence sitting across from him, his eyes settling on her in a curious stare.

Cadence responded to this examination much as I had come to expect of her, staring right back at him, her face as blank as a dead computer screen.

Minerva tore off a piece of her roll and popped it into her mouth, glancing between the two with a growing smile. "Dr. Merton, this is Miss Cadence Turing, a friend of Chance's. She'll be staying with us for the weekend."

Cadence's lips twitched up in a reflexive smile, her head swinging up and down in a nod of greeting. Merton returned the gesture, cheeks reddening.

I cleared my throat and shouted down the table to my guest. "Dr. Merton tends to most of the people around here, Cadence. He's been my family's physician for years, practically an uncle to me."

"Oh, that's very kind of you to say, Mr. Hale." Merton took another long drink of water as his eyes moved around the table. With a tortured gurgle, he choked on the liquid, doubling over in a violent coughing fit. Knocking her own water glass to the floor, Desdemona surged to her feet with a squeal.

The room flew into action. Minerva pounded on Dr. Merton's back, failing to conceal her chortles, while the doctor pulled a handkerchief from his pocket and held it to his face, body shaking, eyes watering. Both Solomon and my father were quick to come to Desdemona's aid, the former more concerned with the water covering his feet, the latter standing and wrapping an arm around her quivering shoulders.

After a few moments of general confusion, everyone settled down, Dr. Merton even redder in the face than he had been before and Desdemona several shades paler, the slightest upset always throwing her weak constitution out of balance.

Minerva took a liberal drink, clearing her throat. "Of course, Chance has never been ill a day in his life, lucky devil."

I gave a stilted laugh, forcing a smile. "Yes, well. I suppose I have always been a picture of health."

"It's all that time spent outdoors when you were younger; made you strong, keeps you virile."

Henry groaned, covering his face with his hand, his mother's suggestive wink not escaping his attention. "Now, Mother—"

"Henry was the same way! Of course, he hasn't kept up with his physical activities the way you have, Chance."

Henry fixed his gaze on the ceiling as he shoveled soup into his mouth almost as if hoping to drown himself in the stuff. I looked around the room for a change of subject. Several topics were running through my mind, none of them appropriate for public discourse, when the dark silhouettes of trees in the night caught my attention.

"Do you remember, Henry, when we were younger, we used to pass messages through that willow tree by the green house?"

Henry's eyes widened and he put down his spoon, smiling. "Good god, I haven't thought about that in years. Yes, we used to climb up it and slip little discs into the knothole at the top, didn't we?"

"Wouldn't it have been simpler to verbally communicate?"

Henry grinned at Cadence. "Simpler, yes, but not very much fun."

"And it kept girls from snooping," said Victoria, dabbing the corners of her mouth with her napkin.

"Oh?" Cadence's brows jumped over her dark eyes. "You couldn't climb trees?"

"I might have ripped my dress." Victoria ran a hand down her front, sniffing. "I find that anything which makes one look less than fashionable is hardly worth doing."

I laughed into my glass. "Isn't that your family motto?"

"You know, it certainly should be."

Benign conversation flowed like warm honey as the meal's courses were brought forward and withdrawn in the graceful dance of fine dining. Even from a distance, Cadence's company delighted me to no end, her cool tones drawing my ear again and again. Though I longed to be beside her, to slide my hand over her thigh, to nudge at her slipper-clad foot with my own, I was, for once, aroused as much by her mind as I was by her body.

After a while, the conversations turned towards system events. My father considered himself an expert on every topic, including the war raging several worlds away.

"If we don't stay neutral on this mess the Charcornacians have created, this conflict will engulf the whole system, mark my words. Neutrality is the only sensible policy."

"But they attacked Whiston with no provocation!" Minerva pierced the air with her fork, almost taking off Dr. Merton's nose in her passion.

"Where was the threat?" Solomon ripped off a chunk of his dinner role and shook his head. "The animanecrons have been living on Whiston, peacefully, for almost two hundred years now. They've shown little interest in colonial conquest or any other aggressive means of expansion. In fact, they've shown little interest in other planets at all."

"Exactly." My father took up his glass of wine. "Kept to themselves, haven't they? Developing God knows what kinds of things; with theoretically infinite life spans imagine what they could accomplish. Charcornac being right next door, they have every reason to be wary of those fraggers' capabilities."

Merton winced at the slur, and I was about to make light of his discomfort when I saw the grimace twisting Cadence's sweet mouth into a disgusted frown.

"As their original creators," father continued, "Halcyon Enterprises can certainly speak to the fraggers' ingenuity and creative capacity, as well as their lack of inherent ethical or moral codes."

"Felix!" Solomon sat forward in his chair, propping his elbows up on the table. "You just said it yourself: who knows what kind of improvements the animanecrons have made to their systems on their own over the past two hundred years? I don't think we can rely on the antiquated data Halcyon possesses to accurately state what they are and are not capable of."

"The Charcornacians say that the animanecrons were trying to expand their trading routes onto human planets," said Victoria. "That more and more of them were leaving Whiston for other worlds."

"Whiston was never a prison, Victoria, it was a compromise." Henry mimicked his father's stance without even realizing it. "The IPC formed the agreement to send the animanecrons to that moon only after they received system-wide pressure to remove them from society. There were never any clauses which prohibited them from coming back if they wished."

"Just what we need," Victoria's lip curled up over her teeth in a sneer, "robots that look like people walking around. It's unnatural."

Henry stared wide-eyed at Victoria, nodding as he reached for his glass. "Oh yes, because so many things today are left in their natural state. What do you think, Chance?"

I shrugged, swallowing my mouthful of food. "Animanecrons don't bother me at all. I'd welcome them back with open arms if the Archerusian parliament would lift this ridiculous immigration ban." My father's face darkened. He'd spent a significant amount of his personal capital lobbying for the ban to pass. I grinned, licking my lips. "Why should we care if a few refugees cross the border? This planet could use all the new blood it can get; or oil, as the case may be."

"I have heard rumors that the Charcornacians are systematically destroying the animanecrons in some places." Belinda leaned back to allow her plate to be taken away. "Shouldn't that alone be cause for censure?"

"You're talking about animanecrons as if they're people, Belinda." My father's voice bubbled on the edge of laughter. "Animanecrons were made to mimic humans; to provide companionship and labor, as machines have done for centuries. But they were never designed to be, nor could they ever be, people; conscious entities with the same level of thoughts and feelings as us. It's impossible."

"If the Charcornacians are really taking steps to control the population size, they are doing little more than recycling outdated machinery," added Merton. "Creating scrap metal, as it were."

Victoria turned to the woman beside her. "What about you, Ms. Turing? Paraesepe is closer to that side of the system after all."

It occurred to me then, as it had before and would again, that Victoria was more dangerous than I gave her credit. She had an unusual knack for creating conflicts, and judging by the slow, deliberate way in which Cadence put down her fork, she had done it again.

"I don't pretend to understand very much about politics," Cadence spoke in a hushed, clear voice, her dark eyes fixed on her plate. "It's a field of mental reasoning that has always puzzled me exceedingly. But..."

The 'but' hung in the air. Each member of the dinner party leaned forward as if preparing to catch the dangling conjunction should it fall.

"...but I fail to understand how refusing to intercede in one life form's attempts to wipe out another can be considered a sound humanistic decision, let alone a sound political one."

The room quieted; utensils stilled in midair, and people stopped shifting in their seats. My father was one of those people. His eyes narrowed. He cleared his throat before placing his fork against the side of his plate. I recognized his pointed movement as a warning but doubted that Cadence would prove as perceptive.

"But you see, my dear," my father stroked his beard, staring Cadence straight in the face, "you, like many others, fail to understand the very nature of animanecrons. They are not life forms; they're machines. Advanced machines to be sure, but machines nonetheless; they're not alive in any sense."

Cadence kept her gaze steady, blinking little and moving even less. "If you define life forms as things that process thought, sensation, and interpret data from within and without themselves, and then act on such inputs in meaningful patterns, then all complex machines could be considered life forms."

Minerva coughed, the sound manufactured and hollow. Her gaze flicked between Cadence and my father, as if panicked, but the quivering around the edges of her mouth told me that she hoped her attempt to alert Cadence to her folly would fail. My father sipped his wine, shoulders tensing even as he jutted them upward, shaking his head.

Cadence plowed onward. "Given that assumption, an entity who has displayed high-level problem-solving skills, logic chains in decision making, independent and inventive responses to stimuli, etcetera...Well, you might say that they are a life form comparable in intelligence to human beings; yes?"

All eyes turned to my father, who sighed and leaned forward, his hands gripping both sides of the table. "What you are so stubbornly refusing to grasp, Miss Turing, is that machines do not think. They are incapable of thought, and certainly incapable of consciousness." His knuckles tightened to white, volume rising with every exclamation. "They are programmed! Every response is pure mimicry! They have absolutely no mind whatsoever!"

"One could say the same thing about you, sir."

I held onto the edge of the table to keep myself from leaping to my feet and kissing her. Everyone else in the room drew in a sharp breath, including my father, who blew himself up to the size of a large, angry balloon.

A chuckle shattered the tension like a rock against a windowpane. We all turned as one body to see Solomon laughing again and louder, clapping his hands, a smile writhing on his lips like a rasher of bacon in a pan. "No, no, she's exactly right! I see what you mean, Miss Turing. It's all a matter of semantics, isn't it? It all depends on your definition of intelligence and 'personhood'."

"I suppose I just find it troubling that any civilized society would stand by on a technicality of birth and allow an entire world to be slaughtered for no reason." Cadence shrugged, relaxing back into her chair with a shake of her head. "But, as I said, I understand very little of politics."

"It would seem you understand a great deal about philosophy, however." Henry's eyes brimmed with admiration.

"A subject as useful to real life as winter wear in the summer."

"You're too much of a scientist, Felix. Just like Solomon." Minerva smiled at her husband, tucking a strand of white-blonde hair behind her ear. "Nothing's worth anything until you can find a practical application for it."

My father neither confirmed nor denied this statement, but let it lie as it fell, ending the whole awkward conversation with alarming grace. Under normal circumstances he would have never walked away from an argument he thought he could win, his retreat adding to the mounting pile of evidence that something unusual was indeed afoot.

Large slices of chocolate gateau and brimming cups of coffee made their way around the table, displeasure rolling off my father like fog, but silence holding sway. He waited until we were all on the verge of plunging into our deserts before tapping his fork against his wine glass and rising to his feet.

"Sorry to interrupt everyone, but I wanted to say a few words. First, thank you all very much for coming tonight. It's always such a pleasure to have my–" The muscles in his jaw rippled, his gaze boring into the top of Cadence's head, "– my family and friends under one roof. I've known most of you all my life. You've helped me through my toughest times, shared my triumphs, and I care for you very deeply. I wanted you all to be the first to hear this important news."

He looked down at Desdemona and offered her his hand. She took it and stood, stepping in beside him as he continued to speak, a violent blush rushing over her face and neck. "The past few months have been some of the happiest of my life; ever since I met Desdemona. I can't bear to think of my life without her and I can't think of a single reason why I should have to face such a future." He extended his arm with a flourish. "Desdemona and I are engaged! We're getting married at the end of the month and, of course, all of you are invited!"

The gentle hum of the incinerator in the kitchen next door was as loud as an AN-GRAV in the dead silence. I groped for the edge of the table and looked over to Henry who was doing the same, his mouth hanging open. Solomon clutched at his glass and Minerva held a steadying hand to her chest. Belinda and Dr.

Merton, in a rare moment of camaraderie, shared a disbelieving stare from the corners of their eyes, and Victoria looked, as she often did when she was jealous, thoroughly disgusted.

My father's face began to harden. I choked on air, struggling to think of something, anything to say before it was too late. A sound like thunder made me jump, and I swiveled round to see Cadence smiling, applauding with vigor.

The rest of the group tried to follow her example, one after the other stuttering out breathless congratulations. I could bring myself to do neither. My father's words had nailed me to my seat. I tried to take in a deep breath. Henry's hand closed around my own, anchoring me and allowing me time to gather up a mirthless smile.

My father's manservant glided into the dining room, oblivious to the stormy seas into which he was sailing, a large case in his outstretched hands.

"Ah, there it is!" My father took the case from him with a wave. "Thank you, Bernard. After all, it would hardly be a wedding announcement without a betrothal necklace, would it?"

He beamed and flicked open the case. A collective gasp pierced the air. Nestled against the dark velvet sat a multi-tiered necklace, the base and chain made from white gold and silver, with fistfuls of sapphires and blue diamonds dripping down from it like frozen rain. My father held the necklace up to the light, the gems' facets refracting and amplifying every ray to its point of utmost perfection. He laid the necklace over Desdemona's collarbone and kissed her cheek.

"That's the Negrescu Necklace!"

I turned to stare up at Henry, who had jumped to his feet as if his chair was on fire. Leave it to him to get excited over history at a time like this.

"I heard it's cursed, you know," Victoria slid one arm over the back of her chair, twisting to get a better look at the piece. "That everyone who's owned it has died horribly or something."

Desdemona crumpled back against my father's chest, biting her lip. "Oh dear! Felix—"

"Now, now, my love, that's just superstitious nonsense."

"Unfortunately," I hissed through clenched teeth.

Henry moved to my father's elbow, eyes never leaving the necklace wrapped around Desdemona's throat. "Sir, shouldn't that be in a museum? The Negrescu Necklace is over four hundred years old! All the great families of the Archerusian System have laid claim to it! It's traveled to most of the spheres between here and the Sunflower Nebula. The hands this has passed through; surely, you don't intend to let it sit in someone's jewelry box? It belongs to the world!"

"Did the world pay for it? No, I did." My father chortled, stroking his beard. "And it will stay with me and not the world until I die or sell it, whichever happens first."

"It's the most beautiful thing anyone's ever given me, Felix." Desdemona stood on tiptoe, throwing her arms around his neck. "Thank you!"

My father kissed her, all pretense of propriety vanishing. I pushed myself back from the table, appetite gone and what I had managed to eat threatening to return.

Solomon stood and shook my father's hand, smiling. "Congratulations, Felix. I hope you'll both be very happy."

"Yes." Belinda leaned forward, her voice breathy. "Indeed, all the best!" She took one bite of her dessert and then, dabbing the edges of her mouth with a napkin, began to rise from the table.

"Belinda?" My father started towards her, his brows drawn up to a point. "Where are you going?"

She clasped her hands together and sighed. "I just thought of the perfect way for us to celebrate this wonderful night. I'm going to make a batch of my special cider!"

Victoria rolled her eyes, hunching down over her plate. "Oh, wonderful."

"Fantastic idea, Belinda," said Minerva, smiling. "If you're sure it isn't too much trouble?"

"No, not at all! I'll just pop out to the kitchen. You all finish your dessert and I'll have it done before you know it."

6

Chapter 6

Bereft of the maternal comfort Belinda's presence always provided, I slid farther down into my chair, mute and sullen. The announcement had quieted the others as well and save for the odd, forced comment we remained silent, lost in whatever thoughts this sudden change had compelled us to contemplate.

In time chocolate cake lay decimated on plates, the last puddles of coffee were growing cold, and we all elected to retire to the sitting room, where more refreshments and other amusements awaited us. I was surprised that Belinda had not yet returned, and I mused aloud that with any luck the kitchen had lacked the ingredients required to concoct her brew. Henry laughed and wrapped an arm around my shoulders as we stood from the table, following the others who were chattering amongst themselves as they headed out into the hall.

My father led the way with Desdemona at his side, who struggled to keep pace with his elephantine stride. He glanced down at her, the edges of a frown peeking out from under his beard. "Dearest, why don't you put that away for now?"

"My necklace?" Desdemona's free hand fluttered over the dripping piece of decadence around her throat. "Oh, but Felix, can't I wear it for a little longer? It's so beautiful and it means so much to me. I don't think I ever want to take it off!"

"Something like that should be worn only on special occasions, Desdemona. It will cease to impress anyone if you wear it like common jewelry." Father unwound her arm from his and nudged her in the direction of the dark room across the hall. "The case is in my study. Just put it back on the shelf behind my desk."

"Oh; of course, Felix." Desdemona shuffled away, her smile crumbling under the weight of her downcast eyes. "I'll be back in a moment."

As Desdemona peeled away from the group to discard her gift as instructed, the rest of us continued across the entryway and into the sitting room, spreading around the various couches and tables like melting butter over a pan.

I hovered just inside the doorway, chewing on the inside of my mouth and watching as Solomon and my father called up some blueprints on the screen embedded into the far wall. Cutting across the room towards them with a sudden lurch, I avoided a frowning Victoria, who doubtless wished to discuss why a betrothal necklace was not currently sitting around her neck. I had to dig deep to find the resolve to carry through with my plan, but for once my distress outweighed my fear of my father.

I strode up behind him. "Can I talk to you?"

My father jumped, looking between Solomon and me with a frown. "What - now?"

"If you could spare a moment, yes."

My father's jaw tightened. I thought he would refuse, but he cleared his throat and turned back to Solomon, nodding. "Excuse me, won't you?"

Solomon gave a small smile in answer and sipped at his port.

I spun on my heel, arms stiff at my sides. The slap of my father's heavy footfalls followed me out into the hall, pausing only to shut the door behind us. The darkness that seeped through the tall windows highlighted the surgical brightness of the electric lights high over our heads.

I faced him with a sour grimace. "You can't be serious about going through with this lunacy."

My father drew himself up. "You best mind your tone, Chance; that lunacy you're referring to is my marriage."

"To Desdemona Eydis? A glorified typist?" I stepped back, pushing my hands through my hair. "You don't know anything about her, Dad; you've been with her for three months!"

"This might be too much for someone who treats their bed like a train station to understand," his chest puffed out as he looked down his nose at me, "but I happen to be in love with Desdemona."

"Oh, so you're in love with her now?" I spat the word back at him. "You're the one who always criticizes me for being too emotional, but now you're in love?"

"I," he beat his fist against his chest, closing the distance between us with a step, "am sensible enough to understand the consequences of my actions. Unlike you," his finger dug into my shoulder, "who, despite my best efforts, is still a weak-minded fool! Letting that insufferable woman con her way into our house–!"

"This is not about Cadence, Dad," I knocked his hand away. "I felt sorry for her. It's called compassion, not that you'd know what that is, seeing how it doesn't fit into a business model or a flowchart."

He sputtered, anger flaming into rage, but I pushed on, my hands wheeling through the air. "Desdemona Eydis is younger than your own son! You don't think that's going to make you a laughingstock from here to the Quincy Moons? She doesn't want you, Dad; she just wants your damn money!"

"And how exactly are you any different?"

His words cut through me like an axe through rotten wood and I stood, split in twain, shaking, closer to tears than I'd been in years.

"All you do is take, Chance." My father paced across the smooth hardwood floors, oblivious to the blow he'd struck, hands behind his back. "Take what you want and then think you can live your life any way you see fit! You've never tried to be the son I needed, to be an heir to this company–!"

"I tried for years, Dad." Ashamed by the tremor in my voice, I avoided his eyes, pressing my lips together. "Maybe I just got tired of never being good enough for you."

"You gave up!" He took a few more slow steps before coming to a stop, disappearing into the shadow of one of the tall trees which lined the outside of the house. "Real Hales don't give up. They fight." He stepped back into the light, stroking his beard.

"Desdemona – she's a fighter. She has more guts in her little finger than you have in your whole body. You know, I have a good mind to give it to her."

My face screwed up in confusion. "What?"

"My money." He stared me down, lips twisting into something like a smile. "Yes. How would you like that, hm? Cut off without a cent? Cut off from your inheritance? After all, Desdemona's been more family to me than you've ever been."

I squeezed the bridge of my nose, trying to ignore his thoughtless words, trying to will the tears back behind my eyes. "Desdemona will not replace your family, father. She can't replace me, and she can't replace–"

My father stared at me, brows drawn up to a point over his red face. I stepped towards him with an outstretched hand. "I understand that you're lonely. I know that there hasn't been anyone since mum, but surely–"

"Don't you dare bring your mother into this!"

I jerked back, one arm coming up in an instinctive posture of defense, but not quick enough to stop the back of his hand from cracking against my cheek, sending me stumbling.

"I do not have to justify my decisions to you, Chance Tobias Hale!" He grabbed my lapels and drew me up onto the tips of my toes, shaking me as he shouted in his tortured, ear-splitting growl. "Everything in this house, every luxury you enjoy; your very existence continues because I allow it! Never forget that!"

A moment of silence passed between us, our eyes locked. Blood pooled in the bottom of my mouth, but I didn't dare spit it out in front of him. I thought I would choke on it.

He dropped me and walked back to the sitting room with

measured steps. I waited until I heard the door open before swallowing, prodding the cut in my mouth with the tip of my tongue and struggling to process what had just happened.

"Chance?"

I jumped and spun around. Aunt Be stood at the far end of the hall, poised outside the sitting room door, a tray of drinks in her hands.

"Is everything alright, my dear?"

I opened my mouth, half-formed words heavy on my tongue like bricks waiting to shatter windows. Prepared to unload all my troubles on her, the concern in her eyes made my heart ache with affection and I resisted, licking my lips and shaking my head. "Everything's fine, Aunt Be; just fine."

"Well, alright then. You better come along." She gestured to the sitting room with the tray. "You know this cider always tastes best when it's hot!"

The prospect of Belinda's cider was the final drop of rain in a thunderstorm that soaked me to the bone. I straightened, tugging the bottom of my jacket as I shuffled back to follow her inside. Belinda had almost completed her rounds when I entered, offering Victoria a cup that she refused with firmness. A quick glance around the room told me that, as usual, no one had partaken of the vile mixture except my father, who sat beside Solomon in deep conversation on the sofa closest to the fireplace.

Belinda took the mass rejection in stride, depositing the drink tray on a side table and hurrying over to the card game that had just been started by Dr. Merton. Merton leaned over to help Minerva read the small print on her cards while Desdemona stared at her own hand with a miserable frown, at a loss for what to play next.

I walked to the side table and took hold of a cup of thick, black coffee. Henry leaned against the bookshelf beside the table, sipping a small glass of water, watching me closely. I threw a mouthful of the stuff back into my throat and managed to swallow with a garbled expletive as the hot drink burnt the top of my mouth and stung at the fresh cut in my cheek.

Henry blinked at me and shifted to stand closer to me. "You alright, Chance? You look like hell."

My head fell between my shoulders, my cheek still tingling where father had struck me. "My father is an imbecile."

Henry's glass clinked down onto the table behind us. His fingertips were cool against my bruising skin. "Did he—?"

I jerked away from him. "Just leave off, will you? You'll make it worse."

Henry's entire frame stiffened. His lips firmed into a straight line, and he drew away, collecting his drink with slow, measured movements.

I took a deep breath, pinching the bridge of my nose. "Sorry."

He shrugged. Neither of us spoke, waiting for the tension to clear.

Always the cooler head, Henry was first to make the effort, sipping his drink and rolling his shoulders back. "Felix couldn't be persuaded to sell the Negrescu to me, could he?"

"My father," I glared daggers into the man's back as I fumbled a nix out of my case, "can't be persuaded of anything, even if it's for his own good."

Henry turned his gaze heavenward. "I should just leave you alone, shouldn't I?"

I rolled my eyes, clapping him on the shoulder and shaking my head. Glib assurances were on the tip of my tongue when Cadence charged into view, coming to an abrupt halt inches from my face, brow furrowed. "Are you and Victoria going to get married very soon or is it to be later? No one can seem to decide."

After a few moments of shocked silence, Henry did me the kindness of nudging me in the back, jolting me into action. I rattled my head from side to side, various syllables stuttering off my tongue, before I could manage, "I beg your pardon?"

"Everyone's been saying that you're going to marry her, and I was just wondering when that would be." Cadence clasped her hands in front of her, fingers tapping a strange rhythm to which she swayed. "I notice she doesn't have a betrothal necklace yet, which would confirm my hypothesis that it is to be sometime in the future, despite the phrase 'practically engaged' being in frequent use amongst my conversational partners this evening."

"Oh, for the love of–!" I was in the middle of tossing up my hands when I remembered one of them was still clutching a cup and the other an unlit nix. I twisted around and slammed both down on the table behind me. "People have absolutely no right to gossip about my personal life! What the hell do they know about it anyway?"

I realized a second too late that my response had been a tad more violent than was called for. Henry and Cadence were staring at me, the former with his glass frozen at his lips, the latter blinking at me as if trying to clear her vision, a smile smeared across her face.

Henry closed his mouth with an audible pop and turned on his heel, pointing towards a bookshelf on the opposite side of the room. "Excuse me, I think I'll just..." he trailed off, striding away as quickly as he could.

Cadence was silent a moment longer before leaning in, hand pressed against her collarbone. "I assumed that everyone knew very little about it. That's why I asked you. But you also don't seem to know anything about it. Should I go ask Victoria? Do you think she will be able to provide me with the relevant information?"

She straightened, located Victoria, and started towards her.

"No, no!" I latched onto her arm with embarrassing speed.

Cadence pulled me with her for a step before she stopped, nose wrinkling.

I cleared my throat, sliding my hand down to her elbow and pulling her against me, lifting my free arm up around her shoulders. "Victoria and I have a certain..." My lips drew down into an exaggerated frown as I bobbled my head from side to side. "...unspoken understanding that at some point in the future we will more than likely end up being at the very least legally married; yes."

Even through our clothes, the heat radiating off Cadence's body warmed me, the sensation more comforting than I had expected. Cadence seemed unfazed by the intimate position I held her in, her head falling back as she gazed up at me. "Fascinating. I would never have thought romantic coupling was such a complicated undertaking in this society."

I wrinkled my nose back at her. "Oh, well, we can't all be as advanced as Paraesepe, now can we?"

She winced, turning away from me. I stepped back, taking her by the shoulders and angling her body back to me. "Why do you want to know? About Victoria and me, I mean?"

"Are you alright?"

The panic in Solomon's voice made me snap around to stare at the two men on the sofa. My father clutched at his stomach, his breath coming out in long, pained wheezes as Solomon's arm curled around his hunched shoulders. He tried to prop himself up, but only managed to lift his head. Sweat ran down his face, his eyes unfocused as he shook his head.

"No, I...I don't think I am..." He squeezed his gut and his entire body convulsed as he slid to the floor.

Everyone leapt to their feet. Solomon vacated his position to allow Dr. Merton to examine my father. We clustered around the man's wracked form, the ladies with their hands at their mouths, the men with their hands at the ready.

Merton checked my father's pulse before prying open his eyelids, his frown deepening. "I need to get him upstairs." He surged to his feet and slung my father's arm over his shoulders, hitching a hand around his hip. "Mr. Hale, come and help me. Mr. Davers, please go ahead and get the door open for us."

Solomon ran out of the room, and I rushed forward to help my father, who was moaning and gasping in pure agony.

"I'll get some fresh water." Minerva strode towards the door. "Desdemona, why don't you help me with some towels?"

"Here, I'll get them," said Henry, jogging past the stunned woman before she could protest.

With the rest of the party trailing behind, Dr. Merton and I struggled up the stairs, swaying like saplings in a storm as we tried to balance against my father's convulsions, his feet twitching uselessly against the carpet.

Depositing him on the bed, the doctor motioned for me to leave. I was about to close the door behind me when Henry and Minerva bustled through, their arms full of towels, bowls of hot and cold water, and the Doctor's medical bag. Then they too were expelled from the room, leaving all of us waiting outside.

The sounds of retching and cursing were audible even out in the hall. It seemed like an eternity before they subsided. Desdemona, pale and shaken, leaned against Minerva, her bottom lip quivering. After what seemed like hours, Merton reappeared, pulling the door shut behind him.

"Is everything alright, Doctor?"

He jumped at the sound of my voice, taking in the sight of so many worried eyes glued on him.

"Yes, yes," He gave a tight smile while adjusting his glasses and clearing his throat. "He's quite alright now. Stomach flu, wouldn't you know; it's been going around the last few weeks."

"He didn't seem sick earlier!" Victoria clutched at her throat and took a large step back.

"This is more of a twenty-four-hour flu, Miss Gad; comes on very sudden like this. But most of the symptoms should be gone by tomorrow. He'll be weak for a few days though; need someone to help him around the house–"

"That's for me to do," said Desdemona in a hushed voice, standing up on her own at last.

Dr. Merton stared at her for a moment before nodding. "Well, the best thing I can suggest for everyone is a good night's sleep. It's very late."

A strange ending to a strange day, our little troupe drifted away to their rooms. The doctor assured me that if I were to hear anything alarming from the adjoining room, I was free to alert him at any time of the night; an offer I found comforting, despite its pointlessness. I slept like the dead, and the walls were too thick for me to hear anything from my father's rooms anyway.

I turned to walk to my mother's rooms and almost tumbled over Cadence, who'd been standing a hairsbreadth behind me. She put her hand on my shoulder. "Are you alright?"

The touch of her hand made me shiver and, for the first time since my father's announcement, I found myself relaxing. "Yes, Cay, I'm fine." I let out a deep breath, gliding my fingers over the back of her hand before squeezing it tight. "Illness just...unsettles me."

"Me too." Cadence frowned. "I'm not very used to it yet."

Her gaze fell to the floor, but her expression did not dim. I was about to pull away when she yanked our entwined hands towards herself, wrapping her other hand around my own.

"Thank you again for letting me stay the night, Chance." Cadence rested our hands against her collarbone and met my eyes, her fingers tapping against my skin. "I feel I've put you out somehow."

"You haven't, I promise. You've turned a dull weekend with family into something altogether more stimulating." I managed a shaky smile and stepped closer to her, gesturing to the house around us with my free hand. "As far as I'm concerned this place is yours for as many nights as you might need it."

Cadence's smile bloomed into an open-mouthed expression

of joy. "Chance! Thank you, I..." She sighed, shoulders rising and falling. "Thank you so much."

We stared at each other for the next few moments, the old wood of the landing creaking under our feet. Her grateful gaze was hypnotic, and I found myself wishing she would look at me like that forever.

I cleared my throat, watching her from under my brows. "Do you need me to come and tuck you in?"

"Goodnight, Chance." She fled down the corridor to my rooms before I had the chance to be offended, waving back at me. "Sleep well!"

I shook my head with a rueful grin, rubbing my chin. Entering my mother's rooms, I discarded my evening clothes without care, tossing them over the backs of chairs, across the end of the bed, and over the dressing table, obscuring the optrics that still sat there after all these years. I sent a prayer up to whoever might be listening that tomorrow would bring fewer troubling events and tumbled into bed, too exhausted to be upset by my surroundings.

7

Chapter 7

I didn't see my father again until he hobbled into the dining room the next morning. Most of the household had finished breakfasting, merely lingering over puddles of coffee and crusts of toast when he and Desdemona graced us with their presence.

Hovering around the man like a hummingbird around a bowl of sugar water, Desdemona helped my father into his seat, taking an old cane from his hand and propping it against the table before moving to fix him a plate out of what was left of the morning's fare.

"How are you feeling, Mr. Hale?" Victoria slathered her last sliver of toast with jam, voice sticky with sincerity.

"Much better today, thank you, my dear."

Desdemona flitted back to the table, taking the seat across from my fiancé-to-be when Victoria flapped her hands at her in excitement. "Oh, Desdemona, dear! I was wondering if I could have another look at that divine necklace of yours. I have got to get one made for myself."

"Certainly; I'll go fetch it." Desdemona paused by my father's chair, hand on his shoulder. "Felix, do you need anything else?"

He shook his head, brow furrowed with the concentration of chewing. Desdemona kissed the top of his head and glided out of the room.

"Miss Turing is sleeping late this morning," said Henry. It was an innocent quip, but the way his brows arched assured me it was anything but.

I glared at him over the rim of my coffee cup. "She's probably exhausted from all the excitement last night."

Henry leaned back in his chair, grin spreading across his face like wildfire. "I was thinking it must be something like that."

I dropped my cup into its saucer with a clatter, glancing at my father and Victoria at the far end of the table, the latter's face growing darker with each passing second. "I meant that going to a party after spending all day traveling must have tired her." I leaned in, stressing every word. "It's only natural that she'd need some uninterrupted rest."

Victoria hummed, her eyes narrowed. "I'm sure you're right, darling."

Desdemona's return saved me from having to deliver an ego-stroking response, distracting Victoria with the prospect of viewing the Negrescu up close. Victoria took the black case with a grin and Desdemona sat down at last, looking over the slim pickings of sustenance that remained.

Passing my napkin over my mouth, I was about to rise and

finish dressing for the day when Victoria's annoyed scoff drew my attention.

"Well, where is it?"

On the table in front of her sat the open, empty case.

Desdemona's silverware clattered against her plate. She snatched the case into the air with a shriek. "It's gone!" Her fingers skittered over the indented velvet. "It's gone!"

"That's impossible," said Henry, standing to get a better look.

"I put it there last night, I swear! It's been stolen!"

"I'm telling you, it couldn't have been!"

Victoria rested her hands on her hips, glaring at Henry. "Well, it didn't grow legs and walk off, did it?"

My father rose to his feet with a roar. "Absolutely damnable!" He wiggled his way out from behind the table and limped towards the door.

Solomon stood and started to follow him. "Felix, what are you doing?"

"Calling the Enforcement Office, damn it all!" My father waved his cane in the air. "Before the sneak thief can get any more distance on us!"

My father missed careening into Cadence by sheer luck, wheeling past her through the door on one leg. She staggered back to avoid the collision and waited a moment before sticking her head around the door and walking to me, a question in her inky eyes. "Has something happened?"

I shook my head, wanting to laugh but not sure why. "We've been robbed! The Negrescu Necklace's been stolen!"

Cadence's jaw dropped and she leaned towards me, grabbing my arm. "Are you sure?"

"Father's gone to call the EO now."

Her nails dug into me. "Enforcement Officers? Here?"

The fear in Cadence's voice made the hair on the back of my neck bristle. I grabbed her hand and pulled it from my aching appendage.

My father shambled back into the room, glaring at Cadence as he said, "Officers will be here in a half an hour. I demanded that a senior detective take the case."

Victoria tossed her hands into the air. "What are we supposed to do until then?"

"We better get dressed, that's what." Minerva rose from her chair, a delighted smile turning up the corners of her mouth. "Shall we gather in the study to receive the gentlemen of the law? That makes the right impression, don't you think?"

We rushed to our rooms, throwing on whatever clothes we thought appropriate for a burglary investigation. Gathering in the study, as Minerva had suggested, we waited in strained silence for the EO to arrive. I wanted to ask Cadence if she was alright, but it was clear from the way she was standing, straight as a rod, her arms crossed tight and high over her chest, that she was not. Victoria's presence behind the footstool on which I was perched also dissuaded me from making such an obvious gesture of concern.

The front bell rang out like a gunshot. The sound of shuffling bodies in the entryway reached us, and we were all straining to hear more when the door to the study flew open and a man strode in.

He flashed a broad smile as he passed and chirped a cheery "Good morning!" to us all. Sitting down at the desk in the front of the room, he began rummaging through the pockets of his second-hand suit, bright green eyes peering down at himself with a frustration his smile did not suggest. His calloused hands emerged from his coat pocket with a thick black pad, which he unfolded over the top of the desk as he spoke.

"I am Inspector Oliver Brisbois of the Arrhidaean Enforcement Office, Twenty-Seventh Northern District, Elite Crime Division, and I have been placed in charge of this investigation. Mr. Felix Hale?"

"That would be me, Inspector." My father grasped Desdemona's hand as he shifted in his chair, directly in front of the desk. "And this is Desdemona Eydis, my fiancé, to whom I gave the necklace."

"Delighted to meet you." Brisbois nodded, tapping twice on the now thin sheet in front of him, his flat screen blinking into life. He turned to me, his broad grin shrinking to a threadbare smile. "I've already had the pleasure of making your son's acquaintance."

I opened my mouth to correct him when his smile tugged at my memory.

"Last month, as a matter of fact," he continued. "Outside the Unatarian Theater."

Henry coughed. The incident came back to me in a flash: Henry picking me up on a warm night, sitting outside the theater with my rambunctious female companions; our commentary on the show, during the show, had not been appreciated.

"Oh." I forced a laugh. "Yes. I think I remember."

"Do you? Surprising, considering how inebriated you were at the time." He returned my laugh with a rough chuckle of his own, turning his attention back to his screen. "You threw a bottle at me; really, a most amusing encounter."

My father's shoulders stiffened. "I must apologize for my son's behavior, sir—"

"I suspect you often do." Brisbois shook himself, stylus hovering over his pad. "Now, Mr. Hale, I understand you were having some kind of party last night?"

"Yes. Close friends and family only, of course."

"Except me," Cadence waved from her place in the corner, "who is neither."

Brisbois looked up at my dove. His raised brows fell in harmony with his gaze, as he looked her over. He stopped at her ankles; folding his hands across his screen while his lips quirked into an amused smile. "And you are, miss?"

"Cadence Turing." She indicated me with a flutter of her hand. "Chance invited me to stay here last night."

"Really? Do go on."

Cadence swallowed. Without warning she leaned down and slipped her hand into my breast pocket, a sudden display of intimacy that drew all eyes to us, including Brisbois' and my fiancé-to-be's, whose nails dug into my shoulder.

"I've just arrived from Paraesepe; looking for work, a brighter future..." Cadence removed my nix case and helped herself to one, tossing the case back into my lap without so much as a nod. "He and I met on the train."

Brisbois rubbed his lips, eyes boring into me like screws. "And he just invited you home, did he?"

She tore off the end of the nix, rolling the tattered stub between her fingers. "We began talking and it became clear I didn't know where I was going to spend the night or when I'd be able to find work." She batted smoke away from her face, grimacing. "Chance was kind enough to offer me his hospitality. Will you need to see my ident papers, Inspector Brisbois?"

Brisbois watched her for a moment and then, with great care, leaned back in his chair. "Not now, no."

He was smiling. Smiling at what was beyond me, but at whom was clear; I began to dislike the man at once. My heart lurched when Cadence returned his sly grin with a full-toothed beam of her own. "Thank you."

Brisbois tore his gaze away from her at length, flexing his shoulders. "Right. Well, that seems clear enough. Mr. Hale, where was the necklace kept?"

My father inclined his head. "On the shelf, just behind you."

Brisbois' stylus flew across the screen. "I assume that you have a standard security system for a house this size; genetic locks on the doors and windows, perimeter sensors, automatic EO call-out, etcetera?"

"I'd be a fool not to."

"Did anyone else know that the necklace was in the house before last night?"

"The gentleman who sold it to me I suppose." My father sunk down in his seat, scowling. "But other than that, no."

"When did you go to bed last night?"

My father huffed, tugging at his moustache as he grumbled, "Sometime around 13 o'clock. I was ill, a sudden bout of stomach flu, put me quite out of sorts."

"And the rest of you?"

We shared bemused glances. Solomon was the first to speak. "I think we all turned in around the same time. 14, half past?"

The inspector nodded, typing away. "When did you all wake up this morning?"

Minerva rolled her eyes. "Most of us were down by 8 o'clock. Cadence, Felix, and Miss Eydis arrived sometime after; I'm not sure when."

"And did you all come down together?"

"Listen here, Brisbois, I'm sure you know your job best, but–"

"I do." Brisbois flicked a speck of lint off his sleeve, olive eyes half-lidded. "But I suspect you're about to suggest otherwise, Mr. Hale?"

My father stood, Desdemona's hand on his arm the only thing keeping him from reaching across the desk and putting his fist in the man's face. "I am suggesting, sir, that this thief, whoever he is, is probably on an off-world freighter by now with my property, while you sit there asking asinine questions about our timetables!"

To my right there was a soft clicking sound. I looked up at Cadence, who did not, at first, appear to be any more interested in the proceedings than she had been before. She stood staring out the tempered glass windows, the slightest grimace of concentration twisting her upper lip away from her teeth.

I doubted that anyone else had heard the muted sound of her tongue popping away from the roof of her mouth, but Brisbois' eyes flickered up at the sound and found its source with ease. He smiled. "You disagree, Miss Turing?"

Cadence turned away from the window, face clearing as her eyes met his. "Yes, I do."

"With which part of Mr. Hale's statement specifically?" Brisbois' smile grew wider. "If, of course, you don't object to such an asinine question."

Oblivious to the power play taking place between the two authority figures in the room, Cadence pushed herself away from the wall, arms falling to her sides. "It's impossible for the thief to be catching an off-world shuttle." She glanced around the room, her speech slowing. "Well, since they never left the house."

Belinda gasped. "Do you mean to suggest that the ruffian has hidden himself somewhere on the premises?"

"That's pretty unlikely, isn't it, Miss Turing?" asked Henry. "Where could he be hiding?"

"I think you've mistaken her meaning, Henry." Minerva paled, but there remained a sparkle in her eye.

Cadence looked around the sea of curious faces and shrugged. "Obviously, one of us must have taken the necklace."

The uproar was immediate and loud. My father objected in the strongest terms to the indignity of the suggestion, while Desdemona tugged on his sleeve, begging him to think of his health. Victoria derided the whole idea with sneers and scoffs, while Henry expressed his concern for everyone's safety, even though his mother seemed quite happy about the prospect of having a thief in the group. Solomon and Dr. Merton tried, in vain, to calm everyone down.

I stayed silent, staring at Cadence, who in turn said nothing and stared at the inspector, who stared back, smiling.

My father, face swollen and red, gripped the head of his cane with such force that his knuckles went white. "How dare you suggest that one of us is a thief, you ungrateful creature? How dare you, madam!"

"I dare," Cadence smoothed out her wrinkled white pants, "because it is the truth."

"She's quite right, I'm afraid."

My father rounded on the inspector with a growl. Brisbois leaned back in his chair, adopting an expression of sincere regret, but holding a quirk in his brows that hinted at something far less remorseful. "It would seem to be the only logical conclusion, sir. Your security is some of the best on Arrhidaeus. From what we can tell, it hasn't been tampered with. That means that either someone here conspired with an outside thief and let him or her in, or, much more likely, one of you took the necklace for yourselves."

"Once you have eliminated the impossible, whatever remains, however improbable, must be the truth." Cadence narrowed her eyes and tapped a finger against her temple. "It's all about using the little grey cells."

"Indeed." Inspector Brisbois twirled his stylus between his fingers, moving it over and under each digit with practiced ease. "Did you steal the necklace, Miss Turing?"

Cadence leaned back against the window. If Brisbois' smile had been disconcerting, Cadence's was a complete bafflement. "No, sir, I did not. I don't care much for jewelry."

"I wasn't suggesting that you'd steal the Negrescu Necklace to wear, Miss Turing."

"You were suggesting that as a penniless immigrant from Paraesepe I need money and the necklace would sell for a considerable sum on any black market in the system." She shrugged.

"I understand. But I didn't steal it. Still, I am the most likely suspect, so please feel free to search my room first."

Victoria's nose wrinkled. "First?"

Cadence slid further down the windowsill and leaned forward, her body forming a sharp 'L' as she supported herself on the balls of her feet. "Inspector Brisbois will need to search the entire manor for the necklace; including our rooms."

My father broke his uncharacteristic silence to bluster. "That is completely unacceptable!"

"I understand, sir. Unfortunately, crime is never acceptable, dignified, or respectful and as such, I can rarely be so." Brisbois turned his attention back to Cadence, nodding. "Thank you for volunteering, Miss Turing."

"Anything to help, Inspector." Cadence drew her hand down her throat, looking much more relaxed than she had a few minutes ago.

"If you all wouldn't mind waiting outside, I should have an additional squadron of men here within the next few minutes." Inspector Brisbois rose from his seat, tapping his screen with one hand to lock it, and headed for the door. "We'll try to make this as quick as possible, but with a house this large, it may take a few hours to conduct a proper search."

"Chance and I," Victoria stressed my name, casting a pointed glance at Cadence, "are going for a walk." She crossed the length of the study in three quick strides. "I need to get my walking shoes."

Brisbois blocked the doorway with his body, smiling at Victoria. "Certainly, Miss Gad. Daniels!" The inspector called into the hallway and waved inwards. A uniformed Enforcement Officer appeared. "Daniels, please accompany Miss Gad to her room; she's getting a pair of walking shoes from her things."

Victoria examined the white-bearded Daniels with a cool stare, shrugged, and led the way out of the study, the old bloodhound trailing behind her at a respectful distance.

Brisbois turned back into the room. "Anyone else?"

"I would like to grab my medical bag, if that's alright." Dr. Merton stood, knees bent as if ready to collapse down again at the slightest word. "Mr. Hale is still not feeling well and I should like to have something on hand if it's needed."

Brisbois nodded and called another Enforcement Officer to the study. The inspector inclined his head towards Minerva, staying the doctor for a moment. "Do you need any medications brought from your room, ma'am?"

"If I can't survive for a few hours without a pill or an injection, Inspector," Minerva fixed such a look of disdain upon him that Brisbois stepped back, "I'd rather you let me crinkle up and die in the sun out there, thank you very much. I'll be fine. Dear," Minerva wobbled to her feet, offering an arm to Solomon, who took it at once, "walk me out to the patio. I'll get a proper tan for once and drive all the men in Zahia mad with desire." She laughed and reached over to squeeze Cadence's arm. "You should join me, my girl. We could both use some color."

"Thank you, Mrs. Davers, I'd like that." Cadence followed the pair out into the hall, sliding past the inspector without a glance.

I toyed with the idea of going after Cadence and the Davers, unexcited by the prospect of a morning stroll with Victoria in her current mood. However, I feared appearing over eager, or worse, overprotective. Even if that was exactly how I felt. It seemed that Cadence reserved her flirtations for everyone but me; an irritating fact, most particularly because it didn't affect my feelings for her in the slightest.

Coming out of the study, Henry's hand grabbed my elbow, tugging me up the hallway and towards the front door. "Come on. Let's go for that walk."

I allowed him to pull me outside without protest, chuckling despite myself. "You? Voluntarily engaging in physical activity?" I pulled my arm free and draped it over his shoulders. "Please, Henry, haven't we had enough shocks for one day?"

"I can be athletic when I want to be." Henry shrugged my arm away as we trotted down the steps and onto the drive. "Besides, would you rather I leave you in the clutches of the green-eyed monster?"

I scoffed, resting my hands in my pockets. "Victoria Gad has never been jealous of anyone in her life."

"You don't know her as well as you think you do, chum." We rounded the corner of the house, taking shelter from the warm morning sun in the shade of the old cherry trees that lined the manor. "You're not just some handsome young thing she's playing with, you know, you're the heir to a fortune, and all the things that go with it." He knocked my shoulder with his own and shook his finger at me. "You're her ticket to the fame-filled life of her dreams; don't think she's going to risk losing all that now."

I rolled my eyes and laughed. "Henry! You make her sound positively scheming."

"She is."

I chose not to press the issue, the atmosphere tense enough

without furthering my best friend's distaste for my intended. He sighed, stopping outside the window to his room and peering in.

I leaned over his shoulder, grinning. "Oh, any officers going through your unmentionables?"

Henry snorted. "Not yet, no." He turned, patting the slim trunk behind him and gazing up into the boughs with a small smile. "You know, it was so lovely last night that I was tempted to climb up and sleep in the trees here like a vagabond."

"Blasted thing." I glared at the offensive softwood in question, kicking it as we passed. "They're all so full of knot-holes and rot, we should really just cut them down."

We spent the rest of the walk in comfortable silence, excepting the odd recital of some poem or monologue by Henry, the landscape transporting him to some other time and place. We were about to turn to the back of the house when my father's voice reached us, speaking in, what for him, were hushed tones. Henry and I slowed our steps, curiosity aroused, and peeked around the corner.

"I would consider it a personal favor, Solomon, I really would." My father paced, waving the end of his cane over the ground instead of using it as the doctor had prescribed.

Solomon sat on one of the long wooden benches facing away from us; arm slung over the seat's curved back. "Of course, Felix, you don't even have to ask. I'd be honored to be your executor. When do you think it will be ready?"

"By tomorrow morning if I'm left in peace tonight. But that's why I'm using the library, of course." My father stilled, bringing his hands behind his back and squeezing them. "I need to come clean about some things, Solomon. I want to be a new man when

I marry Desdemona, with none of those secrets from my past lurking around me."

"And you think changing your will–"

"Rewriting it completely; fresh slate." He swung his cane in front of him and stabbed at the ground. "I need to know that when I do pass on, things are taken care of; that there are no questions about who I was and why I did what I did."

"Have you told Chance about these revisions?"

"In a way, yes." My father looked up, a scowl cutting through the grey hair on his face like a twisted bruise. I resisted the urge to jump back behind the corner. "Damned fool. Never does listen to me."

I chewed the inside of my mouth, unable to look away as my father spat onto the ground. "Your boy may be a bit soft in the head, Solomon, but at least he isn't useless; spending his days drinking, soliciting prostitutes–" He turned on his heel, grinding the grass underfoot. Something beyond Henry's or my range of vision caught his attention, and he squared his shoulders, shaking his cane in the air. "–bringing women like that impertinent hussy into my house just to sneer at me!"

Solomon laughed, but when I looked at him, there was nothing but the ghost of a smile fading on his lips. "You just don't like it when people disagree with you, Felix. You never have." He leaned forward, elbows on his knees, palms up in front of him. "I don't understand why you refuse to give my proposal a second chance."

My father's frame relaxed. He smiled. "Solomon, Solomon!" Sitting beside his old friend and colleague, he threw his tree-trunk of an arm around the smaller man's shoulders. "We talked about this. I can't take any monetary risks on your bouts of scientific whimsy."

Solomon's jaw tightened. "It's called experimentation and research, Felix. Halcyon Enterprises would hardly be where it is today if your forefathers hadn't invested in such things."

"No, I suppose not." My father looked up at Cadence, whom Henry and I now saw approaching from the veranda. "Still, we wouldn't have the animanecron problem if they'd been a little more cautious, eh?" He shook his head and pulled at his beard with his free hand. "I hope they wipe them all out, I really do. Finally remove that blemish from our otherwise sterling reputation for responsible scientific advancement."

Cadence turned her head at the remark, blinking and increasing her pace. In fact, she ended up moving by Henry and me at such a speed that her frame lurched forward and back when she skidded to a halt after noticing us.

"Hello, Chance." She nodded at my friend. "Henry."

"Miss Turing." Henry bent down and kissed her hand, an affectionate gesture, which I was sure, was to annoy me. He succeeded. "Did you get tired of my mother so soon?"

"She was being very flirtatious with one of the young men serving us drinks," Cadence examined the back of her hand for a moment before refocusing, tapping and rubbing the skin in a distracted way. "I felt that they wanted to be alone."

Henry closed his eyes, lips pursing. "Ah. Excuse me, won't you?"

He was off like a shot towards the patio, fully intent on saving his mother's honor, protecting the family from a harassment suit, or both.

Cadence and I stood where Henry had abandoned us. Alone at last. A crooked smile skittered over my lips. "Hello, Cay." I leaned forward, brushing my lips against her cheek. "You're looking lovely this morning."

When Cadence wrapped her arms up under my own and embraced me with such force I struggled to breathe, I fell into her with atypical gracelessness.

"Thank you!" She stepped away, looking me over. "You are very handsome as well."

I was about to mumble my thanks when she reached up and tugged at the elbow of my shirt, her head falling to one side. She smiled. "This shirt suits you; it flatters your arms."

I leaned back, heat flushing through me. "Oh. Really? Well–"

"Aren't you supposed to be taking a walk with Victoria?"

I shut my mouth with a snap and shook my head, watching her from under my hooded brow. "Yes and no," I leaned one arm against the brick wall behind me. "What are you up to?"

"I'm not sure. I seem to be without an activity to pursue."

I nodded and grabbed her hand with a tug. "Take a walk with me then. I know the perfect place to go."

She pulled away and turned towards the house. "But Victoria–"

"–will muddle through without me, somehow," I stepped back and looped my arm through hers, placing her hand on my forearm. "She'll understand; you are my guest after all."

8

Chapter 8

Neither of us spoke as we struck out across the back lawn, Cadence's eyes focused on the ground, a frown of concentration on her face. I didn't want to break her train of thought, whatever it might be, and contented myself with the opportunity to stretch my legs with such attractive company. It wasn't until we reached our destination, with the manor a medium-sized smear in the background, that Cadence spoke, staring up at the aspen trees looming over us.

"What is this place?" Cadence slid away from me, head twisting this way and that as she took in the sight and stepped into a manmade clearing at the grove's center.

"We used to play here when I was younger. Henry, me, even Victoria from time to time; this was our secret hideaway." The sunlight felt cooler and more temperate here, the breeze less intense. I walked to the nearest trunk, sliding my hand over the familiar white bark. "No one comes here anymore, though. Shame, it's such a nice–" I turned around to find Cadence lying face first on the grass, moving her arms and legs over the blades in slow waves. "–spot."

She turned her head to one side, thick bangs falling over her eyes like a blindfold. "Do you think they'll find anything?" Her words were somewhat muffled, seeing as how half her mouth still rested against the ground. "The enforcement officers, I mean."

"I doubt it. They're not known for being the brightest Arrhidaeus has to offer." Lowering myself onto the grass beside her, I wondered how much longer she intended to molest the ground in this fashion.

Cadence rolled onto her back, pushing the wayward hair out of her eyes. "Inspector Brisbois seemed quite intelligent to me."

I stifled a snort, ceasing my search for a nix. "Yes." Picking at the grass, I fixed her with a cold stare. "You two seemed to be getting along rather well."

"Were we? I didn't notice."

I turned away, anxious to conceal my grimace. I did not find jealousy an attractive emotion in others, and I doubted it would flatter me.

Cadence sighed and fell back onto the grass, crossing her arms under her head. "I suppose I just know how to speak to detectives."

"Oh? This talent wouldn't be a hold-over from your seedy, but entirely forgivable Paraesepisian past, would it? Which you still haven't told me about by the way." I rolled up my shirt sleeves and tossed propriety to the wind, lying down in the grass with my arms splayed out around me.

"Not much to tell," she said, shrugging as she worked her flat white shoes off her feet. "I lived an ordinary life populated with ordinary people and we all did ordinary things."

Cadence glanced over at me and jumped at the sight of me at eye level. After watching me with what I took to be mock suspicion, her expression relaxed into a smile. "May I use your arm?"

"What?" I contracted my outstretched appendage with a snap. "Why?"

Cadence squirmed closer, moving across the ground like a lopsided caterpillar. "While the crust of your planet is covered in this monocotyledonous herbaceous plant, the ground is still surprisingly hard, and my arms are getting tired."

By the end of her explanation, she was nuzzled against me, staring up at me with naive hope. She was a queer bird, no mistaking that. But the warmth of her and the pleading smile that blossomed over her pink lips disarmed me in a way that no one had done before. Having her closer wouldn't be a terrible thing. I extended my arm.

She lowered her head onto my bicep with a quiet sigh, sending shivers all over my body. I pulled myself closer to her, resting a hand on her far hip, waiting for any sign that such advances were unwanted, but receiving no such chastisement.

"I know a lot about detectives because I used to sell mystery novels." She tugged at the bottom of her white shirt, giving me a pleasant view of her chest as it rose and fell. "For a job, I mean, not entertainment."

"Just mystery novels? Were you one of those specialty sellers?"

"Yes," Cadence sighed, turning onto her side to face me, brow furrowed and eyes distant with remembrance. "I carried new titles, of course, but most of my stock consisted of old Earth stories."

Smiling, I picked a stray blade of grass off her collarbone and tossed it away, coming back to rub at her skin with my fingertips. "How old?"

She scrunched up her nose, wobbling her head back and forth. "The 19th to 22nd century, mainly."

"Very niche indeed." I cleared my throat when she dropped her head onto my chest, nestling herself closer to me, her warmth enough to set my blood ablaze. Bringing my hand up to stroke her tangled, silky hair, I breathed in the smell of her with half-lidded eyes, murmuring, "And this has given you an insight into inspectors, has it?"

She gave a small nod. "Criminals too."

"Oh, well, naturally."

"In fact," Cadence began playing with my shirt buttons, a frown pushing out her bottom lip, "if the EO really are as unintelligent as you claim, I may be ideally placed to solve the theft of the Negrescu Necklace myself."

I swallowed back a laugh. "Yes! They'd probably appreciate the help."

Her arm went lax on top of me. I closed my eyes and focused on the pleasant heaviness of her body on mine and the sun on my skin.

Something moved across my forehead, and I opened my eyes to find Cadence's hand pushing my bangs up off my forehead, tickling the skin there. Cadence looked up at me with her beautiful summer smile, which crinkled the edges of her eyes and brought out the gentle curve of her cheekbones. It undid me, unraveled me like I was a battered ball of yarn, and I wrapped my hand around the back of her neck, closing my eyes as I leaned in.

"I have work to do."

Frozen halfway to her lips, I struggled to clear my thoughts. "Work?"

"Mmhmm!" Cadence smiled, rolling off my arm and up into a sitting position, forcing me back. She sprung to her feet, shaking out her shirt and pants before twirling around and striding towards the edge of the grove. "Goodbye!"

"Where are you going?" I sounded more peeved than I liked, Cadence's flare for dousing my Arrhidaean ardor beginning to border on cruel teasing. "Cay!"

She spun on her heels, still walking as she shouted back, "I can't just lie around when there's a mystery to unravel! Thank you for the walk, Chance! And your trees, they're beautiful!"

I watched her hurry to the house, a spring in her step, her arms rocking back and forth like a swing in a gale. I opened my mouth. I closed it. Rolling flat onto my back, head banging against the ground, I threw my hands up into the air, whimpering. Life, it seemed, had spiraled out of my control. My father would be marrying a gussied-up dreg, I was about to be cut off from my inheritance, and now I couldn't even manage to make time with the dimwitted refugee I had picked up on the train.

When had things gone so wrong? As a matter of fact, when did I ever let a woman get to me like this? If there was one thing a man like me learned over the years, it was that there were always mountains which were unconquerable. Women who, for whatever reason, refused to be flattered, humored, or otherwise romanced. You couldn't take such things as personal failures. Better to shrug them off and move on to the next conquest, rather than dwell on why the liaison fell flat.

But there was something about Cadence, a quality of hers which left me captivated, trapped and happy to be so.

I liked the girl. I did.

Scrambling to my feet, I rushed back towards the manor, determined to make the pink coloring in my cheeks the result of physical exertion rather than the butterflies which had swelled up inside me at the thought of her.

As I drew near the house, I spotted Victoria and Desdemona reclining in the gazebo on the back lawn. Despite her protestations otherwise, it seemed that Victoria had begun to enjoy Desdemona's company, at least in the same way a cat enjoys the company of a mouse. I considered Victoria and, increasing the pace of my stride, I set my mind on a new course of action.

Victoria lounged against the small set of stairs at the base of the structure, her tight dress leaving little to the imagination as she stretched her legs out in front of her, head upturned to Desdemona, who was perched on the railing above her.

"I've always said that I would never marry a widower without seeing it first."

Desdemona's teeth dug into her bottom lip. "It seems a bit, well, commercial, doesn't it?"

"A woman should look after her own interests, dear. I wouldn't say a vow or sign a certificate until I saw my name in that will."

Blush colored Desdemona's cheeks, the surge of blood

splotching across her thin skin. "Felix has mentioned something about–" She stuttered to a stop when I approached, eyes widening as she twirled her pale hair around her fingers.

"There you are Chance, darling! I've been looking for you everywhere." Victoria smiled, lifting her manicured hand to me.

I turned it over and kissed her palm. She peered at me, eyes narrowing. "Are you alright, dearest? You look positively peaky. Come here and sit with me."

I lowered myself onto the step in front of her, allowing her to wrap an arm around my shoulders and tug me against her legs, her stockings scratching my cheek.

"So, who do you think did it?"

I pulled away from Victoria with a huff. "Vicky, really!"

"Oh, come on," she drew me back, resting her cheek on top of my head and grinning. "You don't think everyone else is talking about it? I think it was Dr. Merton. I always thought he was a shifty sort of man; a bit desperate looking, you know what I mean."

"He wouldn't–" Desdemona stopped, perhaps out of shock at her sure sounding voice, before continuing in a humbler tone, "I mean, he doesn't seem the type to steal. A proper professional like that."

"He wasn't always so professional."

I rolled my eyes, stifling a yawn. Victoria could never resist launching into one of her gossip-dripping stories. I considered leaving, but the sight of Cadence lingering by the corner of the house, talking with Solomon, reminded me why I must endure such things.

Solomon laughed at something Cadence said and leaned forward, rubbing her arm. I pulled Victoria's arm tighter around my shoulders, nibbling on the inside of my cheek.

"Did you know he used to work in District 3 in Römer?"

Desdemona yanked at the hair woven around her fingers, wincing as she shook her head.

"At one of those free clinics; all the patients pure trash; drogan addicts, prostitutes, the lowest of the low. Working for the Hale family must have seemed like a dream after that." Victoria kissed my ear before straightening, head revolving like a periscope. "Where is he anyway?"

"He and Belinda are in the shed looking at some rocks I believe." I began rubbing her leg without thinking, watching Cadence from afar.

Desdemona leaned against one of the wooden columns supporting the roof. "Is that what all that stuff in there is for? Geology?"

"Geology, computer science, botany – it's a scientific hodgepodge." Cadence glanced at us, and I jerked my head away, taking Victoria's free hand and kissing it. "Father always wants his friends to feel at home."

I avoided Cadence for the rest of the day, engaging in idle chit-chat and distracting myself by watching the EO officers through the large windows as they moved from room to room, every so often dusting a window for fingerprints or taking some knickknack away as evidence. They left when the sun began to set, Inspector Brisbois making vague promises about hearing from him soon, even though it was clear from his flat tone that the EO had found little of interest around the house and no sign of the necklace.

Housebound for the foreseeable future, Minerva loaned Cadence more of her clothes, insisting that an evening gown and pant suit were not enough to get a woman through a weekend, dressing her in a simple peach summer dress that hugged her body, accentuating everything that had attracted me to her in the first place.

Dinner dragged on, every topic of conversation exhausted in less than two minutes. My father, almost always an excellent host, had taken the theft of the necklace as a matter of personal embarrassment, and was quite put out the entire evening.

Everyone scattered to take up their individual pursuits after dinner, Minerva and Solomon going to bed early, with Belinda following suit, complaining of a headache. My father occupied the library, citing some work he had to finish, and Dr. Merton, as unpopular a companion as ever, was left to his own devices in the study. When Henry invited Desdemona and Cadence to join him on an evening stroll, Victoria and I, alone at last, withdrew to the sitting room where I began to make love to her as I often did, telling her that her eyes were like emeralds, that the sound of her voice made me quiver, that she was all I could ever think about when I was away. After many compliments of such a nature, she allowed me to kiss her.

But that night's seduction was different, my kisses long and deep, and unable to content myself with her lips, I drew my tongue down her neck and across her chest. I traced swirling patterns down her arms and onto her thighs with my fingertips, while my mind was miles away, buried in the memory of Cadence's eyes, her lips, her damnable, blessed smile, and even her strange tapping, all firing my desire to levels I had never experienced.

Victoria pulled back from me, breathing heavy, and ran her tongue along her lips. "It's awfully exciting having a jewel thief in the house."

I hummed against her skin, nibbling the underside of her jaw. "Very stimulating, isn't it?" Groping the fabric bunched up against her inner thigh, I rested for a minute, trying to catch my breath. "Aren't you the least bit scared?"

"Scared?"

"Well, whoever he is," I kissed her again, flicking her bottom lip with my tongue, "he could come rifling through your room tonight when you're asleep."

"Do you think someone will?"

"It's a possibility." I pressed against her, reveling in the feel of her fingers clawing across my shoulders. "It'd probably be safer to spend the night with someone, safety in numbers and all that."

"Chance!" Victoria's voice rang high and bright in my ear. I sat back. She caressed my neck, smiling. "I thought you said that we shouldn't..." She swallowed the word. "That it'd ruin all the excitement when we finally do get married."

"I'm an idiot, don't you know? You should never take me seriously." I lunged at her throat, biting and sucking at the sensitive skin there with an intensity that surprised us both. "Victoria, if I don't have you tonight, I think I'm going to go crazy."

"You are crazy."

I slid my hand up to her hip, making her swallow a laugh. "Let me take you upstairs, please; let me take you."

It was the first time I had begged Victoria for anything, and I wouldn't have been surprised to find that it was the only reason she said yes at all. She didn't realize that I wasn't asking it of her, but of her body. I wasn't interested in bedding Victoria; I never had been. But I was desperate, not just for sexual release, but for affirmation. I needed to know that I was good enough for Victoria to find the confidence to try for the real prize at least one more time.

9

✦

Chapter 9

I awoke from my coitus induced slumber to a loud banging. Lifting my head off my overstuffed pillow, I looked about through bleary eyes, shafts of sunlight struggling through the heavy curtains. Victoria turned over next to me, grumbling in her sleep. I yawned, pulling the covers over my head, when I heard Dr. Merton shouting in the hall.

"Mr. Hale! Mr. Hale, sir!" Another series of loud bangs ripped through the air. "Sir, can you hear me? Mr. Hale!"

I bolted upright, groggy, but alarmed. Stumbling out of bed, I pulled on my pants and, shrugging into my dressing gown, I groped for my key on the bedside table, where I thought I had placed it the night before. While I searched the room for it, Belinda's panicked voice joined the doctor's outside.

"Should I call an ambulance?"

Somehow my key had gotten knocked to the floor in front of

the door. Sweeping it up with one hand, I shoved it into the lock and rushed out into the hall. Belinda and Merton stood in front of my father's room, faces creased with alarm, still in their pajamas and dressing gowns. Belinda pounded on the door. "Felix! Felix! Say something, Felix!"

I strode over to them, tying my robe shut. "What the hell–"

"Your father isn't answering," Merton moved Belinda to one side, pulling and twisting the door handle, straining against it with all his might. "The door is locked from the inside; I can't get in!"

"Father!" I pushed my ear against the wood, but no sound came from inside. "Dad, open up! Dad!"

"Do you have a key?"

I shook my head at Merton, swallowing to wet my throat. "No, I–" I leapt away from the door, a thought spurring me into action. "There's a connecting door through here, maybe he left it unlocked!"

The three of us raced back into my room, where Victoria had had the good sense to wake up and put on some clothes. I heard her startled voice in the background, but all my thoughts were focused on my father. Twisting the handle of the connecting door, the portal flying open with oiled ease, I rushed into the room, calling for my father, until the sight of him stopped me like a train hitting a brick wall.

Somewhere behind me, Victoria screamed and kept on screaming.

My father lay on the floor in front of me in the same blue striped suit he had worn the day before. The back of his head was a tangled mass of bone, skin, and brain matter, a ring of blood surrounding the wound like a halo. His body twisted like a gnarled tree, bones protruding from flesh, his arms and legs jutting out at grotesque angles. All the skin on his face had been ripped away, leaving only shiny sinew and muscle behind. His lidless eyes stared into me.

I couldn't move, clutching the doorknob with such force that I would find a stinging, purple bruise in the center of my palm later. The doctor pushed past me, kneeling and putting his fingers to my father's neck. The tensing of Merton's shoulders assured me of what I already knew to be true. He looked up at me, breathing heavy. His gaze flickered to the space behind me. "Get them out of here."

I became aware of Belinda and Victoria standing behind me, sobbing. But my limbs refused to do their duty and kept me staring at the thing on the floor. Merton surged to his feet, his voice hoarse. "Get them out!"

My whole body jumped as muscle memory took over. I pulled Victoria to my side, forcing her face into my shoulder so she could no longer look at the bloody pulp on the floor. Belinda had not screamed, but her face was grey, eyes glazed as if she might faint at any moment. I slung an arm around her waist and dragged them both outside, laying Victoria down on the small bench in the hallway and propping Belinda up against the wall.

The clicking of doors echoed around me, frantic voices coming from downstairs. At the end of the hall, Cadence's head appeared from around her door. She took one look at me and ran out into the corridor, hands clenched by her side. "What's going on?"

My tongue sat heavy in my mouth. I reached out to her. "There's... I– I–"

From the corner of my eye, I saw Desdemona tear out of her room and onto the landing, running towards my father's door. Turning, I thrust myself in front of her, pushing her away from the horrible scene. "Desdemona! Desdemona, don't!"

Henry and his father rushed up the stairs, Minerva waiting at the bottom, clutching her dressing gown closed. Behind me the door clicked open, and I moved back to allow Dr. Merton to exit.

He stared at the floor, closing the door, hand lingering over the handle. "I'm going to call the Enforcement Office. I suggest that we all go downstairs and wait for them." The doctor's gaze moved over the crowd. "Felix has been murdered."

Desdemona's cry pierced the air, her hands flailing around her face. She lunged forward, but the shock was too much for her, and she fainted dead away in my arms. I tried to hold her up, but I didn't have the strength to keep myself standing, stumbling under the burden and falling against the wall.

Solomon squeezed my shoulder. I couldn't bring myself to look at him. He said something to me, words of comfort or instruction, I can't remember. Henry took Desdemona without a word, his face blank as he carried her downstairs. Cadence stepped forward to support the unsteady frame of Belinda, brushing a hand against my chest as she crossed in front of me. She followed Henry down, leading Belinda along like a child. The rest of us trailed after them, dragging ourselves away from the scene of the crime in an all too quiet procession.

I have little memory of what happened between the moment when I opened the door onto my father's body and finding myself in the sitting room, collapsed in an armchair by the darkened windows. Like a drunken man coming out of an alcoholic stupor, I became aware of my surroundings by slow degrees. The minutes passed like hours. I waited for some emotion, any emotion, to sweep over me and fill the gaping hole that sucked at my chest. But there was nothing.

Dr. Merton was out in the foyer on the phone, his voice tremulous. When he returned, he went straight to Desdemona, whom Henry had laid out on the large couch, and began to tend to her as best he could. No one spoke. A few times I heard someone crying, realizing with a certain numbness that it was Belinda, a woman who, in my memory, had never cried in her life. I curled deeper into my chair and tried to block out her weeping, running my hands down my face.

At last, the doorbell chimed, and stamping boots skittered into the entryway. Small groups of EO officers marched past the open sitting room door. Inspector Brisbois appeared around the door frame, face drawn, and his sharp green eyes surrounded by dark circles. "Dr. Merton?"

The doctor propped pillows underneath Desdemona's head, her brow slick with perspiration, before he rose to his feet. Brisbois nodded, his tone as conversational as the firm line of his mouth was not. "Good morning." He gestured behind himself to a small group of people wearing green plastic suits. "If you could please show these men to the body, we can get started."

Dr. Merton went without a word. Brisbois leaned back into the room, resting his weight against the door frame. "Ladies and gentlemen, I will be with you in a moment." He disappeared down the hall, a line of officers following.

The room remained silent, except for the occasional sniffle from Belinda in the corner, a handkerchief hovering over her red, wet face. Cadence stood hunched over the sideboard, distant from the rest of us, and I was about to call out to her when Desdemona gave a breathy sigh of awakening, drawing everyone's attention. Minerva, sitting closest to her, leaned over the arm of the couch, fingers brushing against the younger woman's ankle.

Desdemona pushed herself upright, rubbing her forehead. Her eyes fluttered open, and she jumped at the sight of so many people focused on her. "What's going on? Where am I?"

"We took you downstairs to the sitting room, dear," said Minerva, reaching out for the woman as if she might topple over at any moment. "The EO officers have just arrived."

"EO officers?"

"Yes, dear. Do you remember...?" She hesitated. My stomach lurched as I watched Minerva blink tears out of her eyes.

The simple reminder of something happening was all it took to jog Desdemona's memory. She was on her feet in a flurry of arms and legs, shrieking, pulling at her hair as she rushed to the door. "Felix! Felix! Oh my god, I have to–!"

"No, Desdemona!" Solomon bolted from against the wall, using his whole body to block her from the exit. "You can't!"

Desdemona struggled, arms stretching out over his shoulders. "I have to go to him! He needs me! He needs me!"

"He doesn't need much of anything anymore..." Victoria receded further into the corner of the couch.

"Thank you, Vicky," said Henry from behind her, snarling as

he paced from one end of the room to the other. "As sensitive as ever."

"Sensitive? Sensitive!" Victoria shot up onto her knees and leaned over the couch, her yellow hair hanging down in sticky tangles around her face. "I was sleeping next to the whole awful thing!"

"I thought your room was—"

"It is," she slammed her fist against the couch back, realizing her mistake almost as soon as it was out of her mouth. "I was speaking...metaphorically!"

"I think," Solomon started, having succeeded in calming Desdemona by letting her sob into his night shirt, "that everyone should try to remain calm and—"

Victoria spun around, stepping off the couch and unleashing her venom on him without a thought. "Remain calm? When there's been a murder in the house? A bloody, awful murder! Any one of us might be next! I don't—"

The sharp crack of skin against skin roused me from my daze. Victoria stood in front of me, mouth agape, clutching her cheek with both hands. Inches from her was Minerva, face bright red and her body tensed. "Damn it, get a hold of yourself, you stupid girl!"

Minerva turned on her heel, swallowing a few times and pushing her hair out of her eyes. "Solomon is right. The EO is here. They'll be with us soon. We just need to keep our heads and wait." She sat back down on the couch, pausing to look at each of us. "Preferably quietly!"

Screwing my eyes shut, I slid a hand over my forehead, skin

cool and clammy. I choked down another bout of nausea, taking in a shallow breath.

Someone squeezed my knee. I was about to knock their hand away when it loosened, fingertips trilling an arrhythmic beat against my thigh.

"Chance?"

I gave a start and opened my eyes, as desperate for the sight of her face as a shipwrecked man is for the sight of rescue. Cadence crouched in front of me, one knee pressed into the carpet, the other acting as a temporary ledge for a large glass of whiskey. Her dark blue eyes stared into mine with no concern or pity that I could find. There was just the slightest wrinkling of her forehead and a set to her jaw which conveyed a freely offered affection that washed over me like sea water over a wound, cooling and stinging all at the same time.

Cadence lifted the glass and shook it at me, ice tinkling against the sides. "You should drink this; it might help."

I couldn't tear my eyes away from her beautiful face as I fumbled for the glass, gulping the bitter liquid down like a child takes medicine. The corner of her lips flashed up into a hollow smile, which vanished as she rose to look out the window at the EO PTs flying up the drive. I lunged for her hand and held it tight, the smallest ripple of warmth spreading over me when she squeezed it back, covering my hand with hers without even a startled glance in my direction.

For once it seemed that the sensation of eyes on her beat through Cadence's thick skin and she turned to face the rest of the household, brows raised at the stares fixed upon her.

"Would anyone else like anything?"

The sudden clamor of voices was a shock after the long silence. "Bloody Mary–" "Scotch on the rocks, please!" "Bourbon, straight, blessed bourbon–" "–with tonic water!"

Cadence nodded, pressing my hand once more before slipping away. I kept my glazed eyes on her as she stood at the sideboard and mixed each drink with care, measuring out more alcohol for some than others.

The final glass was for Belinda, who hadn't moved from her place by the window. She grasped Cadence's hands when she gave her the drink, pushing them against the crystal. "Bless you for staying so calm, Cadence."

"Glad to see you're making yourselves comfortable." Brisbois stood in the doorway, watching. His usual cool smile missing from his face, his hair a rumpled mess, he stepped into the room, a plastic-wrapped package in his hand.

"From what we can tell," he began with a sigh, loosening his tie, "Mr. Hale was killed sometime late last evening; beaten to death with a blunt object, namely–" He held up the package, blood and another, thicker substance coating what was inside it, "–this book."

Desdemona screamed, covering her mouth with both hands, eyes watering. Solomon threw a hand in the air, the other patting the hysterical young lady's back. "Inspector, really!"

Brisbois dropped the book to his side, ignoring the chastisement. "I'd appreciate it if you all confine your movements to this room or the lawn. I have an Evidence Team on site, and they may be here for several hours, given the size of the house.

"During that time, I'm going to need to ask you all a few questions. I'll be starting with the staff, so it might be quite a while before I talk to any of you. Before I go," silent as he surveyed the room, his eyes rested on each of us in turn, "is there anything anyone would like to say to me now?"

"Who could have done this?"

Brisbois stared at me, as surprised to hear me speak as I was to do so. He rocked back on his heels, jaw tightening. "You may regret asking that, Mr. Hale."

He turned on his heel and marched into the hall, leaving us in a stunned silence. Minerva let out a huff, hand at her collarbone. "Well," she blew some loose wisps of hair out of her face, "what in the world did he mean by that?"

I looked up at Cadence, staring over Belinda's shoulder to the patio outside, her pink lips firmed into a grim line. She had understood the inspector's nauseating insinuation as well as I: if someone from inside the house had stolen the necklace, someone from inside the house had killed my father; one of us was a murderer. Did I really want to find out who?

10

Chapter 10

Solomon cinched his robe around his waist and stroked the stubble on his chin. He shook his head once and then again, spinning around and walking for the windows, throwing them open.

"I need some air."

A general murmur of agreement rose, and several people trickled out onto the veranda after him until only Henry, Desdemona, Dr. Merton, and I were left inside.

I watched as Dr. Merton, preoccupied with his sobbing patient, stroked Desdemona's hair and shoulders, murmuring platitudes in a vain attempt to calm the wounded creature. Surprised at the tenderness displayed by the stand-offish doctor, I had to concede that Desdemona could capture more hearts than just my father's.

The thought sent a jolt of guilt through me, every angry

word we'd spoken the last time we were alone together cruel and pointless. I slumped in my chair, massaging my temple.

"Chance?"

I opened my eyes. Henry stood in front of me, hands hanging limp at his sides. He licked his lips, eyes flickering to and away from my face like a hummingbird. "I...I am so sorry, Chance. Are you alright?" Henry winced, pinching the bridge of his nose. "Damn it, I know you're not, but I don't know what else to say. Is there anything I can do for you, anything you need?"

His concern, touching and most wanted, brought me back to myself. Straightening, I shook my head, trying to pretend the water in my eyes wasn't tears, that I was exhausted, nothing more. I opened my mouth to speak but couldn't trust my voice to hold back the emptiness in my heart.

Henry gripped my shoulder. "It's alright." A tremor in his voice told me that he too was on the edge of tears. "It's going to be alright."

I turned away, taking in a shaky breath and staring outside. Mustering the last ounces of my composure, I spied Cadence, lingering by the gazebo. Bundled up in one of my robes, something she had no doubt rummaged from my closet in the heat of the moment, her skin looked like marble in the glow of the morning sun, hair falling onto her bare neck in curled strands that I could see even from this distance. The sight of her alone made me feel safe and protected from the cruel realities of life that were pressing in around me.

"I think..." I chewed on the inside of my cheek, toying with my bottom lip. "I think some air might do me good after all."

Henry followed my line of sight. A weak smile crept onto his face. He patted my shoulder once more before gesturing back into the sitting room. "If you need me, I'll be here."

I stood up as fast as I dared, legs wobbling under me, and shuffled out the veranda doors. The sun had risen, but the sky was clear and stepping outside was like stepping into a bath of ice water. The cold felt good against my flushed skin, and I quickened my pace. My need for Cadence was now deep and instinctual rather than a passing desire, and I felt foolish for abandoning my pursuit of her. I had no intention of letting my impatience get the better of me anymore. To be in her presence would be more than enough for now.

To my right, someone hissed. I jumped, eyes fluttering open to find Victoria walking beside me, her long negligee tripping her slippered feet as she tried to keep up with me.

"Chance!" My name squeezed its way out from between her clenched teeth. "I need to talk to you."

I shook my head, desperate for a nix and wishing I hadn't left my case in my suit jacket upstairs. "Terribly inconvenient moment just now, ducky."

Victoria grabbed my arm, digging her nails into the sensitive flesh just above my wrist. I came to an abrupt halt with a yelp, jerking away.

"Victoria!" Rubbing at the crescent marks on my skin, I glared into her unapologetic visage. "What the hell was that for?"

Victoria's gaze bounced around the yard. Gnawing her bottom lip, she stepped closer to me, whispering out of one side of her mouth. "I don't think either of us should mention anything about last night to that pig of an Inspector."

"Why on earth not?"

She scanned the back garden again, as if anyone would care about our sexual intrigues now. "I have my reputation to think of," she tucked a lock of hair behind her ear, shivering in her less than appropriate outdoor attire. "And it's bad enough being involved in something like a...a..."

"A murder?" I spat the word at her and she flinched. I gritted my teeth, fists clenching at my side. "Well, I am so sorry that my father's violent death might adversely affect your social standing, Vicky; we have to tell him!"

Victoria threw her hands into the air, snarling. "Why does he need to know?"

Her obduracy cut through what little patience I had left like a hot poker through flesh. I grabbed her shoulders and jerked her to me. "Because we're each other's alibis, damn it!"

Her mouth hung open as she stared at me like I was some creature from the abyss, daring to lay a hand on her in anger. She scoffed, shaking herself free of my grip. "Oh, are we?"

I lunged towards her, arms outstretched. "What the hell—"

"I am a very sound sleeper, Chance." Victoria retreated another few steps, resting one hand on her clavicle as she locked eyes with me. "After my head hits the pillow, why," her eyelashes fluttered, cartwheeling her free hand through the air, "I don't know if I can vouch for what did or did not go on."

My arms fell to my sides, and I bit down hard on the inside of my mouth. "I could say the same, you know."

Victoria's smile was the glint of a knife in the dark. "Do I really look like the kind of person who could beat a man to death? The inspector would never believe you."

"I guess you're lucky he doesn't know you like I do." I forced my muscles to relax, and I turned, shaking my head. "You win. I won't say anything."

The bottom of her negligee rustled against the grass as she stepped towards me and held my shoulders. "Thank you." She laid her face against my back, breathing out a sigh. "I am sorry, you know. I rather liked your father."

I slid out from her grip without a word, more determined than ever to reach Cadence. During Victoria's negotiations, she had disappeared behind the gazebo. I rounded the small white structure with long strides, pushing hanging honeysuckle out of the way. Cadence was propped against the back wall, her hips pressed against the gazebo floor.

"Cay." I sighed her name, feeling more relieved than I had a right to.

Cadence jumped out of her skin at the sound of my voice, jerking up from her reclined position and turning away, covering her face with her hands.

It wasn't the reaction I had been hoping for. My brow furrowed. "Cadence?"

Her shoulders shook and though I heard her muttering under her breath, the words were unintelligible. As I edged closer, I realized that she had abandoned the lingua franca in her distress, a series of rough clicks and trills emanating from her that was not Common Tongue.

I placed my hand on her arm, wary of disquieting her further. "Cadence, darling, are you alright?"

Cadence whimpered, pressing my hand into her skin. Even in the cool morning air, the heat of her stung. I moved around her, peering into her downturned face. Eyes staring at the ground, framed prettily by wisps of her black hair, she swallowed hard and gave a firm nod.

"Yes."

She rolled her eyes and took a breath, forcing a smile onto her lips. "Yes! I'm fine!" Closing her eyes, the tortured smile evaporated like a drop of water in the desert. "Not fine, I'm not fine, someone's been killed after all. But...relatively. I mean, I'm not dead right now, and I feel very good about that!"

She opened her eyes, shoulders falling as she met my confused stare. Moaning, she fell forward, wrapping her arms around me, burying her face in my chest. She was heavy for a woman with so slight a figure, but I absorbed her sudden embrace without pause, holding her tight as I stroked her tangled mass of hair. I understood all too well that people like Cadence and I could be strong for only so long before we needed to stop pretending.

We stayed there for a few moments, Cadence still and silent in my arms. I kissed the top of her head, drowning in the scent of her.

She shifted against me, head rolling to one side. "This is bad, isn't it?"

"I'm sorry."

She pulled back, the palms of her hands resting against my shoulder blades. Her dark eyes searched mine, brow furrowed.

I brushed her cheek with my thumb. "I'm sorry for dragging you into all this, however unintentionally I might have done it."

Cadence shook her head, gaze falling to the dew-covered grass under our feet as she released me. She wrapped an arm around her stomach, cradling her face in her free hand. "Do you think–" Moving her hand over her face, she bit down on her thumb, taking another step back. "Do you think Inspector Brisbois will want to see my ident papers now?"

I squinted at her, grimace twisting my lips. "I don't know; probably. Why?" A silly thing to be worried about at a time like this, I was about to remind her that as a stranger to the house she would be a prime suspect, when the words died on my tongue.

The EO's arrival yesterday had made her so nervous, so guarded, almost afraid, until Brisbois told her not to bother with her ID and travel documents. That same fear was in her eyes now and I reminded myself that I knew next to nothing about the singular woman standing in front of me; even though I had assumed very much indeed.

Lowering my voice, I reached out to her, looking about for any of the others within hearing distance. "Cadence, is there something wrong with your ident papers?"

She slid her hand up from her mouth to her forehead, shoulders hunching in around her. "I can't tell you, Chance. I've been enough of an inconvenience to you already." She clicked her tongue off the top of her mouth, throwing her hands to her sides as her eyes searched the skies above us. "I wish I could just go home."

I chewed the inside of my cheek, trying to sort through the seldom experienced emotions Cadence put me through. My heart beat hard in my chest. As miserable as I was, the thought of losing Cadence filled me with a wretchedness I couldn't bear. I licked my lips and leaned forward, taking her hand in mine.

"Cay." She looked at me and I almost lost my courage. Taking in a deep breath, I pulled her close. "I know I don't exactly come off as the dependable sort," I put my other hand on top of hers, "but if you're in some sort of trouble, I will move heaven and earth to help you, I swear. You can trust me."

Cadence's eyes went wide. She looked from my face to our entwined hands. After what felt like forever, she lifted her other hand and, with just a stutter of hesitation, placed it over mine.

"My ident papers are fake."

I nodded, squeezing her hand. "Alright. Where did you get them?"

"Janus Station." Cadence tapped the back of my hand. "A man sold them to me. They cost almost all my money." She stared at the ground, her brow wrinkling. "That should mean they're good forgeries, though, right? If they cost that much? That makes sense, doesn't it?"

"It does, yeah." I cleared my throat, walking around her and pulling her further behind the gazebo, away from prying eyes. "So," I mustered a weak smile, "what's your real name, dearest?"

"Oh, Cadence is my real name!" A smile burst across her face like a sun flare. "We don't have last names on Whiston, so I had to make that one up; but I'm still Cadence."

I scoffed, smirking, my mind rejecting the implications of what I had just heard like an organ rejecting poisoned blood. "On Whist-?"

The rapid flow of new data pouring through my synapses clicked and merged with what was already there, dropping the truth of my guest's origins fully formed into my mind like an atom bomb. I looked at the hand I held and threw it away like it was a snake, wiping my palm down my front as I turned, shaking my head. "No, no, no - you told me you're from Paraesepe. You said—"

"I lied."

I spun around to face it. Its inky blue eyes, bright in the shadow of the gazebo, searched my face. A sad, half smile wilted on its lips. I watched, mind wiped blank by confusion, as it lifted its hand to my shoulder and squeezed, fingertips warm even through my robe.

Jerking away, I threw myself against the side of the gazebo, the only thought running through my scrambled mind being, *'Don't let it touch you'*.

Panting as if I had just raced around the entire estate, my body shook, beads of salt water on my chest growing clammy in the cool air. My head heavy, my heart aching, all I could think was, *'Dear god, please, please don't let it touch me'*.

The acidic taste of vomit and alcohol mixed at the back of my throat. I gagged, forcing it all back down as I croaked, "You...you're not one of, of them, are you?"

It pulled its hand back towards its chest, holding it to itself as if it'd been slapped. There was something in its bioengineered eyes, a simulation of an emotion called 'hurt'.

"Yes, I am an animanecron. I'm also Cadence." It shook its head, raven black hair swaying. "I'm not ashamed of what I am. I only lied to protect myself, not to hurt you, Chance. I ran because I didn't want to die; if the EO catches me, they'll send me back." Its shoulders began shaking again. "I can't go back. The...the things they'll do to me, I—" Its voice was soft, anguished. It bit its lower lip, pressing a hand to the top of its forehead. Its eyes screwed shut.

The sensation hit me like a bucket of cold water. I wanted her, needed her with a desperation I'd not known, to look at me. I needed to see Cadence's beautiful blue eyes meeting mine. Because it was Cadence. Somehow. It was the magnificent creature who'd caught my eye on the train, whose smile lifted me into heaven, whose mere presence here had given me strength after my father's earth-shattering passing. It was Cadence. My Cadence. It had to be.

The feeling was there. Then it was gone. The cold water turned lukewarm, and I was left clammy and damp.

Cadence stepped towards me, hand outstretched, her eyes avoiding mine. "Please, Chance, could you–"

I leaned back from her, staring, my lip pulled back from my teeth. "Did you kill him?"

Her head whipped up, eyes wide. "Chance!"

"Did he figure it out? What you are?"

Cadence's jaw snapped shut. Gripping the gazebo, as if something like her would need steadying, her face slid back into its usual impassive expression, lips parted and eyes half-lidded. It felt inappropriate to breathe, which was when I realized she wasn't.

From beneath her half-closed lids, she watched me, as still as death and with a detachment that struck me, for the first time, as truly alien. Was this what had first attracted me? In my heady passion, I deemed it exoticism, but in the thrall of this new, icy fascination my desire for her seemed to be a freakish quirk, a perversion, the consequences of which I dreaded.

Cadence took in a breath, blinked, and then exhaled. "If your father discovered who I am, he didn't tell me." Rolling her eyes, she gave a sharp shrug, her composure cracking as she glared at me. "And even if he had, I wouldn't have killed him! Do you go around killing people who find out who you are?"

My whole body relaxed, my belief in her answer comforting me more than perhaps it should have. I turned my back on her, drawing my hands down my face.

Swallowing down my toxic cocktail of emotions, I shook my head, massaging my throat and neck. "You have to leave."

"I can't. If I run, Brisbois will chase me. I'll be caught and sent back to Whiston."

A mirthless laugh tore itself from my throat. "Do I look like I care?"

Cadence walked around to face me, throwing her hands up into the air and matching my scowl. "Why does this matter so much to you, Chance? I'm still the same person I was five minutes ago!"

"No, no, it's not – it's just – you're not!" I sputtered, eyes darting around us as if I might find the words that would explain to both of us the things I felt and why hanging in midair. "You're not a person!"

Cadence tilted her head to one side, her hands on her hips. "What am I then?"

"You're a machine!"

"So are you!"

"What?" I tore my hands through my mangled hair. "What the hell does that even mean?"

Cadence waved at me. "When you things are opened up you look like machines too, just different kinds of machines."

I shut my eyes, rubbing my forehead as I groaned. "It's – it's different, damn it."

The fight drained out of me. I was too tired, too wrecked to stay angry for any length of time; it wasn't worth it. I sucked in a long, deep breath of air, hoping my limbs would stop shaking on their own.

"Are you going to tell him?"

Dropping my hand, I stared at her. Cadence shifted her weight from foot to foot, arms limp at her sides. "Inspector Brisbois; are you going to tell him who I really am?"

I looked at it, its skin catching the glow of sunlight, my eyes drawn against their will. She was so beautiful. The thought was there before I could stop it. Bile rose in my throat as I shook my head, grimacing.

"No. No, I won't say anything." I jabbed my finger towards her. "But if your forged papers don't pass inspection there's nothing I can do for you."

Cadence clasped her hands in front of her hips, her head bobbing in agreement. "Thank you."

"Don't thank me." An all too realistic expression of pain flitted across her face, and I dropped my gaze. "Just...stay away from me, alright?"

"Alright." Cadence hesitated before starting forward, careful to give me a wide berth as she went around me.

Several steps behind me, she stopped. I closed my eyes, praying that she wouldn't speak, that she would keep walking and never come back.

"I'm sorry, Chance. I'm very, very sorry."

Staring at the thick grass under my bare feet, I waited a full minute before seeing if she was gone. Alone, I succumbed to my body's weak desires, collapsing onto the grass, morning dew seeping into my clothes as I cradled my head in my hands, concentrating on breathing.

11

Chapter 11

Henry said nothing as he sat down next to me on the lawn. How long I had been in that prone position I was unsure, but Henry seemed content to sit there with me until the planet crumbled beneath us. He began picking at the grass, tying the blades together into a chain. As much as I wished for his guidance and comfort, I had decided not to tell Henry what I had learned about Cadence, seeing how fond of the girl he was and wanting, as always, to spare him pain. Revealing Cadence's true nature would be kind to neither of them. I never was an altruistic man, but I nevertheless had no desire to become a cruel one.

As the better part of the morning wiled away, Henry induced me to stand and come inside the gazebo, where Minerva joined us. Conversing with Henry, drawing him out of himself by asking after his studies and work, all the while she held my hand, squeezing it now and again and giving me a smile.

A little after midday a servant brought out some cold sandwiches and water, apologizing as she explained that it was all the
EO would let her take from the house. Having missed breakfast,
most everyone helped themselves to at least two of the sandwiches, Desdemona and I being the only ones who refused food.

Cadence made a point not to talk or look at me the rest of
the day, my wishes having been made clear earlier, but I found
that I could do little else than stare at her when I was sure others weren't looking. Everything about her was artificial, I knew,
and the feelings I had for her had to be wrong given that fact. I
couldn't want a machine.

The sun began to set, and we moved back into the sitting
room, waiting to be interviewed by Inspector Brisbois. One by
one everyone was called into the study, returning after a half
hour or so with the same shell-shocked expressions, the smallest smidgen of displeasure coloring their cheeks. Even Cadence
looked disquieted, though I assumed by the fact she returned at
all that her forged papers had passed inspection. Relieved by her
return, a warm sensation bloomed in my belly at the sight of her,
which I was quick to stamp out.

Soon, everyone had been seen but me. Staring out the sitting
room window, I watched the last few rays of sun paint the orange
clouds pink when Henry fell into the seat next to me, hands
balled up into fists.

"I don't like the way Brisbois is asking questions." He shifted
against the chair, gritting his teeth. "I don't think he's going in
the right direction at all."

"I'm sure he knows what he's doing," I sighed, sinking down

further in my seat, managing a smirk. "He certainly didn't become inspector because of his good looks."

Henry snorted. There was a pause while he composed himself, but it wasn't long before his hand pressed into my hunched shoulder. "How are you doing, chum?"

"Oh...surviving."

"Mr. Hale?"

I lifted my head to see a walrus mustached EO officer standing in the doorway. He gestured down the hall. "This way, please."

Henry gave me another pat on the back as I hurried to my feet, following the officer out of the room and down the hall, smoothing my rumpled hair and clothing. He knocked once on the study door before opening it, ushering me inside with a nod.

"Mr. Hale," Brisbois, standing behind my father's desk, turned, swiping an array of windows and documents off the front screen and onto the desktop panel, clearing his view. "Please, sit; I'm sure you must be exhausted."

One of the room's plush leather chairs had been pulled in front of the desk. I collapsed into it with a grunt. Brisbois walked to the sideboard, smiling. "Is it presumptuous of me to offer you a glass of your own brandy?"

I rubbed my forehead, chuckling. "Oh, very; I'd accept it anyway, if that helps."

He poured a liberal amount into one glass and a small puddle into another. Resting his back against the front of the mahogany desk, he leaned forward with a tight, sympathetic smile, handing me the larger glass. "How are you feeling?"

I took the drink, smothering a hysterical laugh. "I don't know if I'm feeling anything right now. Just..." I swished some brandy around my dry mouth, lowering the glass onto the armrest, "...shock. Pure bloody shock. I still can't believe this is happening."

Brisbois swallowed his own mouthful of brandy with a nod, crossing behind the desk and easing himself into his chair. "Can you think of anyone who would want to hurt your father like this, Mr. Hale?"

I shook my head hard, my mouth agape. "No, no one! He was—was—" I stuttered over a positive description of my father, the lie too much for even my grief to sustain. Turning away to stare at the floor, I brought my glass to my chest, speaking with slow deliberation. "Inspector, my father was not the easiest man to get along with. Quite frankly, we never got on very well ourselves. He was demanding, and patronizing, and a genius businessman; I'm certain he made a few enemies in his time. But I honestly can't think of anyone who would want to murder him."

Brisbois sat there for a moment, staring at me, assessing my character and doubtless finding me wanting. But at the time I couldn't think of anything except the way my heart had stopped when I saw my father's head smashed open on the floor.

An EO officer knocked at the door and Brisbois walked to the open portal, accepting a small diskette from the woman. He let the door swing shut behind him, tapping the disk against his palm, olive eyes cutting into me like shards of glass.

"Money can be a strong motivator for crimes like these, Mr. Hale. You'd be surprised how easily men will kill for it. And your father was a very wealthy man."

The hair on the back of my neck began to rise. I narrowed my eyes, shrugging. "Yes, I suppose he was."

Brisbois strolled back to his seat. "Do you know where your father kept his will, Mr. Hale?"

"I know he had a copy of it on the docu-disk in the top drawer there." I gestured to the desk, sipping my drink and wincing at the harsh flavors. "The official one is at his solicitors, I think, in Römer."

Brisbois made no move to validate my statement, leaning forward and meeting my eyes at last. "Do you know who benefits from his will?"

I watched him, crossing my legs. "I do, I believe."

"Your father must have loved you very much."

"I don't know how he felt about me; I never did." I cleared my throat, scrutinizing the desk's leg as my streak of honesty continued. "If my father left me anything it was because he was a stickler for tradition, the family name and all that. If he'd had another son, I'm sure he would've had no hesitations in passing me over."

"You've certainly hit the nail on the head there, Mr. Hale." Brisbois' stared at me in mock surprise, his eyes bright, but his lips pulled tight across his face.

I licked my cracked lips, eyes darting about the room. "I'm sorry?"

"Your father was going to remarry, wasn't he?"

I shrugged again in an impatient yes. Brisbois' arms fell to his sides. "It was possible that he may have had another child. And even if he didn't, one could presume a sizeable portion of the estate would go to the new Mrs. Hale."

"I suppose. Look, what exactly are you asking me?"

"I'm asking you if you killed your father, Mr. Hale." Brisbois tilted his head, the slightest smear of a smile crossing his face. "I rather think you did." He threw open a document window on the right-hand screen, adjusting his jacket over his narrow shoulders. "What I really want to know is why. I think I know, but I'm sure I don't understand the whole breadth and depth of the situation. It'd be best if you explain yourself."

At Brisbois' accusation, the world stopped spinning, the momentum flinging me off into space. I couldn't breathe, but I heard my heart beating hard against my breast and I wanted to throw up. It was too much, too much after everything else that had happened. Too much after my finding my father's broken body, too much after Cadence's revelations – too much to bear.

"He was my father."

The inspector's hands hovered over the input keys. "That's your reason?"

"No, that's not my bloody reason!" All at once I rushed back into myself, the force alone carrying me onto my feet and towards Brisbois. I slammed my glass onto the desk and felt it crack, a small river of brandy flowing over my hand. "Are you insane? He was my father, you–you contemptuous little prick! He may have been a complete bastard, but he was my only family in the world! What reason, in all the stars above, could I have for murdering him?"

"He was a complete bastard: a demanding, patronizing man who was hard to get along with, who was going to marry a woman whom you intensely dislike, and to whom he was expected to entrust much of his estate, new children or no, leaving you, I believe the expression is, tits-up in a snow drift, so please don't tempt me to arrest you, Mr. Hale, by calling me names!"

Brisbois was on his feet, face inches from mine. "I have witness statements," he swiped a document onto the left-handed screen, "confirming that the door between yours and your father's room was the only way in or out of the crime scene. Both hallway doors were locked from the inside and your father's key was found directly under his body." He moved another window onto the screen. "You were overheard joking with your good friend Mr. Henry Davers about hurrying your father into the grave just the day before!"

"That is completely–!"

"Your father's will is missing!"

My anger dissipated like snow in summer, leaving me with a lukewarm puddle of despair in the pit of my stomach. "What?"

"Last week, your father traveled to District 12 and had his will voided. Told his solicitor he was making a new one. And the docu-disk on which he stored his own copy–" Brisbois snapped the drawer open and shut, "–is conveniently gone. Vanished. Probably destroyed." He loosened the knot of his tie. "You're going to pretend you had no idea about that either?"

"This..." I stepped back, shaking my head, staring at the ground but seeing nothing. "This is a nightmare."

"It's just beginning for you, Mr. Hale. The only reason you're not in restraints right now is that I'm lacking the proper evidence." There was a brusque rap at the door and Brisbois stood, striding towards it. "But once I find what I need, you'll be spending the rest of your life in the Anteries Penal District, I promise you."

Brisbois yanked the door open and an EO officer stepped over the threshold. He whispered into Brisbois' ear, garnering a nod from the inspector, who tossed his head back in my direction before walking out of the room.

"Get him out of my sight."

I was bustled out into the hallway, where several servants pretended to not have been listening at the door, hurrying about their business. In a daze, I wandered into the entryway, feeling my way along the wall before succumbing to horror, collapsing against the plaster and sliding to the floor.

Dr. Merton stood in front of the stairs several yards away, an EO officer at one elbow and Brisbois waiting at the other. The man's eyesight seemed to be failing him further as he squinted and pulled the pad in his hands closer and farther away every few seconds. "I'm sorry, I can't quite see where I'm supposed to– oh, oh yes, thank you." He signed the screen in a flurry, handing it to Brisbois with a sigh.

Brisbois and the EO officer hurried out the open front door, where I saw Cadence standing just inside, staring at me even though I had been oblivious to her presence. Even Merton hadn't noticed her, jumping when he looked up to see her there. He was about to chastise her when he followed her line of sight to my crumpled form.

"Mr. Hale?" He rushed over, crouching beside me. "Mr. Hale, are you alright?"

A scrapping noise at the top of the stairs made us all turn to see a stretcher being pulled out of my father's room, something bulbous and heavy weighing it down, hidden under a white sheet.

Merton swallowed, turning back to me. "Here, come away. I just signed for the release of the body; they'll be taking it now.

Please, come outside. You need some air." He attempted to pull me to my feet, but my muscles refused to perform their designated functions, and we had considerable difficulty getting upright.

"Miss Turing, would you mind helping me, please?"

Cadence ran towards us. The threat of her assistance was all the motivation I needed, waving her away as I pushed myself up onto my feet and leaned against the man at my side. She followed behind us as we struggled back to the dining room and out through the veranda doors. Everyone else was outside already, talking in hushed tones, and my ignominious appearance caused quite the stir.

Henry took the steps up from the lawn two at a time and helped the doctor sit me down in a lawn chair. He knelt next to me, hand on my arm. "What is it? What did Brisbois say?"

My hands shook as I slid them across my slick forehead, the words cracking over my tongue. "Oh god, Henry! He thinks I killed my father."

Everyone began talking at once. The din pounded at my aching head like a mallet against a drum. Henry collapsed into the chair beside me. "That's absolutely ridiculous! How could he–?"

"He's certain." I dropped my hands from my face, arms hanging limply off the side of my chair. "All he's lacking is the evidence he needs to arrest me."

"And I will find it."

Brisbois' voice sent an electric shock through me which racked every muscle. I twisted around in my seat, eyes bulging. He stood in the doorway, leaning against the jamb with a grim smile. "We're leaving now, ladies and gentlemen. We have all we need. I may be in touch over the next day or so to conduct follow up interviews, so please," he gave a final wave before walking back inside, "no one leave this house."

His footsteps diminished. In short order, the sound of gravel crunching beneath the boots of other officers in the drive became audible, their PTs humming to life.

"Now, Chance." Belinda crouched beside me, tilting my face towards her. "Chance, darling, I don't want you to worry. We all know you had nothing to do with this, nothing."

I looked around at the faces surrounding me and felt less than certain of this. My head fell into my hands.

"I think he needs some time alone." Merton gestured to the group. "We could all use some rest; it's late."

One by one everyone passed me and went into the house, talking amongst themselves once more. Henry tapped the back of my chair. "Do you want me to stay?" I shook my head. His hand rose and fell, the vibrations tickling my back. "Alright. I'll be in my rooms if you need me."

For a moment, there was nothing. But then, I felt it – felt her standing behind me, eyes fixed on me. I don't know if there was something she wanted to say, something she wanted me to say, or if she wanted to make sure there was nothing I needed. But she waited there for several long minutes, without touching me, without speaking aloud any sentiment or question.

When Cadence left, I felt the hole of her there; and I almost, almost called out to her to come back.

12

Chapter 12

The first furtive rays of light slipped past the linen curtains, illuminating my mother's rooms with a dim glow. Turning over in bed, I clamped my eyes shut, but sleep had not and would not come, forcing me to face this first morning of a new world.

I tried smothering myself with a pillow, confident that losing consciousness and sleeping were almost the same thing.

After spending a few hours trying to get out of bed, even someone of my stubbornness had to admit defeat. Inside I had nothing left – no glib remarks, no chipper spirit equipped to battle the unthinkable event that had wiped me clean.

Accepting failure seemed to be the key to the rest I had sought all through the fitful night and I fell asleep at last. Nightmares awaited me in the depths of my subconscious, visions of a hellish existence in prison and my father's disappointed visage merging with Cadence's driving me back to reality.

I struggled awake and turned onto my side, groaning at the effort and rubbing my half-open eyes to banish the image of Cadence's face. It was with a distressed bellow, a frenzied flailing of limbs, and a painful thump onto the floor that I realized I couldn't rub her face away because it was there, lying on my pillow about an inch away from me.

"Goddamn it, Cadence!" I started to stand but remembered that I was naked, sending me scrambling for some bed sheets with which to cover myself. "Why– What– Do you even–" I regained my mental and physical balance enough to jab a hand towards the door. "Get out of my room!"

It hadn't occurred to me that my sudden awakening might have frightened Cadence as much as it had me. She jumped up from the mattress when I fell, clambering off the bed, and was now cringing behind a large metal lid, held in front of her like a shield.

"I brought you breakfast!"

I looked down to see a silver cart at her hip, which had various meats, breads, and jams arrayed across it. There was also a pot of tea, steaming, which had been under the lid.

"But you were asleep, and I didn't want to wake you because of everything that's happened, and I'm sure you need your rest, but I also couldn't just leave, so I was waiting for you to wake up." Frowning, she dropped the lid onto the cart with a smack. "And don't shout at me!"

I held up a hand, the other still clutching onto my makeshift robe. "Alright, alright."

My head ached and the food looked fresh, so I scuttled over and helped myself to some toast, glaring as I chewed. A thought occurred to me, and I glanced back down at the cart. I hadn't had breakfast in bed since I was a child, it being one of the many luxuries my father didn't believe in, but even so, I couldn't remember ever seeing a trolley like this being used for it.

"How did you get this upstairs?"

"The cart lift."

Sighing, I grabbed another piece of bread and sat on the mattress, tying the sheet tighter around my waist. "Why are you bringing me breakfast?"

"Everyone else had already been down. I didn't want you to miss out."

"Right. Now, why couldn't you just leave the cart and go?"

Cadence sat down next to me, hands falling into her lap. "I need to talk to you. I think I can help." She stared at the floor, threading her fingers together and tapping them against herself. "With your father's case."

I didn't know how to respond to such an offer, so I took another bite of toast instead. After a few more moments of silence, Cadence turned to me, hands rising and falling in her lap. "Inspector Brisbois is certain you're the murderer, yes?"

My toast threatened to fight its way back up my gullet. I forced it down with a grimace, nodding.

"I'm not." She put her hands, still wound around each other, over mine. "I don't think you did it at all."

I looked from her to her hands and back again, hopeful that this would signal my discomfort to her. "Why not?"

"I've seen killers. They don't look like you."

The bottom fell out of my stomach. Closing my eyes, I put the half-eaten bread on the bedside table. I had been trying not to think about what Cadence may or may not have seen or done in her escape from Whiston and the Archerusians who were so intent on destroying her kind. To have her shove her tragedy in my face with such calm left me with a sudden urge to hold her.

I bared my teeth at her. "That's very nice of you to say, dove, but the 'I don't look like a killer' argument probably won't sway the Inspector much." Drawing back my hands, I stood, heading for the teapot.

"That's not how I can help!" She squirmed to the edge of the bed, smiling. "I can investigate! Or, rather, we can investigate. On our own! I have a lot of theoretical experience with mystery solving and crime and you're not a complete idiot, so I thought you might like to try."

"Theoretical experience?" The dark brown liquid spilled into my cup as I scoffed. "You mean your book shop? That wasn't another one of your lies?"

There was a long pause. "No." She fidgeted against the mattress, smoothing down the front of her skirt. "Well, not really; I didn't sell them in the way you think. I was an entertainment installer. I would modify animanecron models with drives and programs and the like and then download leisure data into their systems – in my case, mystery novels."

"And this gives you experience solving crimes?"

Her smile vanished, eyes narrowing at my unimpressed tone. "I have over ten thousand texts stored in my system, all accessible at any time, searchable and readable." She stood, folding her arms across her chest. "Some of the most intelligent detectives in the world and their most challenging cases are in my head. I've been able to study their work at length over the last hundred and twenty years of my life and with that accumulated knowledge, I should be able to solve anything. In theory."

"No offense, Cadence, but I don't really want your help." A large gulp of tea burned its way down my throat, and I winced. "You shouldn't even be here."

"I agree. But I am and I'd like to do something useful." Cadence dropped her arms to her sides and shrugged, eyes flickering over me. "Besides, you've been kind to me. Invited me to stay in your home."

"I only did that because I wanted to bed you, ducky."

"Oh, I know." She smiled, head tilting to one side. "But it was still kind."

The cup clattered onto the tray, splashing my hand with scalding liquid. Ever since I had found out what she was, I had been anything but kind; I knew that. But rather than hold a grudge, Cadence focused on all the good things about me, and I hated her for it. I didn't want her to look at me as if she understood who I was when even I wasn't sure.

"Please. Leave."

Cadence took a step towards me. "But, I–"

"Good god, just go!" It felt good to yell and I put even more power into the next shout, pouring all the anger and frustration and pain of the last few days out onto the person who deserved it the least. "I don't want help from a talking calculator! I don't need pity from something like you!"

I grabbed her face with one hand and pulled her towards me, fingers pressing into her cheeks so hard they would've left bruises on real skin. "You're a walking hunk of scrap metal. You don't feel pain, you– you interpret data. You don't understand what it's like to be human, to have a heart; to have a father, let alone lose one!"

"Don't talk to me about loss!"

Cadence ripped my hand from her face and shoved it into my chest, knocking the wind out of me. Collapsing onto the edge of the bed, wheezing, eyes watering, I still saw Cadence clear enough, her hair caught in the corner of her mouth, her lips trembling, the lines of her face drawn taut in rage.

"I've lost everything! My family, my friends; my whole world is being butchered by you hateful, empty monsters and you soulless things don't even care!"

She rubbed her palms against her cheeks in small circles. Screwing her eyes shut, her volume dropped as she regained some semblance of control. "I thought you were different. I thought you were a better man than your father, but I was wrong. I'm sorry." Her hands fell from her face and she turned to leave. "Sorry to have bothered you."

I lunged at her, grabbing her arm before she could move any closer to the door. "Did...did you just get angry at me?"

She shook me off with an exasperated cry. "I am angry at you, Chance!"

I straightened up, blinking at her. "I didn't think you could do that."

Cadence clasped her hands together, rubbing them against her forehead as she fumed. "Of all the stupid, close-minded–!"

"What would you do if I kissed you right now?"

"You do know that I'm five times stronger than you, yes? Since you seem to know everything about my kind." I shrugged, an innocent gesture on my part that infuriated her further. "I would slap you, idiot! Hard!"

I kissed her. Hard. I pulled her flush against me, sliding my hands under the hem of her flimsy white shirt, fingers roaming over her lower back while my lips fought for purchase against her own. She burned, like a tongue of fire.

She could have thrown me across the room, but for all her rage she must not have wanted to do me any permanent harm. Prying me away, she jerked her head free from my kiss, and slapped me. With all the power she put behind it, it was more like a solid fist to the jaw, forcing me to hold on to her even tighter to keep upright.

I pulled myself up and kissed her again, keeping my eyes closed and focusing on the sensations pulsing through me at this most intimate contact. My heart raced, and only partly from fear, and, with a last shudder, I let myself enjoy the moment as I would any other.

And I did. Despite everything that she was and everything that I was afraid she might be, I felt no different kissing Cadence than I had kissing any other human being. Except that, of course, I felt ten times more aroused by her lips than I had by any others in my history; even with the throbbing bruise forming on my cheek.

A sense of clarity and direction reclaimed me. I released her, for some reason expecting to be caught up in a desirous embrace.

When she hit me this time, I had nothing to hold onto and fell to the floor with a thwack. Cadence's hands were clenched, her knuckles turning an even paler shade of white. Eyes clamped shut, she looked very much like a toddler at a toy store: beyond frustrated, but with no way to express it. She stomped one foot so hard that the vibrations rattled the paintings on my wall.

"What the hell is wrong with you?"

I sat upright, wobbling and punch drunk, rubbing my jaw. "Nothing, apparently, though I was worried there for a while."

The door slammed shut behind her.

The morning faded away before I tried to find Cadence again. I hoped she'd had enough time to cool off. My jaw stung and while I was fully aware that I had deserved it; I still didn't fancy the idea of getting hit like that ever again.

I padded barefoot down the hall to my rooms, apology well-rehearsed. The door stood open, but feeling the need to reacquaint Cadence with my well-mannered side, I knocked twice before stepping in.

My treasure was not there, but she had been. The room was a whirlwind of borrowed clothes and bath towels, toiletry items and teacups. She had even gone through some of my dresser drawers, pulling out several pieces of clothing I assumed she intended to wear at some point, the thought making me flush and smile.

I was about to exit and continue my search elsewhere when I spotted a thin white rectangle face down on my bedside table. Recognizing the optric for what it was, I also recognized that all my own had remained in their proper places. I studied the thing from a distance, teeth cutting into my lower lip.

When Cadence had escaped through the Charcornacian blockades, she could have only taken a handful of things with her. This optric was one of them; a picture important enough to take up space in the bag you were packing for survival.

Casting furtive glances all around me, I tiptoed towards it. I picked it up, tapping the screen twice. The optric came to life with a bright flash and I found myself staring into a familiar face.

Cadence sat in the middle of the group, a person leaning in on either side of her. Two older men had opted to stand in the back, crouching over and smiling with manic brightness. Half-eaten sandwiches and empty glasses littered the table in front of them and a bland digital sky hung behind. Whiston's surface was uninhabitable; they'd had to burrow deep under the regolith and into the caverns the moon was honeycombed with to create a sustainable colony. This pixilated painting of blue and white was the only sky Cadence had known.

Her face turned to one side, mouth open in a laugh, she leaned towards the red-headed woman on her left, whose brown skin was dotted with tattoos and symbols I didn't understand. The young man to Cadence's right had an arm thrown around her shoulders, waving at the camera.

It was the kind of family I had dreamed of having, and it had been hers.

I sat on the disheveled bed, staring at the optric almost without seeing it. What did she think of when she thought of them? Were they dead, lost to a war they hadn't asked for? Or even worse, left behind? Forever.

Cadence's black hair, draped loose around her face and shoulders, stood out like embers in a dark room, but the brightness of her eyes was unmatched. Round marbles, a dark, endless blue, the lines of her smile had rippled up into those eyes, making her whole face glow like a cheery fire.

The whole scene radiated warmth. Is that what Cadence thought of when she thought of them? Warmth? Love?

I stayed staring at Cadence's optric for a solid hour before I had composed myself enough to continue my search. With her words ringing in my ears, I searched the house for her, calling her name in a pathetic way that I am quite glad she was not around to hear. Just as my frustration reached its peak, one of the maids suggested that I might look for her out by the swimming pool.

I hadn't thought to make the long trek out to the pool for two main reasons. First, I was certain that Victoria would be there, and I had had my fill of her. She often spent the later hours of the day sunning herself and I couldn't imagine why she'd let something like a murder interrupt her bronzing. However, I also hadn't bothered looking for Cadence by the pool because I had assumed that she was unable to swim.

The pool, nestled at the far back of the estate, was linked to the manor by a winding, flower-lined path. As I strolled down it, I tried to work out how it would be possible for a creature like Cadence to take to the water and stay afloat. The best I could come up with was that her frame, while made of metal, must be mostly filled with air, and therefore displace more water than she weighed.

Excited to see this phenomenon in action, I ducked under some willow branches to find Cadence several feet away from the pool, sitting at one of the tables scattered about the area.

The pool had never been my favorite part of the estate and I was intrigued that Cadence had gravitated to the spot. It was a quiet clearing, bordered by white marble statues of various seafaring folk and creatures, silent and stoic, watching all who sank or swam with the same bland indifference.

Victoria was stretched out in her usual spot on the far side of the pool, next to the columns which held up the diving boards. Her skin radiated heat, sharp green eyes hidden behind thick sunglasses. By comparison, Cadence looked like one of the statues surrounding her, skin so pale I fancied that the sunlight might reflect off her skin if hit at the right angle. The effect was enhanced by the fact that, unlike Victoria, who shifted and breathed, Cadence was completely still, as if made of stone.

Walking towards Cadence with a small hitch of hesitation, I racked my brain for what to say. Sitting in one of the ornate metal chairs, Cadence's legs stretched out in front of her, and a floppy straw hat covered her face. Stopping beside her, I hoped that the sensation of another living thing so close would alert her to my presence, but it seemed that no such sense existed within her.

"Cadence?"

Wringing my hands, I was wary to touch her again without her permission. Maybe her auditory receptors shut down when she wasn't at full power.

"Cadence, are you alright?"

Her chest rose and fell; a sigh.

"I was taking a nap." She uncrossed her feet, slouching even further into her seat. "Now I am being annoyed by you."

I gestured to the chair opposite her, hopeful that annoyed was a step down from enraged. "May I sit?"

Cadence lifted the brim of her hat. If her voice had sounded less than angry, the daggers she glared into me indicated no such change in feeling. "It's your chair; sit in it if you want."

I swallowed and sat, feeling like an awkward six-year-old at his first formal event. My clothes itched and I had to grip the table to keep myself from squirming. I took a loose nix from my pocket and got it going, taking a few steadying gasps from it. At a complete loss for how to begin this conversation, it didn't help matters when Cadence dropped her hat back over her face, resuming her former position.

Clearing my throat, I put out my barely smoked nix and folded my hands on top of the table. "I didn't know that ani-manecrons took naps."

Cadence plucked the hat off her face, crunching the crown between her fingers. The glare was absent from her eyes, replaced by the detached blankness of which I had grown so fond.

"Every sentient being takes, and furthermore, enjoys naps." She pushed herself up in her seat, swinging her long legs under the table as she turned to face me. "Next to sex and showering, napping is the most enjoyable physical activity a living thing can engage in."

"I'm so relieved you had sex on that list." Smiling despite myself, I tapped the center of the table and woke up the Servo. The small screen blinked to life. "One iced lemonade and one Pentra-chan Whiskey."

Cadence folded her hands on top of the table, lifting an eyebrow. "Please?"

"Please," I added quickly, embarrassed by my lack of tact and embarrassed for being embarrassed at being rude to a machine.

The drinks appeared from the depths of the center column,

condensation dripping off the glasses. Grabbing mine, I gulped down half of it by the time Cadence finished thanking the Servo.

"Listen, Cay–"

"I didn't like you kissing me like that, Chance." Cadence examined her frozen lemonade, frowning. "It was rude and clearly unwanted and you're lucky I expressed my distaste for it on your face and not elsewhere."

I crossed my legs, casting a frightened glance at Victoria. Her chest continued to rise and fall in the steady rhythm of sleep. I moved my chair closer to Cadence, keeping my voice low. "Yes, you're absolutely right. I'm sorry; I don't know what came over me. It's one of the things I want to apologize for."

"It was not how I wanted our first kiss to go at all." She shook her head, stirring the slush around the cup with her drink's rainbow-colored straw.

"Well, I–" My mind dropped out of the track of my rehearsed apology, hands seizing around my glass. "I'm sorry, did you just say...?"

Cadence's wide eyes stared into mine as she sucked at her iced lemonade. I sat back, struggling out a laugh. "You wanted to kiss me?"

"Well, not at that particular moment, no." She tapped the sides of her glass. "But I had considered the possibility of such a thing occurring. As you said earlier, you did only bring me here because you wanted to sleep with me."

The remembrance of my confession shot through me like a pneumatic hammer to the shin. I bit down hard on the inside of my mouth, drawing a hand across my forehead. "Ah. Yes. I did say that."

"You also said I was a talking calculator." Cadence dropped her hands onto the table, her gaze to the top of her shoes. "And a piece of scrap metal. And that you didn't want my help. That you wanted me to leave."

"Yes, I remember. I'm..." Swallowing the lump in my throat, which must have been my pride, I placed my hand on top of hers. "I'm sorry I said those things, Cadence. I didn't mean them. The truth is, I'm not very good at asking other people for help."

"From what I've seen, you're not very good at asking for any-thing–" Cadence pulled one hand away, bringing her lemonade closer to her, "–from anything. Especially not politely."

"I'm afraid that's only one of my many faults." I spun my glass round on the table, staring into the whiskey which remained. "I'm cowardly, conceited, and a sluggard of the first degree. I cer-tainly don't deserve your help. During my tiny blip of existence in this universe," my shoulders sagged, "I haven't added one bit of anything to this world, good or bad. But my father did; for better or worse, the world is different because he lived in it. And he didn't deserve to die like that."

I heaved out a sigh, feeling every one of my twenty-seven years and twenty more besides. "I suppose what I'm saying is, if your offer of help still stands, I would gladly accept it. But not because I deserve it; because for everything he was and wasn't, it's my father who does."

The breeze weaved its way through the trees, branches rustling all around us. I had said too much, leaving myself hol-low. But when Cadence squeezed my hand with all the tender-ness of any living thing I had ever known, I rushed back into myself, like waves tumbling back onto a beach. I had done something right at long last.

"I would be honored to help your father." She gave me a crescent moon smile, wavering and small, but just as bright as any other, patting my hand. "And I'd be happy to help you too, if you decide you deserve it. We machines are well-versed in usefulness. It wouldn't be hard to teach you."

"One impossible task at a time, please." I mustered up a smile and ran my hand through my hair. "Let's focus on solving a crime, shall we? How exactly do you propose we go about it? I don't know about you, but my sleuthing skills are a bit rusty."

Her smile vanished into thin-lipped concentration as she leaned back in her chair. "I was considering that just before you came out."

"Excuse me, but you were napping just before I came out."

She glared again, the effect ruined by the way she slurped her drink. "I was doing both. I am equipped with over seventy multi-core processors and all of my scripts have been written to ensure that parallel processing can be executed flawlessly."

I was alarmed to find that I understood what she had said. Some of those computer science courses at university had stuck after all. "But of course; how silly of me."

"Personally, I feel it would be prudent to begin with examining the motives and personalities of each person in the house and trying to narrow our pool of suspects."

"Inductive reasoning, good idea," I sat back, propping my feet up on the rim of the table. "Shall we start with someone random and go from there?"

Cadence crossed her legs, the pink skirt she had changed into falling off her knees. "Why not start with me?"

"Why would we start with you?" I scoffed, waving away her weirdness. "It's obvious you didn't do it."

"Is it?"

"You'd hardly be offering to help me catch the murderer if that murderer was you."

"Of course I would!" She leaned forward, shaking her head. "It would be the only smart thing to do. It keeps suspicion away from me while placing me in a prime position to plant evidence against whomever I like, including you, Chance."

"Alright then," I crossed my arms over my chest, smirking. "What's your motive?"

"Well, let's think." Cadence rested her chin in the palm of her hand; the movements of her jaw making her head bounce up and down as she spoke. "Felix was a bigot. I might have killed him because of all the awful things he said about my people. Or it could be that he had discovered who I really am and threatened to reveal my secret; I had to kill him to protect myself."

A little flower of doubt began to bloom in my mind. "Did you kill him?"

"No. I was asleep in my room with my door locked like everyone else." She blew a stray hair away from her eyes, muttering. "Well, almost everyone."

"Good." I trod on that flower of doubt with the hobnail boots of trust and felt all the better for it. "I didn't do it, so who's next?"

"Hold on," Cadence straightened in her seat, bringing her hands down flat against the table. "A good detective cannot have enough data at his or her fingertips. I think it'd be best if you told me everything that happened to you since the night before the murder until you found the body."

I began to shrug but arrested the motion when I realized what that span of time included. The corner of my mouth crept up into a one-sided grimace as I gnawed the inside of my cheek. "Everything?"

"In detail, if you please."

I ran a finger along the inside of my opened collar. "Well, after dinner, I..." My instinctual reaction, honed from years of juggling women like so many colored balls, was to lie. I had one ready, something about being exhausted and going upstairs to read, when it occurred to me that just this once, the asker may not only forgive me for the truth but deserve to hear it.

I squared my shoulders and tried to meet Cadence's gaze, but still the words stuck in my throat, coming out in small stutters. "Victoria and I spent some time. Together. We– we were downstairs in the sitting room. Alone. We were there, until ten or eleven. And then we went upstairs. To my room. Together."

She didn't even blink. I leaned back in my chair, gripping the table. "Just how much detail are you looking for here, Cadence?"

"You're doing fine." Cadence flashed a toothless smile at me before resuming her blank stare. "Did you and Victoria have sex?"

I concentrated on my drink, wishing for an entire bottle of the stuff. "We did, yes."

"And did she spend the rest of the night with you or go back to her own room?"

I glanced up at Cadence. She was as unmoved as ever, though my pause elicited a sharp rise of her brows. I pulled back from the table, hands falling into my lap. "No, she, uh, she slept with me."

Cadence sat back and nodded. "That's good, a much better alibi than mine. Was the connecting door unlocked when you went to sleep?"

"No, I made sure to lock it." I wiggled against the hard seat, my brow furrowing. "But you can unlock it with either my father's key or the one I had, from either side of the door."

"Alright. So, you woke up the next morning?"

"I woke up because Merton and Belinda were trying to get into my father's room, and it was locked. I came out to see what was going on, we tried to get the door open, but couldn't. I remembered the connecting door, forgot that I had locked it the night before, and just pulled it open."

Swallowing, I leaned forward and rested my forearms against the table. "He was just..." I closed my eyes, squeezing my hands together. "My father was lying on the floor by the door."

"Did you lock your own door that night?"

"Yes, I always lock my door. Don't need over eager servants waking me up before I'd like."

"And it was still locked when you woke up in the morning?"

With most of the morning an indistinct blur, I was about to answer her with a shrug when a thought struck me. "Yes! Yes, I'm sure it was. I remember having trouble unlocking it. I usually always leave my key on the bedside table, but in all the—" I looked up at Cadence and, as well as she had taken this Victoria business, thought it best to avoid describing the frenzied way we had made love that night.

Shaking my head, I rubbed the back of my neck. "Well, I must not have the night before because it was on the floor in front of my door. I probably dropped it."

Cadence's eyes narrowed. She gave a grunt and slumped down in her seat, focusing her attention back on me. "Okay then. If we're talking about suspects, what about Henry?" Her expression softened and she frowned, bottom lip puckering out. "I know he's your friend, but I think it's only fair that we include everyone, don't you?"

"No, no, of course," I nodded with enthusiasm, relief buoying my mood. "But I should say that I don't really see Henry as the murdering type."

"You know him better than I do; but humans can do strange things under the influence of certain stimuli. He was very upset about the Negrescu Necklace."

"Henry was put-out about the necklace, but I think he'd steal it before killing for it. Of course," I rubbed my bruised jaw, wincing, "he did mention he was worried his father was going to be fired from Halcyon Enterprises."

"Ah ha!"

I stifled a laugh. No one I'd known had ever said 'Ah ha' aloud before, let alone in the impassioned way Cadence let loose the exclamation. She jabbed her finger into the air. "Perhaps he was trying to protect his father's career!"

"Perhaps," I swung my feet off the table, shaking my head. "Though Henry's never been overly concerned with his father's career or their family's social standing. If anyone was going to kill Dad for that, it would be Solomon Davers himself; or even Minerva."

Cadence's brow furrowed, her mouth missing her straw. "I

understand why Solomon would want your father out of the way. And he's clever; he could figure out how to get away with it. But Minerva. She seems a very calm, level-headed sort of person – sickly also."

"I love Minerva to pieces," I shifted in my seat, biting my lower lip and clasping my hands together, "and she's treated me like her own son since I was a child. But she loves fiercely. She'd move heaven and earth for Solomon if she thought it would make him happy."

"You know," Cadence smirked, bringing her fingers up to her lips as if uncomfortable with this unplanned display, "for someone who is entirely self-centered, you have a real talent for reading people, Chance."

Flattered, despite her reference to my less than positive quality, I responded with a shy half-smile of my own. "Thanks, Cay."

"I like that name; no one's ever called me that before!" Her smile wavered under the influence of self-consciousness. "I'd have one for you, but we're not very good at nicknames. They're difficult to process."

"Oh, that's alright! 'Chance' doesn't really shorten to anything anyway." I reached out and touched her hand. "I'm glad you like it."

Cadence's smile widened and she tucked her hair back behind her ear. "Very much so."

After a moment of silence, she cleared her throat, an action I was certain had no physical benefit for her and must therefore be a pre-programmed response. To help her recover from unease?

I stared at her, grinning like an idiot child. Heat rushed into my cheeks.

I blushed.

I spun away, desperate to cover the pinkish glow she must have already seen. Hard pressed to remember the last time I had been relaxed enough to blush in front of anyone, I took a moment to marvel at the situation that had made me react in such a way.

"Watching you two gabbing on, one would think you were old friends." Victoria's voice rang out clear and strong, like steel striking steel. Long practice allowed me to hide my wince as I looked up to see her observing us from her bed of grass, sunglasses perched on top of her head.

"It's so sad you'll be leaving, Cadence, once this whole mess is cleared up," Victoria rose from her spot of repose and walked towards us. "But I'm sure you have better things to do then hang around a house of sorrow like this." Crossing behind me, Victoria placed her hands on my shoulders. "What were you two talking about?"

I was at a loss for how to answer, but Cadence was, as always, light years ahead of me, sucking down the last of her drink before replying, "We were trying to figure out which one of us is most likely to be the murderer. We haven't gotten to you yet."

I had to talk to Cadence about her unfortunate habit of telling the truth. Victoria squeezed my shoulders tight. "You know, dear, your humor is very unbecoming." Her voice was as cold and bitter as a blizzard, tinged with a reproach I recognized all too well.

Cadence blinked at her, one side of her mouth sliding upward. "Yes. I'm beginning to realize that."

Victoria sighed and moved around me, running her hand through my hair. "Join me for a swim, Chance?"

"Not today, love." I brought her hand to my lips, placing a light kiss in the center of her palm. "I'm not really feeling up to it."

"Oh, you poor, poor dear," Victoria pressed hard kisses onto the top of my head. "I wish there was something I could do to help." She crouched down, pulling me round to face her, fingers stroking my cheeks. "Just know that no matter how long you're in prison, I'll wait for you, Chance. I love you that much."

I grabbed her wrists and yanked her hands off my face, her nails scratching me on the way down. "For god's sake, Victoria, I didn't kill my father!"

"I know that!" She bounced to her feet, eyes wide with shock, but her lips a thin, angry line. "But it's not looking very good for you, is it?"

"Well, thank you so very much for the vote of confidence!"

From the forgotten space to my left, there came a long crackling noise, like someone chewing gravel. Victoria and I turned to find Cadence sucking at the last few pools of lemonade at the bottom of her cup, determined to taste every drop.

Looking up, she smiled. "This was really good." She shook the empty glass, straw rattling from side to side. "May I have another?"

Victoria pounced on her without hesitation, arms akimbo, and eyes blazing like wildfire. "I have to say, Miss Turing, I think it's shameful the way you're taking advantage of Chance. If he wasn't such a big-hearted idiot," she shot an incensed glower in my direction, "you'd be left to sell yourself on a corner in Römer somewhere – a job you've shown a real flair for in the last few days."

"You'll have to tell me where the best corner is, Victoria. I always listen to the voice of experience."

A loud bark of laughter burst from me like water from a dam. The sound surprised me into immediate silence, and even Victoria had been struck dumb, her mouth agape, breath coming out in sharp sputters.

I stumbled to my feet, forcing myself to laugh once more. "Cay's a real card, isn't she, Vicky?" I patted my gasping lover on the back. "I think I'll head back to the house, sun's a bit much for me, what about you, Cadence?"

Cadence reclined in her chair, gaze shifting from the enraged Victoria to me and back again. "What about me?"

I drew a hand down my face, frustrated that subtext seemed to be one of the few things beyond Cadence's considerable grasp. "Didn't you have something to do back at the house, pet?"

"No. I–"

I adopted a look of panicked desperation that proved much easier to read. Cadence's face cleared and she turned back to Victoria, nodding. "Sinc, yes. I'd forgotten. Belinda was going to show me the crystals in the garden." She flashed a smile before resuming her unflappable calm, and stood, striding with purpose back towards the house.

I watched her go, slipping my hands into my pockets. Then, because I am a man who will never burn a bridge that leads back to a willing woman, I stole a kiss from Victoria and hurried away.

13

Chapter 13

"I think I would like to kiss you again," I said, out of breath from my jog across the yard. Grasping Cadence's arm, I steered her to the right. "Not that way, m'dear, this way."

"Why do you want to kiss me?" Cadence stopped short and I stumbled over my own feet. "And I thought you said we were going back to the house?"

I slid my hand into hers, holding it tight. "No one has ever told Vicky off like that. Ever. It was sensational and I loved it." I kissed the back of her hand with a cartoonish smack. "And I told Vicky we were going back to the house because that way, if she wanted to look for us, she'd have a place to start. We are, in fact, going to the garden, over here."

I tugged her again and she allowed herself to be pulled, falling in step beside me. "Oh! You lied."

I cast a glance over my shoulder. "Not very convincingly, I'm afraid."

"I think it was very good." Cadence sighed. "I could never lie like that."

"Really?"

She nodded, bending down to pluck a white wildflower as we walked. "Animanecrons have some difficulty with lying. I understand what it is," her long fingers stroked each petal in turn, "but we generally don't see the point."

"Are you saying that animanecrons don't lie?" I scoffed at the assertion, flinging my hand back towards the pool. "But you told me you were from Paraesepe! And just now, you told Vicky that—"

"It wasn't a lie." Cadence spun the curled stem between her fingers. "Belinda really does want to show me the crystals." The stalk pin wheeled to the ground. She sighed again. "I can lie, if I have to. I just don't like to." The edges of her lips curled into a small smile. "I mean, even humans don't enjoy lying, right?"

I stared at the top of my shoes. "No, we don't enjoy lying."

Cadence and I soon arrived at the small gardens, which were, as I understood it, my mother's only addition to Hale Manor. They had been kept up in her absence, and in those heady days of summer the tall shrubs that lined the cobbled pathways were blooming and the small, thin trees reclaimed their green coats.

Cadence gestured towards the side of one of the paths with her hat, staring at the shimmering colored stones nestled between the flowers. "Are those Belinda's crystals?"

"Yes; Aunt Be helped design this place. Those are from her personal collection; crystals are her specialty, you know."

At the center of the garden, stone benches and fountains were strewn about as if tossed by a playful giant. Reclining on one of these granite seats, Cadence balanced her hat on the far edge and smiled up at me. "Should we keep going?"

I squeezed into the corner of the bench, anxious to prove to her that further physical advances from me would be made only when appropriate.

Cadence looked at me and, without a word, scooted closer until our feet touched. "Who do we have left?"

"Well," I extended my arm behind her, careful to confine it to the bench's back, "I think we've run through everyone who was really close to my father, except Belinda."

"And Desdemona."

I snorted. Cadence slid down in her seat, crossing her arms over her belly. "She was going to marry him; I'd say that makes them pretty close."

"Please," I sneered. "It was a passing infatuation, a bizarre manifestation of his first mid-life crisis. Even if he had gone through with it, he would've divorced her within the year, I'm certain of it."

Cadence shrugged. "Maybe she thought she would be in his will already. Or perhaps she found out she wasn't going to be, and she was angry."

My face lit up with a triumphant grin as I snapped my fingers. "That would explain why it's missing!"

"What?" Cadence stopped pushing her flat shoes off her feet, jerking to attention. "Your father's will is missing?"

"Brisbois thinks the murderer must have destroyed it for some reason." I held a finger to my lips. "Henry and I overheard

Solomon and my father talking about it earlier that day; my father was completely rewriting the will. Perhaps Desdemona killed him because she thought he had already changed it in her favor!"

"Then why would she destroy it?"

My mouth hung open. "Ah. I see your point." I huffed and rolled my shoulders back. "She still could have killed him though."

Cadence ignored my final words, chewing on her bottom lip. "Belinda's a bit of a problem too."

"What makes you say that?"

"Well, from the limited number of interactions I've had with her, I'd definitely say she's the murdering type."

I paused halfway through shrugging off my jacket, a grimace pulling my lips taut. "That's an awful thing to say, Cadence!"

"Killing someone's an awful thing to do, Chance!" She pushed herself up, her brow furrowed and lips pursed. "Anno, it's not as if I'm saying she's a bad person."

Draping my jacket over my knees, I shook my head, sneering. "Murderers are generally not good people, Cay."

She opened her mouth as if to disagree, but, after a moment, she shut it again, teeth snapping together. Swallowing and blinking, her body relaxed back into the crook of my arm. "I didn't say she was a murderer. That's the problem, you see? I think she's capable of it, but I can't fathom any reason in the world why she'd want to kill your father."

"Good. Belinda's been a part of the family since before I was born." I shifted under her, unable to decide where to put my hand before tossing propriety to the wind and curling my arm around her shoulders. "She and my mother grew up together and she's always been there for Dad and me."

"We're left with Dr. Merton and Victoria then." Cadence nuzzled against me, her elbow digging into my spleen. "Would you consider Merton a friend of the family as well?"

"Not really." I leaned into her, trying to dislodge her joints from the more vulnerable areas of my body. "It's hard to become a part of people's lives when you only see them when they're ill. Not the best memories, you understand?"

"Any reason he'd want to kill your father?"

"No." Staring down at her, breath shallowing as the heat of her warmed me, I found the sensation so fascinating that it was hard to focus on the conversation at hand. "I can't see mumbling Merty murdering anyone anyway; he's a cowardly little man."

Cadence grunted, fingers tugging at the lock of hair tucked behind her ear. "And fear has never driven humans to kill?"

Her optric flashed before my eyes. The universe would be hard pressed to find someone more unqualified than me to judge whether Cadence had a soul, but there had been a certain brightness in her eyes in the optric that, while not gone, was now dull – tarnished.

I cleared my throat. "I suppose you're right, though. Merton doesn't seem a very likely murderer, leaving us with Victoria."

"Do you think she could kill someone?"

"I must admit, it's all too easy to imagine her as a murderer," I squeezed Cadence's shoulder. "But she doesn't have any kind of motive, however blood thirsty she may be, so we'll have to mark her off the list as well."

Cadence smiled. "I beg to differ. You told me yourself: Victoria can assume that she will soon be your wife."

I nibbled at the inside of my cheek, shivering in the sun. "I don't know about soon." Pulling her closer, I brushed some hair from the corner of her eye. "But yes, I suppose so. What does that have to do with anything?"

Cadence rested her head on my shoulder. "I just wonder if Victoria might have been a little overanxious to be the wife of the head of Halcyon Enterprises."

"You mean she wanted to marry my father too?"

Cadence looked up at me wide eyed, a small smile stretching her lips. She patted my knee. "Your father is dead, Chance."

I bristled under her obvious mockery. "I hadn't forgotten, Cadence, I – oh. That's a bit of a stretch, isn't it?" Pulling away, I rubbed my bottom lip, squinting. "Do you really think Vicky would kill my father just to make sure I inherited?"

Sighing, Cadence slid back to her side of the bench, grabbing her discarded hat. "You'd know better than I." She cast a cool glance in my direction, slumping in her seat and dropping the hat over her face. "You're the one who's going to marry her after all."

Shooting her a useless glare, I stood, sulking as I stretched out my cramped muscles. "You're not honestly going to nap again, are you? When there's a killer on the loose?"

Cadence lifted the straw hat from her face, shrugging and shaking her head. "None of us are going anywhere, are we?" She reclined, hat descending once more. "Trust me, no investigation was ever hurt by the detective taking a nap. Who knows, maybe the answer will come to me in my sleep."

"Detective," I gave a snort and prodded her leg with the toe of my shoe. "Getting a bit ahead of yourself, aren't you? You haven't done any actual detecting yet."

But Cadence would not be baited. I shoved my hands into my pockets, scowling. "Shouldn't we go interrogate someone? Or maybe you could distract everyone while I search the bedrooms for some damning evidence."

"Chance, sit down and be quiet or go away and be noisy elsewhere."

With a loud humph, I stalked off towards the house, feeling as piqued as I dared. Cadence could nap if she wanted to; I might not have possessed her crime solving expertise, but I knew that every investigation started with asking questions, and that's what I resolved to do.

An opportunity presented itself as soon as I walked through the front door, the sounds of an argument floating around the entryway. I followed the tendrils of sound to their source like a starving man to a fragrant plate of food. The voices came from the sitting room, its door shut tight. Like an old biddy at a keyhole, I leaned against the wood, straining to hear inside.

"I tell you I'm fine!" Desdemona's voice played along the top of her register, the door doing little to muffle its cracking. "I don't need that stuff anymore!"

I was surprised to hear Dr. Merton's voice answer her, soft and plaintive. "I know you don't need it, Dezzie, but I think it might help—"

"I said no, Douglas!"

I jumped back from the door as it swung open, screeching on its hinges. Desdemona's pale hair hung around her face, her eyes bloodshot as she stormed out of the room, squeezing her temples. "Please, can't you just leave me alone? Can't everyone just leave me alone?" She ran down the hall, turning and stumbling up the stairs. The door to her room crashed shut.

I waited a moment before strolling into the sitting room, hands in my pockets. "Everything alright, Doctor?"

Merton started as I entered, glancing around the room as if he'd forgotten something. He flexed his hand in and out of a fist, sighing. "Yes, perfectly fine. Poor thing's just a bit hysterical. Understandably, of course."

He dropped a small vial of burgundy liquid into the medical bag at his feet. Following my line of sight, he smiled, waving to it. "I was trying to give Desdemona a light sedative; calms the nerves. Would you like some? I'd be more than happy to–"

"No, no thank you, Doctor." I collapsed into the plush love seat across from him with a grunt. "No need of your potions today."

He shrugged and returned to his bag, latching it shut before walking to the door.

"Actually, I was wondering: do you remember the last time you saw my father? On the night he was killed, I mean."

Merton stopped, turning to look at me, his brow furrowed. I leaned forward, spreading my hands in front of me. "I was just curious if he was still feeling unwell from the night before."

Merton seemed to consider the question and find it harmless enough to answer, taking several steps back into the room and adjusting his glasses. "I believe when I last saw him, he was heading upstairs from the library. I had just come from Miss Tanith's room – she had been complaining of a headache – when I noticed him on the stairs. I called out, asked if he needed anything, but he said he was alright and told me to go to bed. That was around eleven, I think."

"Did he seem alright?"

Merton's brows rose and fell. "Yes, fine. Quite his usual self."

I watched him a beat longer than necessary, trying to intimidate the truth out of him. But he gave no further answer, just peered at me, grimacing.

"Thank you, Doctor."

Merton inclined his head and walked again through the door, this time making it all the way into the hallway before turning around and clearing his throat, back hunched, head bowed. I glanced up at him and he crossed his arms, rubbing the inside of his wrist with his thumb.

"I wanted to say, Mr. Hale, how terribly sorry I am that this happened. I admit to feeling almost responsible for the way things have turned out for you and your family. I–I couldn't alleviate your poor mother's suffering, may she rest in peace, and–and now..." His dark brown hair fell into his eyes, and he shoved it back, deflating, rubbing the back of his neck. "I suppose it's silly, but I can't help but feel I'm bad luck to you."

I pressed my hand to my chest, smiling. "I appreciate your concern, Doctor, but believe me: I don't blame you for a thing. I know you've done all you could."

Watching him leave, I pondered my next move. Getting to my feet with a spring in my step, I proceeded to the servant's quarters, an area into which I had never ventured, seeking to interview the household staff. Alarmed by my presence, and with the fear of dismissal palpable in their looks, the staff proved reticent to the point of obnoxious and I learned next to nothing.

The realization that as the head of the household I would have been well within my rights to fire the lot of them unnerved me. Ambition had never been counted among my many sins, the pursuit of it leading to the accumulation of responsibilities; fetters I had always avoided. Now it seemed that the shackles of accountability were cinched tight, a noose around my innocent neck, with no reprieve forthcoming.

On my way upstairs, a young maid mustered the bravado to demand the return of my breakfast dishes. Enamored of her boldness, I promised to send them down at once. However, the cart, sitting where I had abandoned it beside my bed, refused to be moved. I bent down to see what the trouble was and found a scrap of cloth caught in one of the wheels. Tugging the scrap loose, I slipped it into my jacket pocket, thinking that I would dispose of it in the kitchen incinerator later.

With the dinner hour drawing near and the sun setting, I began to worry that Cadence, still not returned from her somnambulate indulgences, would be unable to find her way back to the house in the dark. Throwing a light coat over my shoulders, I stepped out onto the patio, resolved to head out to retrieve my guest, when Victoria skidded around the corner, taking the stairs up to the porch two at a time.

"Hello, Vicky!"

She looked up with a start. Even the dim light couldn't hide the deep scowl on her face. She spun on her heels and stomped back the way she came.

"Vicky?"

She took the steps down to the lawn as quick as she dared in her high heeled shoes, struggling to maintain an air of dignity, and gripping the wall next to her as she went. "I've decided I'm not speaking to you, Chance!"

I smirked, hopping down the stairs after her. "Clearly your mouth and your brain are at war with each other, darling."

Victoria turned at my snide remark, missing the last step and pitching forward. I reached out and grabbed her shoulders, but she knocked me away, leaning against the house and sputtering.

"Now," stepping back, I thrust my hands into my pockets, "what have I done to deserve this cruel and unusual punishment?"

"Isn't Miss Turing around somewhere?" Victoria stuck out her chin, casting exaggerated glances around us. "I'm amazed she's not underfoot at this very moment, following you about like a stray dog."

Victoria... jealous? After all this time? I had too high an opinion of her intelligence to think her ignorant of my many trysts in the past, and yet, she had, up until this point, shown no inkling of jealousy. Still, I knew how to respond to such outbursts, and it took me less than a moment to adjust my demeanor, sighing and rolling my eyes. "Oh, I know. It's awful, isn't it?"

Victoria stared, arms falling to her sides. "What?"

I rested my hand above her shoulder, shaking my head and shrugging. "Poor thing is just so helpless, you know? If I'd known all this was going to happen, I wouldn't have brought Cadence here at all; now I'm stuck with the clingy woman."

Victoria's armor melted away, her body slumping against the wall. She attempted a glower, but it lacked all conviction. "I got the impression that you rather liked being clung to, Chance, dear." I squeezed her arm and saw the smile in her eyes. "That you were enjoying your chance to play the knight in shining armor."

I closed the gap between us with a step, tutting. "Please, my darling–" I laid a soft kiss on one corner of her mouth, "–sweet–" my lips brushed the opposite corner, "–vivacious Victoria," I pushed myself against her, lifting her chin up and resting my forehead against hers, grinning. "You know I much prefer playing the dashing rogue."

I kissed her full on the mouth, running my tongue along her bottom lip before cupping the back of her head with my hand and pulling her deep into my embrace. The setting sun warmed my back, save for the slender bands where Victoria wrapped her arms around me. I drew away, smattering kisses on her cheek and chin.

Her face flush, she seemed otherwise unmoved by my affection, a smirk twisting her lips. "That's because you do it so well."

"Yes, I do, don't I?" I nuzzled the tip of her nose, my smile shrinking. "The truth is Vicky, you were right. I'm just terribly upset about this business with my father. I'm in really big trouble this time and I don't know how I'm going to get myself out of it."

Victoria gave a soft, unconvincing coo of pity, cradling my face in her hands. "Is there anything I can do to help?" She slid her hands down my neck and chest, settling on my hips and squeezing. "Any way I can...take your mind off your troubles?"

"Mm, I can always think of things like that. But you could help me another way too."

"What's that?" All traces of the bitter, envious Victoria had fled, replaced by a happy, delusional young woman.

"Brisbois is so damned certain I'm the killer, but there has to be something, some little detail that can get me clear of all this. Was there anything you could tell him about the night my father died? Anything useful that you noticed?"

"No, I'm sorry, pet. I slept straight through the night. After all, I was so exhausted after we..."

She wound her tongue around her lips, digging her light green nails into my hip. I fought the urge to pull away, something in the pit of my stomach growing heavy, and forced myself to kiss her with a growl, raking my hand through her hair and not stopping until oxygen became an issue for the both of us.

I eased back, swallowing, leaving Victoria to gasp in the cool evening air as she shook her head. "No, I wasn't any use to the Inspector at all. But you know what I did see?"

I tilted my head to one side, lifting a brow in question.

"Well," Victoria threw her arms around me again, "when he was interviewing me, Brisbois got a call and had to step outside to take it. I was walking around the room, stretching my legs and I saw a picture of Desdemona on his screen." She closed her eyes as if the memory pained her, groaning. "And she looked awful, just awful, and terribly young; it must have been from years ago. Anyway, you won't believe it, but it was a mug shot!"

The weight in my stomach solidified into lead. Victoria giggled, grinning wide. "Apparently, our Desdemona used to be a drogan addict and stole some jewelry to pay for the habit; picked the lock on a cabinet in some house in District 12, grabbed the stuff and ran! So, I guess we know who stole the Negrescu now, don't we?"

I struggled to nod, my mind miles away, back at the morning

before, when I had pounded in vain on my father's locked door, trying to wake the dead. Could Desdemona have picked the lock, snuck inside, and killed him? Had my father found out about her less than savory past and threatened to leave her, forcing her into desperate action?

"Are you alright, Chance?"

I couldn't bring myself to look at Victoria's face, staring instead at her shoulder. "Yes, dearest, I'm fine. It's just a shock, isn't it?"

"Oh, not really! You said that she was a worthless little tramp, and you were right!" Victoria pulled me close to her, pushing her face into my neck. "It's a shame you can't throw her out of the house right now, but soon it will all be yours. And we can enjoy it together, just like we always talked about."

"I can't wait, dove."

Victoria looked up at me, head falling to one side. She smiled after a moment, patting my back. "I think I'll head inside; dinner should be ready soon."

I worked up a smile in kind and stepped back, waving to the house. "I'll catch you up."

She blew me a kiss as she moved up the stairs, disappearing onto the porch. At the sound of the door latching shut behind her, I let out a huff, shaking out my rumpled clothes with a shiver.

I turned and walked into the twilight, more intent on finding Cadence than ever, when I saw, with a start, that she had found me. Standing by the far corner of the patio, leaning against the brick, I could tell she must be looking in my direction, but any details of her face were blotted out by the deepening shadows.

"What were you doing?"

"Trying to get some information out of Victoria," I started towards her, missing the flatter than usual tone of her voice. "I think—"

"I don't like her."

I stopped, brow furrowing. "That's fine; the feeling's mutual."

Cadence's eyes were unnaturally bright in the darkness, illuminating her deep frown like a torch. She turned away, pressing herself flush against the brickwork, arms crossed over her stomach. "I don't want you to be alone with her."

I jerked back, shaking my head, trying to clear out the static of surprise and find my words, a smile splitting my face. "Cadence, are you... are you jealous?"

She rolled back her shoulders, sliding down the wall. "No. That would imply that I felt some sort of exclusive attachment to you which, hila, would be silly."

"Not that silly."

Taking in a deep breath, her head fell to one side as she glared. "If she is the murderer, she could be dangerous. Besides, it's traditional for the two detectives to work the case together. If we go off on our own, we might miss something the other wouldn't. So, you should stay. With me." Her smile, born of triumphant reasoning, dimmed, her eyes narrowing. "Not Victoria."

I swallowed down a peal of laughter, tongue pinched between my teeth. "Alright, Cay, alright. You're the expert, I suppose." Stepping closer to her, I placed my hands against the wall on either side of her head and leaned in, my voice a rough whisper.

"I wouldn't mind if you were jealous, you know. I'd think it was sweet."

Cadence, darling Cadence, so stoic and unflappable, slipped for a moment, breaking eye contact to glance at my arms before shaking her head. "Unfortunately, I am not jealous, therefore, not sweet."

"You really are though." I brushed the front of my body against hers, my lips at her ear. "Very, very sweet."

A soft, suckling kiss on the underside of her jaw would have proved my point, but that was the moment when Belinda's voice cut through the stillness like a chainsaw.

"Chance!" Her shadow thrown down against the grass, Belinda's footsteps clattered across the porch above us. "Chance, dear!"

I pulled back from the object of my desire with a sigh. Cadence stared at me, one side of her mouth cocked upwards in a cheeky grin. The sight of her sent a throb of pleasure through me that made my knees buckle. Having no time to inquire after her pleasing expression, I grabbed her wrist and tugged her up onto the patio with me.

Belinda, relieved rather than puzzled at our sudden appearance, ceased her hand wringing. Eyes red from crying, she still held herself tall, reaching out to me for comfort.

"There you are, dear. There was a call for you from the EO Medical Department. They said they moved your father to Drexel's Funeral Parlor, per his solicitor's instructions. You can go in and make the arrangements tomorrow, if you feel up to it."

My seductive bravado crumbled like so much dried sand, smile disappearing as my shoulders hunched. Cadence stepped forward, hand on my arm. "This would be your opportunity to view the body, yes?"

"I suppose so, but–"

"You feel up to it." She swept past us, undoing the clasps of her shirt in preparation of her changing for dinner. "I'll meet you out front after breakfast, and we can head out then."

Belinda shook her head, waiting until Cadence's heavy foot falls had faded away before speaking. "I don't like the way that woman talks to you, Chance. You're the head of this family; you deserve to be treated with respect."

I clicked my tongue against my teeth, wrapping an arm around Belinda's shoulders and kissing her cheek as I led her inside. "Don't worry about Cadence, Aunt Be. She's just trying to take care of me."

14

Chapter 14

The morning dawned drizzly but warm, a presage of the monsoon season soon to come. Cadence sat beside me in the back of the PT, fingers at her lips as I told her everything I had gleaned from my solo investigations: from Dr. Merton and Desdemona's argument in the sitting room to the illuminating results of Victoria's snooping.

Absorbing all this information with the quiet voracity of a sponge, Cadence kept her questions until I had finished, hand falling into her lap. "What's drogan?"

"It's a drug; a liquid that you inject into any major vein, like the ones in the arm. Users get frenzied on it – very strong, very dangerous. It's instantly addictive; the high makes you feel like a god, apparently."

"Do you think Desdemona is still using this narcotic?"

"Not a chance. My father may have made some bad decisions

as far as Desdemona was concerned, but he hated addicts of all kinds. She would have had to take regular drug tests to work at Halcyon Enterprises anyway." Cadence looked at me, eyebrow raised in question. "That's where they met."

"So, it's possible to stop using drogan?"

"Possible, but hard. I think they have some rehabilitation clinics down south."

Cadence leaned back in her seat, crossing her legs. "These files the EO keep sound extremely useful. I wonder if I could get Inspector Brisbois to let me see some of them."

"And just how would you manage that?"

Cadence smiled, running a hand through her hair. "Ask nicely, of course."

Grimacing, I turned to look out the window, squirming as the first pang of jealousy hit me like an iron bar to the stomach. I was almost certain that acts of useful flirtation were beyond my preprogrammed prize, but I had seen the way she and Brisbois had been carrying on and found it hard to ignore the obvious attraction between them, counterfeit or no.

Drexel's Funeral Parlor, where the most affluent citizens of Zahia came to rest, stunk of formaldehyde, synthetic flowers, and overworked electronics. We spent our first hour there sitting in the funeral director's office, talking at great length about my father, a subject upon which the director seemed to consider himself an expert, despite having only met the man as a corpse. A grim little man with smooth palms and knotted fingers, furry eyebrows hunched over his dulled brown eyes, he wriggled as he spoke.

With all the arrangements and forms done away with, we

were escorted to the mortuary to view the body before it came under the director's ministrations. The director balked at this request at first. He insisted that it was hardly customary to let the family view the body before it had been properly seen to, explaining that the whole experience may be upsetting. But after a while he relented, accepting my explanation that due to the circumstances of my father's demise, I felt I had not yet truly had an opportunity to accept his death and that this would help. Talking all the while, he cycled between empty condolences and practical cost estimates with ease.

"Am I right in remembering that your father requested a burial, rather than a cremation, Mr. Hale?"

"Yes. He wanted to give his loved ones something to go back to and pay their respects."

Father was conceited like that; I kept the thought to myself.

The director gave a heavy sigh, as if the weight of my father's life had been thrown solely across his diminutive shoulders. "Well, that will be somewhat more difficult and costly to arrange..."

"Money isn't a problem," I said for what must have been the fiftieth time.

The man shook his head from side to side with such vigor I was afraid it would pop off. "No, no, of course not, sir, I didn't mean to imply, by no means, yes; indeed, why should it be a problem?"

The director fell silent as he unlocked the slab-like doors which led to the mortuary. The hermetic seal broke with a whoosh, the doors sweeping open across the linoleum floor. The air inside was stale and cold and tasted like candied plastic, over-sweet and thick. Unlike the rest of the funeral home, decorated in the expected blacks, grays and occasional pastels, the mortuary was painfully bright, every steel surface polished to perfection.

A row of metal beds stood in the center of the room, all empty except for one. I stared at the body, covered by a thick white sheet as if that alone could restore the dignity lost in death, and recognized my father's familiar shape.

"The EO returned your father's personal effects as well, sir." The director handed me a large bag, sealed at one end. "I would be more than happy to dispose of them for you."

His blue suit was visible through the plastic, as were the dark brown specks which stained it. I would have liked nothing better than to hand the gruesome package back and let them burn it all, but Cadence stared at the bag with undisguised excitement. Passing it from hand to hand, I swallowed hard, nodding. "Thank you, but I think I'll deal with these myself."

"As you wish, sir. I will leave you for a moment." He extended an arm towards Cadence. "Would you like to wait out in the hallway, miss?"

She glanced back at me, brow furrowing, before shaking her head. "No, thank you. I'd quite like to see."

He shrugged and departed, shutting the doors behind him.

With all the masculine bravado of which I was bereft, Cadence flung the sheet away, exposing my father's body to the unflattering lights. His jaw was fractured, jutting out to one side in a grotesque scream. His open eyes, covered in a grey film, bulged out from his skinless face, a sharp contrast to the purple and green flesh everywhere else. With the back of his skull collapsed, the rest of his head looked like a deflated balloon.

I saw where the EO medics chipped away at the bone and removed his brain.

"I'm going to be sick."

Cadence leaned over the body, waving towards the wall. "There's a sink over there."

I dry heaved over the deep sink for the next few minutes, holding the sides for balance as my head swam. Haven eaten no breakfast in preparation for this moment, there was nothing for me to throw up, but my throat still burned as it spasmed. I ran the faucet, bringing handfuls of water up to my mouth and sucking up the liquid as I shook. Behind me, I heard Cadence moving around, humming and tutting.

"I'm afraid nothing's jumping out at me," she said at length. "He was killed with several blows to the back of the head. The skin on his face has been scrubbed away. But with what, and for what purpose, it's impossible to say. Initially I had assumed his broken bones were further injuries sustained during the initial attack, but," a crackling that made me gag and clutch the edges of the sink sounded, "there's no bruising around the breaks in any of his limbs, nor is there significant blood pooled into the breaks in his neck. So, they must have been inflicted postmortem; again, for some reason which is indeterminable at this time.

"He was still in his day clothes, which means he hadn't had time to undress for bed before he was attacked." Her footsteps echoed in the empty room, followed by the squeal of a seal being ripped open. "I don't see anything immediately helpful in his personal effects either."

I walked back to her, grateful that Cadence had re-covered the body now that she was done with it. She stood by one of the empty metal beds, tipping out the contents of the plastic bag. Tossing the bag to the floor, Cadence moved her hands over the jumble of items with a frown, pushing some things aside and picking up others for examination.

My eyes were drawn to the folded suit of clothes. Some dispassionate F.O tech had marked the blood stains with black circles and written a small number beside each one. With shaking hands, I lifted the jacket up by its shoulders, the fabric swinging and twisting as it dropped open. It looked several sizes too small. My father had been a large man in life, but his clothes had shrunk now he was gone. My gaze moved over the fabric with reluctance until the flapping left sleeve drew attention to a dark stain on its elbow.

Picking at the sleeve with the tips of my fingers, I pulled the fabric closer. The dark stain wasn't a stain, but a hole in the jacket itself. A small, jagged tear, frayed strings swayed around the edges, the lighter stripes running off into the hole like train tracks off a cliff. The gap tugged at something in my memory.

"Hold on a moment," I put the suit down and began digging through my pockets. Cadence paused in accordance with my request, looking up through half-lidded eyes.

I pulled the tattered piece of cloth I had found the afternoon before out of my breast pocket and held it up to the light. The fabric was a perfect match to my father's suit, a dark blue with lighter blue stripes. Laying the scrap over the hole in the jacket, it fit like the final piece of a jigsaw.

"Chance!" For once, Cadence looked as impressed with me as she should have been, mouth hanging open, her bored eyes now wide with excitement. She jabbed her finger at the ripped segment. "Where did you get that?"

"It was stuck in the wheel of that cart that you left in my room." I turned the swatch over in my hands, rubbing it between my fingers. "How the hell did it get there?"

Cadence's face went blank quicker than a shut-down screen. She started tapping the table in a quick, eccentric pattern, running her tongue across her lips. "I don't know."

My brows came down hard as I stared at her, one corner of my mouth pulled up over my teeth. "You're lying. You definitely need to practice if you ever want to get away with it."

Cadence cleared her throat and looked away, still tapping. I shook the fabric at her. "This is important somehow, isn't it?"

"It is. But it's dangerous to theorize in advance of the facts." Bursting into a laugh, Cadence slapped her hand against the table, leaving a dent in the thick metal. "Cy, I'm pretty sure it means you're off the hook though, Chance, I am pretty damn sure about that! I have to check on some things back at the house, let's go!"

All the way home Cadence refused to share her conclusions with me, insisting that to do so would not only confuse me, but ruin the suspenseful flow of narration. Literature never being a strong subject of mine, I nevertheless realized that what she meant was that she didn't want to spoil the surprise.

When we arrived back at the manor, Cadence marched

through the foyer and into the hallway on the right, coming to a stop in front of the back wall. To her left was a shabby staircase which led to the staff's quarters. In the opposite corner a small, brown button sat.

Cadence depressed the button and the dumbwaiter's door slid open with a creak. Taking a step back, hand at her chin, she gazed into the opening as if waiting for it to speak. After a minute, Cadence dropped down on all fours and crawled inside. It was a tight fit for a woman of her size, and she soon scooted out again, fingers tapping against the ground. Crawling partway in again, she moved her fingers along the welded edges of the shaft.

Jumping back with a small grunt, her skin pricked by the imperfect seams, she sucked at her fingertips and sat back on her haunches, staring down the hall. "The kitchen butts up against this wall here..." Cadence laid her hand against the wall, "and the dining room is on the far end..."

She pursed her lips, looking up at me as she patted the dumbwaiter. "Who has the room closest to this?"

"Henry, then his mother and father, and then Dr. Merton," I said, pointing out each room in turn. "Why?"

Cadence stared at the ground, frowning as if it had insulted her. She made a clicking sound, one arm shooting into the air. "Well, the proximity alone is certainly suggestive."

"Proximity? To the dumbwaiter?" I took her by the hand and hoisted her up, still surprised by her substantial weight.

"Are you certain that Henry doesn't have any violent tendencies?"

"He can be particularly vitriolic about resurgence era modernist poetry, but other than that, no."

Throwing her hands into the air, Cadence headed down the hallway to his room. "I better ask him myself."

"Ask him what, if he's a psychotic killer?" I grabbed her arm, shuttering forward as she dragged me along before noticing my attempt to stop her. She glared at me and shrugged.

With a sigh, I released her, shaking my head. "Alright, alright, we'll go see Henry. Let me do the talking though. He's liable to think you're a bafter if you go about it your way."

Cadence blinked at me, drawing away from me slightly. "Bafter?"

I spun my finger next to my temple. "Bafter, you know – crazy? Just let me handle this."

There was no answer to my knock and, seeing as the door was unlocked, I let myself into Henry's rooms. He wasn't there and it occurred to me that he might be out on one of his constitutions, curled up on some grassy knoll with a pad and a stylus. If that was the case, we would have little chance of finding him until he decided to wander home.

I had said as much to Cadence when a manservant caught sight of us in the hall and informed us that if we were looking for him, the young man had gone out to the shed some time before.

The shed, my father's workroom whenever he brought technical projects home from the office, was a squat, brown thing around the side of the house, hidden from view by some well-placed trees. Originally a greenhouse, it still retained several flowering specimens to which the groundskeepers tended. Over time it had been taken over by more scientific equipment, such as relays, test models, microscopes and chemical distillers.

Nix dangling from between my lips, I pushed the door open and strolled in with Cadence close behind. Henry sat at the work bench closest to the door, underdressed by his standards: a thin cotton t-shirt and a pair of well-worn corduroys making him look almost common. The computer hummed under the desk, Henry using it to access the vertex on his small black pad, screen glowing beside his microscope. Staring down the lens, tongue sticking out one side of his mouth, he concentrated on the dissection of a large purple flower propped up on the tray.

"Henry, love – talk to you for a moment?"

He peeled back the outer layer of stem with his tweezers, revealing the pale pith beneath. "I'm a little busy, Chance. But I suppose it can't wait?" Looking up from his work at last and, seeing that I was not alone, he attempted a smile. "Oh. Good morning, Miss Turing. Did you sleep well?"

"I was up most of the night thinking."

Henry gave a hum of approval and returned to his scope, picking up a tiny scalpel and cutting at the plant. "A woman after my own heart."

Cadence gasped, eyes widening as she pressed her hand to her collar. "I'm not after it, honest!"

Henry sat up from the scope, blinking and twirling the scalpel between his fingers. "N-no, I just meant–"

"What is that?" She pointed at the purple-headed specimen on the table.

"It's a flower of the Aconitum genus." Henry pushed back

from the table so she could get a better view. "You may know it by names like Monkshood or Wolf's Bane."

Rocking back and forth on my heels, I patted Henry's back. "Henry is a bit of an amateur botanist when it takes his fancy – only scientific bone in his body, really."

"Please, Miss Turing!"

Cadence, too self-possessed to jump at Henry's sudden cry, did jerk the stalk away from her face, brows jutting up over her round eyes.

Taking a deep breath, Henry shook his head, reclaiming the plant from her. "Sorry; but this plant's very poisonous. You generally have to ingest it, but there's no point in being careless."

"Flowers can kill you?"

Focused on the pad in front of him, Henry missed the suspicious tone of her question. "Quite a few can, actually; if you know what you're doing."

Cadence's pointed stare bore into me. Rolling my eyes, I dropped my hand onto Henry's shoulder. "Henry, you didn't kill my father, did you?"

Cadence scoffed from the other side of the table, hands on her hips. "And how was that subtle?"

"Alright," Henry swiveled in his chair, pushing it against the workbench and staring up at us, arms slung across his belly. "I've seen you poking around the manor, asking everyone strange questions. What are you playing at?"

"Inspector Brisbois thinks Chance is the murderer, but we know he's wrong, so we're trying to figure out who did it instead because I don't think Brisbois is doing a proper job of it, and I don't want Chance to go to prison." A perfunctory smile flashed across Cadence's face before she leaned down and met Henry's gaze with a stern frown. "So, did you kill Felix?"

"No, I did not." There was more amusement than anger in Henry's voice as he slumped further into his chair. "Why would I?"

"You were very angry with him the night of the party. And you told Chance you were worried he was going to fire your father and ruin your family's reputation."

"Miss Turing..." Henry probed his cheek with his tongue, collecting his thoughts. "If you're really set on going through with this, you should know that looking for someone who was angry at Felix Hale is like looking for someone Chance has made love to – very easy to find. I didn't like the man particularly, but I don't know many people who did, his own son included."

Beginning to take offense, I wagged my finger at him before I realized there was little point. "That's fair."

Cadence straightened with a huff, prodding at some of the pins holding up her tangled hair. "I don't suppose you saw anything particularly revealing then?"

Henry spun his chair back around and pulled himself under the desk. "Everything I saw or heard or thought, I told the inspector." He peered down his scope, shrugging. "Which wasn't anything; I was asleep downstairs."

"Can't you think of anything unusual or strange about that night? Anything at all? The slightest detail might be important."

Henry looked up, forehead wrinkled, eyes slits of annoyance. "It was bloody hot in my room, does that count?"

Cadence jumped like one of her circuits had shorted. "Hot?"

"That room's always been stuffy–"

"He didn't say stuffy, he said hot. I have to go back to the house." She threw up her hand, wiggled her fingers, and was off. "Bye, Henry!"

"Miss Turing." Henry watched her go, brow still furrowed, but the corners of his mouth edging up towards a smile. He turned back to the table with a shake of his head, bending over his work after a cursory glance in my direction. "Aren't you going to follow her?"

I leaned against the desk, folding my arms over my chest. "Do I look like a lapdog?"

"Do you really want me to answer that?" Stylus perched in one side of his mouth, Henry began to laugh. "Honestly, Chance, I haven't known you to spend this much time with a woman...well, ever. Especially considering that you haven't even slept with her yet." He plucked the stylus from between his lips, twirling it at me like a wand. "Could it be that your heathen heart has been softened by our fair angel from Paraesepe?"

"Stuff it."

Looking around, unsure of what to do next, I caught the scent of Cadence's perfume lingering in the air and stood. "I better head in."

"Did you hear your mistress' whistle?"

"I'll make you eat that stylus."

Going back the way I came, I stubbed out my nix underfoot and tried my best to ignore what Henry had implied, uncomfortable with the thought of becoming attached to anyone in a serious, romantic way. I had only seen a relationship like that work once.

As I swiped my finger and opened the front door, I was surprised to find one half of that pair standing just inside, hands clutched at her sides.

Minerva must have been walking the grounds, as she often did in the morning, her boots now caked with mud. She turned when the door opened behind her, scowling and pushing a wisp of pale blonde hair up out of her face.

"Oh, Chance, it's you." Turning back into the entryway, she shook her fist at the ground. "You see, you lazy things? You're causing a traffic jam!"

I hugged her shoulders, resting my head next to her own. "What seems to be the trouble, Min?"

"Your FASCs don't appear to be working, dear."

"Oh, it's probably just some mud or sticks or something that's jamming them up." I stepped around her into the entryway, where I noticed Cadence paused by the stairs, watching with apparent interest, but making no move to join us.

Poking at the FASC door with my foot, I continued, speaking over the pathetic whirring sound as the caterpillar machines tried to emerge. "Happens more often than you might think. If they can't self-clean whatever's on them, they just refuse to do any more work."

Minerva shifted from foot to foot, throwing her hands up in the air with a huff. "Well, I do hate to track mud in all over the place."

Bowing, my arms outstretched, I smiled wide. "I suppose I'll just have to carry you around the house, then."

Minerva threw her head back and laughed, swiping at my arm. "Don't make offers if you're not prepared to follow through with them, young man."

Laughing with her, I offered her my arm to steady herself with while she bent and removed her boots. Kissing me on the cheek in thanks, she headed off to her room, exchanging passing pleasantries with Cadence, who slipped what looked like a fistful of burnt cloth into her pocket.

Waiting until Minerva was well out of sight, Cadence strode towards me. She leaned forward, one hand on my shoulder, her lips at my ear. "I know how your father was killed."

"What? You're joking!" I shook my head and pulled away. "You don't joke, do you? How did you—"

"Your father," she gave my shoulder a squeeze before taking a step back, eyes moving around the room, "was killed right about where you're standing, I'd say. The murderer attacked him, perhaps following him from the library."

Her gaze darted down the hallway behind her, towards the kitchen. "He or she cleaned up the blood, cleaned up themselves, and then moved the body upstairs to your father's room, locking the door from the inside. They unlocked the connecting door, entering your room while you and Victoria slept, found your key on the bedside table, and let themselves out through your door. Locking it from the outside, they then slipped the key back in under the door. Brilliant."

Tapping my foot against the floor, I waited until it was clear that Cadence had run her train of thought into its station. I ticked my head to one side, heart throbbing. "Are you going to tell me how you know all that?"

"Eventually." She drummed her fingers against her chin, brow furrowed. "You're so impatient. After all," she started pacing around the entryway, "we still don't know the 'who' and that's the most important part." Stopping by the staircase, she pivoted on her heel to face me. "Did you know your father very well?"

I chewed the inside of my mouth, taking a hesitant step forward. "What do you mean?"

"Would you know if he had any secrets – things he wasn't proud of?"

"Please – I'd be the last person he'd take into his confidence."

Sighing, Cadence ran her tongue along her upper lip, thinking. "Did he keep a diary or any kind of personal record of his life?"

"Not that I know of. He always said he'd write an autobiography one of these days. But if he had anything like that, it'd be up in his room."

A sly grin spread over Cadence's face.

15

Chapter 15

"Couldn't Inspector Brisbois arrest us for this? It is a crime scene after all." I shifted my weight from foot to foot as Cadence worked her programming magic on the EO lock sealing my father's door, my eyes sweeping both ends of the hallway, vigilant for any sign of movement.

Cadence had the lock's faceplate stuck in one side of her mouth, tapping away at the buttons inside with her fingers. "I'm most certain that he could, yes."

"And we're going inside anyway?"

The lock popped off into her hands, slipping away from the frame as if all that had held it there were spit. Cadence smiled, humming as she put the machine back together and handed it to me, brows raised high under her thick bangs. "Look at it this way: if we don't go in, you'll probably end up arrested anyway."

"You're so comforting." Sneering, I reached around behind her and opened the door.

We scurried inside, careful to close the door behind us. The afternoon sun streamed through the windows, making it unnecessary to turn on any lights that might alert others to our presence. I stood in the middle of the room, staring at the ground under my feet while Cadence puttered around.

"What are we even looking for?"

"Anything. Who is this? She's wearing a lovely ring." Cadence stood by the bedside table, an optric in hand, displaying it to me like it was a trophy.

The woman in the picture had long blonde hair of exactly my shade, curling around her heart shaped face, which was split into a laugh. Her wide smile reached up into her green eyes and they sparkled like sea foam. She had one arm thrown around a Belinda twenty years younger than she was now, who pointed off to one side of the frame, a fruit drink tipped back in one hand, her face glowing.

I swallowed the lump in my throat, letting it drop into the pit of my stomach, and managed a smile. "Oh, that? That's my mother. Both she and Belinda are wearing those rings, the diamond shape and the nautilus; it's the crest from their college, the Römer University of Advanced Science."

"I wasn't aware that you had a mother."

I sat down on the bed, leaning onto my side. "Where do you think I came from? Human beings aren't manufactured, you know."

Cadence scowled, brows falling into a hard line over her eyes. "Sarc, I'll have to bear that in mind." She shook her hair out of her face, walking towards me as she refocused on the optric. "Where is she now?"

I picked at the loose threads in the bedspread beneath me. "She's gone."

"I see. I remember your father mentioning something about that. Is she somewhere off-planet? On holiday?"

"I don't mean she left, Cadence, I mean she's dead." My voice was loud and thick with hurt. I sighed, lifting my head. "She died a long time ago."

"Oh, my god." Cadence crumpled down onto the bed next to me, hands going limp and releasing the optric she had been clinging to. She shook her head once, and then again, harder, curling her arms around her waist. "Oh, I'm so, so sorry. I..." Looking at me from the corner of her eye, she turned away, rubbing the back of her neck. "Apol, I didn't understand the turn of phrase."

Her head wilted on her neck like a rose bud touched by frost, hair coming forward over her face like a curtain. "That is so very, very sad. Forgive me, I feel terrible for having pried."

Her sincere grief cut me to the quick. "Oh, Cay, it's alright, really. I was only a child when she died." I sat up, putting my hand on her shoulder. "Sometimes it's like I barely remember her."

"But when you do, it hurts even more that she's gone." Cadence dug her fingertips into her cheeks, shaking her head. "Please, forgive me; I'm not very used to death. It was a new experience for me when my family was..." She lifted her fingers, pulling quotation marks down through the air with complete seriousness, "... 'gone'."

"Do animanecrons not die?" I searched her face, eyes dancing along the lands and grooves of it. Cadence had been alive much longer than I, I knew that now, and I imagined that she had experienced more of the universe in her span of existence than I could ever hope to. But to think that her life had never been touched by death before proved equal parts heartbreaking and wondrous.

"No, not generally. Our physical formats can wear out, but it's traditional to be moved to another model before that happens; consciousness remains intact. There are very few who choose to..." She waved her hands in front of her, biting her lip. "I don't think there's an entirely human word for it. We call it 'nestati qurumaq'." The words hissed and clicked like electricity going through a switchboard. "It means something like 'fade away'."

I swallowed hard. "I think I understand."

Cadence avoided my gaze, picking up the optric from where she had dropped it, holding it as if she were afraid it would shatter and be lost forever. "What happened?"

"She got very ill and eventually her body just gave up on her. Dr. Merton was attending to her at the time, and Belinda and my father did what they could: cooking special food for her, preparing her medicine..." I took the optric, caressing the lines of my mother's face as I had done many times with my own copy. "There was nothing anyone could do; she just got sicker and sicker until it was too late."

Cadence ghosted her hand over my back. "And now your father was going to remarry."

"Yes." I put the optric face down on the bed between us and

stood, pushing my hand through my hair. "Where should I start looking?"

For a moment, I thought Cadence wouldn't allow me to end the conversation with grace, but whatever platitude she was about to assail me with she swallowed down, waving towards my father's dresser.

I pulled out and emptied each drawer in turn, doing what I imagined was a more thorough search than what had been conducted before. Opening my father's underwear drawer, I grimaced. "Well, I'm certainly seeing a whole lot of nothing."

Emptying the drawer took little time, but as I went to pull out the last pair of briefs, I found they wouldn't come. Giving another tug, I lifted them up and away from the drawer, but to no avail. Stuck on something I couldn't see, I pulled the drawer out as far as I could and peered inside.

A loose thread was stuck under the bottom of the drawer, which would have been an impossibility of physics, except now that the drawer was empty, I just could make out the edges of a compartment into which the thread disappeared. A small nick in the wood looked as promising a place to start as any, and when I worked my fingers into the space, the bottom panel popped open.

Confusion growing, I laid the panel on the top of the dresser and slid my hand into the revealed space. My fingers brushed against something soft, and I pulled it out, holding it to the sunlight.

It was a cloth bag, a blue and white pattern of flowers decorating it, with a thin twine draw string hanging uncinched. Taking several steps back until my knees hit the end of the bed, I sat down, my mouth dry. "Is this trash or a clue? I don't think I know the difference."

Cadence strode towards me, mouth agape. "Where did you find that?"

I gestured to the drawer, focus fixed on the trinket. She moved to investigate for herself, showering me with acclamations and missing the signs of my growing distress. I had always assumed that there were things about my father I didn't, and would now never, know, but I had never expected those things to require such a secretive hiding place.

Coming up empty at the drawer, Cadence returned to me, rubbing her hands together. "You're getting good at this! What's inside?"

"Nothing; it's empty." I shook the pouch and tossed it to her.

"How curious!" Cadence dropped it on top of the dresser, staring at it from a distance. "Why would your father keep an empty bag stuffed under a false bottom in his intimates' drawer?"

"I love that you just called them intimates, I really do." I grinned, her strangeness reviving my good humor. "Honestly, Cay, how extensive is your Common Tongue vocabulary?"

"Extensive enough." Cadence dusted off her hands, frowning. "Such an ugly language."

"I beg your pardon?"

"There's so much room for misunderstanding. Con, Animatum is much more precise." She plucked the bag off the dresser, brow furrowing as she examined its insides. "Look at that," she said, passing the bag back to me with a nod, "it's frayed at the bottom. Whatever was in there must have had sharp edges and moved around in the bag every time your father opened the drawer."

Cadence wandered around the room, eyes focused on the ground, and I watched her with a smile, leaning back on the bed to admire her backside when she got down on all fours and began crawling over the carpet.

"Why do you do that?"

Her head shot up, fingers stilling. "What?"

"You stick little sounds at the beginning of your sentences."

Sitting up on her haunches, her smile faded. "Do I?"

I nodded. One side of Cadence's mouth slid downwards and she squeezed her knees. "Bugger."

Falling forward without further explanation, she resumed her stilted movement across the carpet, picking at the floor here and there. Forced to stop when she reached my foot, still planted on the floor at the edge of the bed, she swiped at it, but I kept it where it was. She looked up at me and I returned her stare. Sighing, she hit my foot again, this time while saying, "They're emotion tags, okay?"

I moved my foot out of her way, allowing her to search under the bed as she continued. "You may have noticed that my range of facial expressions isn't as wide or nuanced as yours, nor is my vocal inflection particularly varied."

"I wasn't going to say anything, but yes."

"It's not just me; most animanecrons are like that. So, we use verbal tags at the beginning of sentences to highlight the intended emotional tenor of the exchange." Cadence stood, pushing a loose bang behind her ear. "I didn't realize I was doing it when I was speaking Common Tongue though. I suppose it's just habit now."

"I can see where it would be quite helpful." The bottom section of her tattoo peeked out from under her shirt as she crouched by the corner of the dresser. "One of these days you'll have to teach me all of them."

"If we're together that long."

My heart stuttered in my chest, and I turned away, grimacing at the thought of her leaving. A few days ago, I had been suffocating under Cadence's presence, but the more time I spent with her, the more natural it felt to have her around. I would miss her if she left.

"How did you get here?"

Held between Cadence's fingertips was a docu-chip about half the length of my thumb. She picked some threads, which matched the color of the empty bag, off its sharp contact points, placing each on the dresser before laying the chip flat in the center of her palm.

"Where did you find that?"

"Behind the dresser." Cadence jerked her head back towards the large wooden piece of furniture, pulled several inches away from the wall. It had taken five men to carry it into the room in the first place, and my mind rebelled at the notion that Cadence had moved it by herself. I accepted it when she nudged the whole thing back into place with her hip.

"Do you have a computer I can use?"

I nodded and gestured towards the room next door. Cadence had the system in my mother's room up and running in a flash, the translucent screen glowing bright. Reaching down to the input port, she slid the chip in with care, patting the drive and performing her customary thanks before turning her attention to the screen.

Buzzing and humming, the computer chewed on the chip like a child with gum and spat out the docu-chip's contents in one dizzying moment, words flooding the screen at such a rate that Cadence had to jerk her hand up to slow the flow, swiping back up to the top of the very first document.

Standing behind her, I placed my hands on her shoulders and squeezed. She leaned into me, caressing my biceps and moving her fingers down my arms with a firmness that made my skin hum.

Cadence rested her hands on top of mine, fingers tapping against me. "All I want to do is take you for hours and hours, until we're both so exhausted we can barely breathe."

I stared at her, mouth moving but useless. "Cadence, I...I..." Glancing back towards the open door, I crouched next to her. "Do you really think that's a good idea, darling – with everything that's going on?"

Cadence stared at me with wide, terrified eyes. "Huh, what?" She fixed her gaze on the space just above my head and I could see her spooling through the events of the last few minutes in her mind. Closing her eyes and opening them again, she put a hand on my shoulder. "I was reading from the chip, Chance."

"Yes, I know you were," I countered, shooting up into a standing position. "I just thought that we maybe shouldn't read things like that out loud; you know, if this is really a clue and everything."

She gave me a tight smile before returning her attention to

the screen. I collapsed into the nearest easy chair, taking a moment to catch my breath before dragging my seat up next to hers.

The chip held ten or fifteen long messages, all following the same basic pattern. Opening with a few short sentences of overacted despair, they then detailed fantasies of the most intimate nature, the section which Cadence had read aloud proving to be rather tame. Each letter ended with a promise to see the reader again and a vow to be together in the end. They were all between a man, 'F', who could only be my father, and a woman, who was referred to only as his 'beautiful serpent'.

"That sly dog; love letters!" I reached across Cadence and flicked at the screen, scrolling up to the top and highlighting the date. "These are almost twenty-five years old." Scrolling back to the bottom, I highlighted the parting note, which read 'Your own Beautiful Serpent'. "It's funny, I don't remember my mother ever going by that."

Cadence leaned back in her chair, gesturing at the screen as she spread her long legs in front of her. "Why would you assume your mother wrote this?"

"Well, they were married at the time."

She glanced from me to the screen and back again, rubbing the tips of her fingers together. "The people in these letters are parted. They miss each other, they hate the person in their way..." she waved to one particular graphic segment, brow arching, "...and they long to consummate their relationship with repeated and, may I say, creative acts of physical intimacy. Strange sentiments for a husband and wife to exchange."

The implications of her argument dawned on me. I bit the inside of my mouth hard. I had been little more than a child when my mother died, but I loved her with the same fierceness of any son, and the knowledge that my father had been communicating like this with some other woman made me wish he was alive again so I could punch him right in the face.

Cadence ejected the chip, examining it by the fading light. "Someone didn't want these found; I'm certain there were more. Destroyed, probably. But by whom?"

"My father certainly wouldn't have wanted anyone to know about them, that stuck-up, hypocritical, sanctimonious ass. When he and Solomon were talking about changing his will, he said that there were things he wanted to clear up; he wanted to be able to marry Desdemona with a clean slate, as a new man, all that rubbish people say when they think they're in love." I gestured to the chip. "Maybe this is what he meant."

"I'm going to talk to her." Cadence stood, directing a shake of her hands and a few clicks to the computer in thanks, and walked towards the door.

"Desdemona?" I got to my feet and started to follow her. "Can I come?"

"No." Stopping on the other side of the bed, she examined me. "She knows you don't like her; she won't talk around you."

"I can be civil, I promise!" Feigning hurt feelings, I placed a hand to my chest, a put-upon glimmer in my eyes. "I won't even glare."

Cadence turned forward again, tapping her foot. She dropped her hands to her sides. "Fine. You'll stand. Far away. In a corner. Being non-threatening."

I walked behind her and dipped my fingers under her hair,

caressing the nape of her neck, my lips twisting into an indelicate smirk. "I love it when you're authoritative with me."

16

Chapter 16

Desdemona was downstairs in the study, curled up on the long couch at the back of the room. Her bare feet tucked under her, she clutched a brown leather pillow to her chest, watching television on the main screen behind my father's desk. A commercial for pheromone spray oozed out of the speakers at a murmur while we entered, Cadence leading the way.

"Hello, Desdemona."

Desdemona pulled her attention away from the screen. "Oh, hello, Ca–" She winced, squeezing the cushion to her as she squirmed. "I mean, Miss Turing."

Cadence lifted her hand, waving it in time with her shaking head. "Please, Cadence is quite enough for me." She sat on the other end of the couch, mimicking the woman's posture as much as she could, sans cushion. "To be honest, I find all the miss-ing and mister-ing around here a bit strange."

Desdemona's lips twitched upward for a moment. "I thought so too, at first. But you get used to it." She turned her gaze to me, eyes wide as ever, the edges pink from crying. "Hello, Chance."

"Hello." I shifted where I stood, uncomfortable standing but too awkward to sit down. "How are you?"

"Alright, I suppose, considering." Desdemona shrugged, turning back to the screen. "You don't need to worry about me. I'll be fine."

"It's all been a terrible tragedy for everyone here." Cadence took a deep breath in and sighed, resting her elbow against the arm of the couch. "I feel like such an interloper in all this. I wish I had known Mr. Hale better."

The name roused Desdemona out of whatever pit of self-pity she had been wallowing in, straightening as she stole a glance at Cadence. "I wish so too. Felix–"

She pressed her thin lips into a wavering line, but instead of crying, Desdemona reached down and muted the TV with a firm jerk, throwing the remote across the sofa cushions and turning towards Cadence. "Felix was just the nicest man I've ever met," she said. "He could be stubborn and pushy sometimes, I guess, but he was really always looking out for people. He was very loving and bright, and I admired him more than any man I've ever known."

I watched Desdemona with renewed interest. She looked older sitting there, her formless blonde hair pulled away from her face in a tight ponytail, a plain brown and olive dress draped over her. It was an astonishing revelation, to think that she believed everything that she had just said about my father; that she may have truly liked the man.

"How did you two meet?"

"I got a job at the Halcyon Enterprises offices in Römer as a secretary for one of the production managers." Desdemona tilted her head to one side, staring at the cushion in her grasp with a smile, squishing the fat corners between her fingers. "We were in a few meetings together. Felix was always very encouraging and friendly, especially for the head of a big company. He really made me feel important."

I sat in the chair kitty corner to her. "What were you doing before?"

"Nothing, really." Desdemona didn't look up, crossing her arms over the cushion and gripping the inside of her elbows. "I was just sort of drifting. Didn't know what I wanted to do, until I met Felix."

That was one way to describe my father: a huge boulder in the stream of life. You couldn't take him head on; he would force you to pick a direction, one way or the other.

Desdemona relaxed into the cushions behind her, head lolling back. "I made some mistakes when I was a kid." She began rubbing her arms, pale lips trembling. "Made some bad decisions, you know? But Felix never cared about any of that. He understood."

"We've all made mistakes," Cadence nodded. "They're easier to forgive when we remember that. I'm sure even a man as..." She twisted towards me, eyes widening as she blanked on an appropriate descriptor. I shrugged, at a loss myself and she blinked a few times before turning back. "...as wonderful as Mr. Hale made mistakes, right?"

"Felix? Mistakes?" Desdemona sat up, smiling and sniffling

back those tears which had threatened to fall. "Oh no, he wasn't like that. Sure, he had some regrets, but–"

"What regrets?"

It was bizarre, bordering on humorous, to hear Cadence's and my own voice in concert like that. Desdemona started, nails jabbing into the defenseless cushion. "W-well, you know, just...just things! Like..." She met my eyes and looked away. "He talked a lot about Verity... how much he wished his first marriage hadn't ended so badly."

"What on Arrhidaeus do you mean by that?"

"Who's–"

"My mother, her name was Verity," I snapped at Cadence, my fingers digging into the arms of my chair as I waited for Desdemona's answer.

Desdemona licked her lips as she shrugged, voice shallow. "I don't know, that's all he'd ever say – that it had ended badly."

Cadence looked between us. She straightened, steepling her fingers in front of her. "It's very hard to lose someone, isn't it?"

To her credit, Desdemona held my gaze as we both nodded at the platitude.

"Death is always a 'bad end' to a relationship," Cadence continued, folding her hands over her knees. "Especially premature death, as was the case with both Felix and Verity."

I turned away from Desdemona and she sighed in relief. Cadence cleared her throat and leaned back in her seat, attempting nonchalance. "I hope Inspector Brisbois makes an arrest soon. I wish I could have been more helpful to him, but I'm afraid I was asleep through everything; I didn't see anything or hear anything, makes me feel very useless."

"Oh, you shouldn't," Desdemona reached over and squeezed Cadence's arm. "It's not your fault."

"I'm sure you're right." Cadence smiled, patting Desdemona's hand. "Were you able to tell the inspector anything important?"

"No, I wasn't either. Just that I saw Felix going to bed at around eleven."

"You actually saw him?" I jumped on the fact, eager to turn up something concrete, while Cadence shot a glare in my direction.

Desdemona nodded, settling back into the cushions. "I have trouble sleeping, so I usually sit-up quite late, reading, browsing the vertex, sometimes even drawing. Felix stayed up late too; well after eleven, anyway; I don't think I've ever seen him go to bed before fifteen or one. Anyway, I heard some noises out in the hall – some grumbling and talking – and I poked my head out and saw Felix going into his room."

Shaking her head, Desdemona pulled at her lower lip as she spoke. "He looked so tired, so I didn't call out to him. I figured he needed his rest after being so sick. Now I wish I'd said something."

"What makes you say he looked tired?" Now it was my turn to scowl at Cadence, whose excitement was hard to miss. "Did he turn around; did you see his face?"

"Well, no, it was just..." Desdemona moved her butterfly-like hand across her forehead, eyes fluttering shut. "I don't know why I said that. I just remember thinking that he must be tired. But he didn't turn to me or anything; he just shuffled into his room. Perhaps that was it; Felix didn't usually shuffle."

Cadence frowned, turning to look out the window. A long

minute passed in silence, and with no more questions forthcoming, Desdemona's attention was soon recaptured by the television. She lifted the remote and unmuted the sound, gesturing to me. "Have you ever seen this one? The animation's pretty silly, but it's always been one of my favorite flickers."

Blocky figures waddled across the screen. A frowning frog in a tweed waistcoat sat in a prison cell, bemoaning his fate to a mole and rat on the other side of the bars, who were holding bowlers in their hands, looking mournful.

The scene struck my memory and I edged forward in my seat. "This is *The Wind in the Willows*, isn't it?"

"Yes!" Desdemona's face broke out in a smile and she scooted closer to me. "We've just gotten to the part where the weasels have taken over Toad Hall and made a mess of everything!"

Cadence turned back to us, brow furrowed. "Weasels?"

"Little furry rodents that bite, dear," I answered, not bothering to look at her, entranced by the animal drama on the screen. "My fa–" I swallowed the formality, casting a glance towards Desdemona's eager face, "–Dad, he used to read me this story when I was little. Every time I had a nightmare, I'd get to hear about Rat and Mole and Mr. Toad."

On the screen, Rat and Mole had just reached Badger's house, the fussy Wiseman character of the piece, who refused to be disturbed by Toad's troubles any longer. "I always wanted to be Mr. Toad, even though he gets into all that trouble; at least he was having fun."

Cadence rose from her seat, crossing in front of the screen as quick as she could. "I'll leave you two to it then!"

"No, you don't," I grabbed her wrist as it swung by and

tugged. Cadence allowed the motion to pull her down onto my lap, her blue eyes staring into mine, a curious tilt to her head. Slinging an arm around her hip, I leaned back in my chair, jutting my chin towards the screen with a smile. "Stay and watch; it'll be educational."

The three of us passed a charming hour in my father's study, the story bringing to mind some of the good moments I had shared with my dad and allowing me the luxury of forgetting a few of the things I had learned about him of late.

The front door chimed, which we elected to ignore, not curious in the least who might be coming to interrupt our blithe times with Mr. Toad. There was a knock on the study door as the credits ran, and after a customary 'yes?' my father's manservant, Bernard, bowed into the room.

"So sorry to bother you, sir. But Inspector Oliver Brisbois has just arrived, sir, and insists on speaking with you. I did try to impress upon him the unsuitability of the hour, sir."

I glanced up at the clock on the wall and was surprised to see that it was nearing dinner time. Cadence and I shared a glance, but I put on a brave face. As I thanked Bernard and asked him to tell the inspector I would be right out, Cadence slid off my lap, giving a small wave to Desdemona before following me out of the room.

Pushing through my dread, I approached Brisbois in the entryway, a stalwart EO officer his sole companion, and managed a broad smile. "Inspector Brisbois! How nice to see you again."

Brisbois gave a curt nod, twisting his face into a scowl. "Mr. Hale, I did say I would be back for some follow-up interviews, and I'd like to conduct those now, if you don't mind."

I made a great show of checking the clock above the door and wincing. "It is rather late, old boy; wouldn't you prefer to wait until tomorrow?"

Brisbois took a deep breath, probing the inside of his cheek with his tongue. "Clearly not, seeing how I have come all the way out here now."

I shrugged, gesturing back into the house. "Well, I think everyone is pretty scattered about, but I'll do my best to wrangle them together. Miss Eydis is in the study–"

"That's fine, I'll start with her." He strode past, brushing my elbow with his arm. "Please gather everyone else in the sitting room."

Deeming it unwise to antagonize a man with a taser gun, I did as he requested. Brisbois interviewed me second this time, asking the most banal questions about what my father had had to eat the night of the party, how long he had known Desdemona, even if I knew whether he liked to sleep in pajamas, all his previous threats of putting me away having vanished.

While the majority of those whom he had finished with decided to go in for dinner, I opted to wait until Cadence had her turn. We sat side by side on a small love seat while the others filed in and out, one after the other. Brisbois, it seemed, had decided to save her for last.

Minerva, second to last, stalked back into the sitting room, ruffled and annoyed, with Brisbois following close behind.

"Miss Turing?"

Cadence rose to her feet, smiling at Minerva as their paths crossed. Minerva threw herself into the vacated seat next to me with considerable force, looking back at Brisbois with narrowed eyes. "What that man needs are three days with a fast woman."

I wrapped my arm around her shoulders and squeezed, taking a long drag of my nix as we watched the inspector usher Cadence out the door, the two of them conversing at the threshold before disappearing down the hall. Minerva patted my chest. "It's too bad Cadence has already become so attached to you; they make a pretty pair. But you've got your hooks in her, haven't you?"

I chuckled, smoke curling away from my face. "To be perfectly honest with you, Min, I'm not sure who has their hooks in whom."

Minerva cackled, wiggling her finger at me. "Good, good! You need someone who can knock you off balance now and again. Keeps things exciting; certainly works for Solomon and me." She leaned back with a sigh, fiddling with her wedding necklace. "I only wish Henry could find someone like that. Someone to shake up his life and leave it in beautiful shambles; it's what he really needs."

"Is that love, then?"

"Of course! If love doesn't ruin all the ideas you've ever had, then it's not a very good love at that."

I considered the statement, nodding. "Min, can I ask you a question?"

"Of course, my dear, anything."

"Were my father and mother in love?"

Her fingers stuttered over her collarbone. She stared at me for a minute, more curious than surprised, and folded her hands in her lap. "I'll give you an answer; but first I need to know: are you looking for comfort or honesty? Sometimes they're the same thing, but where matters of the heart are concerned..." She finished the thought with a shrug.

"I'll take honesty, if it's all the same to you."

"Good choice." Minerva cleared her throat, turning to face me with squared shoulders and a thoughtful frown. "Your father and mother married because it was a good, sensible match. They were both from well-respected families, both young and ambitious; they had a lot of similarities and I do think, for a while anyway, they were at least very good friends." Her gaze fell, moving over the patterns in the carpet. "Are you sure you wouldn't rather ask Belinda about all this? After all, she knew them better than I did."

"Yes, but you'll tell me the truth." I threw my arm over the back of the couch. "Belinda's always looked through rose-colored glasses where Dad's concerned."

"I don't think they ever loved each other." Minerva's body relaxed back as if a great weight had been lifted off her. "They had a chance, a real chance, but I don't think they ever quite," she snapped her fingers, "sparked."

Leaning forward, she rested her elbows on her knees. "When your mother came to live here, I remember thinking how beautiful she was, beautiful inside and out. She was so..." She grunted and shook her head. "It's hard to describe. Verity was like...like the sun. She was so alive, so warm. I think that brightness butted heads with your father's more somber attitude towards life. They were never quite on the same page. But still, they could have learned to complement each other."

"What got in the way of them sparking?"

"Well," Minerva crossed her legs, reluctant but committed to telling the story. "A few years after they were married, just after you were born, Halcyon Enterprises ran into some serious financial troubles. To this day, Solomon won't tell me why or how, but I'm certain your father made some ill-advised investments that never paid off. He wasn't the type to cut his losses, so he just kept throwing good money after bad and it all spiraled out of control."

I made a mental note to go back through my father's financial records and try to find evidence of this spiral for myself. Minerva continued, drawing her hand back through her flaxen hair. "Financial strains can be hard on the best of marriages. Coming from a wealthy family, your mother still had a sizeable fortune of her own, under her own name. When Felix asked her to use it to bail out the company, she refused. He pushed." Minerva clucked, grimacing. "You know how your father pushed." Shrugging, her hands flopped into her lap. "Things were never the same after that. And then, of course, she became ill – rather sad."

"Do you know of anyone else my father might have...?" I cleared my throat, squirming, and tried again. "Is it possible there was another woman at some point?"

Minerva jerked upright, scoffing. "Where did you get an idea like that?" One corner of her mouth tugged down into a frown, her hand at her stomach. "To be honest, I never saw your father as the type of man romantic enough to have an affair. But..." She placed her hand over mine as she thought, giving it a hard squeeze. "No, there's no one I can think of at that time; no one new in his life. Just the same old group of friends."

We were interrupted by the reappearance of Cadence and Brisbois at the door, the latter shaking her hand, smiling. "Thank you very much for your time, Miss Turing. It's been a pleasure, as always."

"Of course; I'm sorry I couldn't be more helpful, Inspector."

"Not at all," he waved her concern away and took her by the shoulders in a show of familiarity that I resented. "You have a keen mind and a good eye for detail. We could use more people like you in the Enforcement Office."

Cadence swung her hips from side to side, holding her hands together in front of her. "Well, I don't think those shiny blue uniforms would suit me very much, Inspector; but I appreciate the compliment."

Brisbois allowed himself a delighted laugh before turning to me, his smile fading into a concealed grimace as he gave me a lazy salute. "Mr. Hale, I'll keep you informed of any developments as they arise." He bowed to Cadence, the sparkle in his eyes returning, before heading back out to the front door.

"My goodness!" Minerva, grinning from ear to ear, got to her feet, shaking her head and patting Cadence on the back as she passed out of the room. "If that man was any sweeter on you, he'd get cavities."

Cadence laughed, sparing me a glance at last. I rose and walked over to her, taking her by the elbow. "What happened?"

"Nothing, really. He just asked me a lot of questions about your father and Solomon, strangely enough."

I frowned at this apparent change in tactic and glanced down, trying to gather my thoughts. It was then that I noticed the small data key clutched in her hand. "What's that?"

Bouncing onto her toes, she shook the key in front of me.

"Copies of a few EO files! There are some things I want to look over."

"How on Arrhidaeus did you get those?"

"Like I said before," Cadence patted the back of my head, lips split in a sticky sweet smile. "I asked nicely."

17

Chapter 17

I cajoled and begged; wheedled and demanded; bribed, promised, and tried every trick I knew to discover what Cadence had done to get those files; I might as well have been trying to move the planet off its axis.

My dove's furtive ways were not only in conflict with the partnership we had begun to build, but they also hurt. After all, my father was the murder victim; didn't I deserve an equal share of information? Whatever Cadence had uncovered, I needed to know what light it shed not just on the case, but also on the man himself.

My father and I hadn't always shared the antagonistic relationship of my adult years. When I was a child, he had gone out of his way to spend time with me, to learn about my interests and aspirations, and to show me an open, unconditional love that had made up a great deal for growing up motherless.

Everything changed when I turned eleven. My father became a task master, a lecturer, a figure of authority to be feared above all others. His criticisms were harsh, his dismissals of my personal interests swift and uncompromising. Anything that did not fit with his image of the perfect heir to the Hale legacy had to be severed from my soul like a diseased limb. Foisted upon my young shoulders was not just the responsibility of my inheritance, but the guilty burden of being a disappointing son.

We were not close, and had not been for some time, but his death revealed to me sentiments not easily admitted about our relationship. Lost without his presence, the things I discovered about him and the inner life he had led, his human failings, all were making me feel closer to him, even if they simultaneously angered me. Solving his murder was a way of solving the mystery of my father as a whole. Perhaps he and I had not been so different after all.

But to explain any of this to Cadence was impossible, and so my frustration grew. The next morning, when she sent word that she would not be joining us for breakfast due to some 'private business,' I was as disenchanted with her as I had ever been.

I wolfed down breakfast without tasting it, my mind awhirl. Proving a poor companion for polite company and my close friends alike, I resolved to leave Cadence be and refused to inquire about her the rest of the morning.

Belinda and Henry went off to play a round of lawnball, while Victoria and Desdemona indulged in some vertex shopping in the study, and the rest of the house was engaged in one type of chore or another. I wandered into the library, which is where I spent most of my time at the manor. The cavernous room, with its rows and rows of dusty shelves, was almost always quiet, a quality even a social person such as me longed for on occasion. It was also the coolest place in the house, an oasis on increasingly hot days, outfitted with a special air conditioning system to keep the story cubes from overheating as they charged on their hundreds upon hundreds of stations.

The cold also stopped the 'relics', as my father had called them, from molding or turning to dust. I had never understood his devotion to the cumbersome books, dry and rough as they were. They had a certain antique beauty, but story cubes were too elegant and simple not to favor. Palm-sized three-dimensional blocks, they held holographic collections of words and pictures which were projected in front of one's face with a reader, all navigation handled by eye and finger movements.

Regardless, the books remained the pride of my father's collection, filling both sides of the tall shelves which lined the edges of the reading alcove. In the far-right corner of the library, they clustered around the chairs and desks like a group of rumpled tramps on a street corner.

I walked to the alcove, hoping to take a quick nap on one of the couches, when I heard signs of life ahead of me. Peeking around the corner of a shelf, anxious to avoid certain members of our party more than others, I at first saw no one. The table lamps glowed, and piles of books were stacked on top of the chairs and tables where I knew they didn't belong, but I could not find their manipulator. After a moment, the muffled sounds of footsteps on carpet reached me and soon Solomon appeared from between the far two shelves, mumbling into the side of a tall stack of books he held in his arms.

Placing the books on the floor next to the love seat, he was about to return the way he came when I knocked on the shelf and stepped out into the space. "May I join you, sir?"

Solomon pivoted back in my direction, smiling at the sight of me. He rubbed his lower back and nodded. "Certainly!" Perusing the chaos he had created, he cleared his throat and adjusted his glasses. "If you can find any place to sit, that is."

"Is there anything I can do to help...?" I followed his gaze, my brows drawing up to a point. "...whatever it is you might be doing?"

Solomon cracked a tired grin, relaxing his weight back onto his heels. "Brisbois told you about your father's missing will, yes?"

"He thinks I did something to it to keep Dad from taking away my inheritance."

Solomon gave a derisive snort, rolling his eyes heavenward. "Idiot."

Sighing, he shook his head, slipping his hands into his pockets. "Well, your father was revising his will the night he died. He mentioned to me that he'd be working on it in here, you see," he threw his hand towards the books all around him, grimacing, "and I thought that maybe he had misplaced it, or that it slipped behind some of these blasted things."

Scratching his neck, Solomon stared at the stacks without seeing them. "I can't shake this feeling that there was something important about this new will. And if I don't find it, your father will probably haunt me 'til I die. He could be a right bastard like that sometimes."

I leaned against the shelf, grinning. "Yes, he really could be."

Solomon turned to the bookcase behind him. I took a step

further into the alcove, shoving my hands into my pockets. "Sir, can I ask you a question?"

"Of course," he waved me towards one of the less cluttered sofas, starting towards it himself. "And it's Solomon; you're my boss now, remember?"

"That's sort of what I wanted to ask you about." I sat down on the plush footrest across from the couch, threading my fingers together as he cleared off a pile of books to make room for himself. "Was it true that my father was going to fire you?"

Eyes widening, Solomon lowered himself into his seat, careful not to disturb the adjacent stack of books. "How did you–? Oh, well, I suppose it doesn't matter now. No, he wasn't going to fire me. But I was going to leave just the same. Your father was a brilliant businessman, but he was no scientist. The projects I was pushing were too radical for him: too much uncertainty, not enough profit. I wanted to go somewhere where I could pursue my research, that's all, nothing personal." Taking a deep breath, Solomon cocked his head to one side, voice quieting. "Now that I think about it, I was probably the closest thing he had to a friend."

"Well, he did know how to alienate people."

"I don't think he ever intended to alienate you." Solomon held up his hands, chuckling and sitting back as I stared at him aghast. "I know that he did! I would never be so foolish as to call Felix Hale a good father, but..." He pursed his lips, running a hand back through his dark hair. "But you were his son. And he did care, you know."

Tears pricked the corners of my eyes. I sat up and cleared my throat, turning away. "Thank you." Standing, I ran my hands over my legs, mumbling. "I suppose I'll let you get back to it. If you find anything–"

"You'll be the first to know."

I strode out of the library and into the sunlit hallway, a lightness in my chest that had not been there before. Crossing the entryway, I glanced up at Cadence's door, still shut. Stopping just past the foot of the stairs, I stared, tapping my foot. I took a step forward and froze. I took a step back, watching the door as if it were a dangerous predator.

After a full minute of this, I jogged up the stairs with new resolve. Cadence may have been the one running this little detective agency, but I was the co-founder, in a manner of speaking, and she couldn't keep me in the dark; I wouldn't allow it.

Pushing the door to my rooms open without any warning, I marched through the bedroom and into the small work cloister at the far end. Cadence sat at my console, a long, official-looking document in the middle of the screen. Jumping at my sudden appearance, she jerked her fingers in front of the screen, shrinking the document and bringing up a host of others.

"Ala, Chance! Couldn't you have knocked?"

"I did, you must not have heard me," I said, finding it necessary to pause as I took in the sight of her. Rummaging through my dresser had provided her with one of my faded yellow polo shirts and a pair of jeans, baggy on her, which now sat cinched around her hips.

I cleared my throat, determined to keep my focus, and lowered my brow, frowning as I spread my hands in front of myself. "Now, Cadence, I don't want any more of this sneaking around behind my back, alright? I've had enough. If we're really partners in this, you have got to start treating me like it and trust me."

Pivoting to face me, she curled her arm around the back of the wooden chair, resting her chin on top of it. She made my blood rush to all the right places and I hated her for it.

I pointed to the screen behind her. "First things first: tell me how you got those files from Brisbois. I promise, I won't scold or lecture; depending on what you did I may or may not be physically ill, but–"

"I stole them."

There would come a time in our relationship where nothing Cadence said would surprise me anymore, but as it was, my jaw dropped and I jerked back. "You stole confidential EO files?"

Rolling her head onto its side, she massaged the back of her neck, sighing. "While Brisbois was questioning me, I asked him for a glass of water; he went down to the kitchen to get it, and when he was gone, I got onto his system and downloaded the files to a data key I had in my pocket."

"That..." I moved my gaze from her to the screen and back again, "...is incredibly illegal."

Cadence shrugged and swung back to the screen. "I needed them."

That seemed to be enough of an explanation for her. I was hard-pressed to be too disapproving; after all, she'd done it to help me. Stepping behind her, I leaned against the back of the chair, rubbing my eyes. "What sort of files are they?"

"A few things I thought might be pertinent to the case. What have you been up to all morning?"

Relating the facts I had gleaned from Solomon, I laid out his purpose in the library as well as his side of the story about his rumored departure from Halcyon Enterprises. She absorbed it all quietly, interjecting a few questions here and there, but not sharing any revelations the information produced, if any. I realized that I had yet to tell her about the previous evening's conversation with Minerva and gave her the full details of that exchange as well.

Cadence craned her head back to look up into my eyes, her frown seeming to take on a comical tilt from that angle. "Minerva says your mother became ill soon after this financial trouble occurred?" I nodded. Cadence's scowl deepened, brows rising and falling in a troubled ripple. "That is disturbing."

I moved my hands to her shoulders, where I began folding and unfolding the cuffs on her sleeves. "Is it?"

She lowered her head between her shoulders, dragging her tapping fingers down her cheeks. "Well, more suggestive than disturbing. Like this," she swiped a long document up onto the screen, "Desdemona's arrest file."

"My, my." I took control of the screen with a flick, scrolling through pages of charges which stretched back to Desdemona's adolescent years. "She's quite the juvenile delinquent, isn't she?"

"Yes, but that's not the interesting part. The interesting part is that she never committed a crime alone. There's always this other party mentioned," Cadence highlighted a line under a charge for vandalism: "'Accomplice captured: see record D6C5M5'. I can't get to the file, obviously, but from what I can piece together, it's a man – a lover of some sort. They were both remanded to a rehabilitation clinic in Cayeux. But there's only one record for a completed program."

"So, she got clean, and he didn't?" I straightened, pulling at my bottom lip as I processed this new information. "I wonder if they've kept in touch."

"Speaking of clinics," pushing away from the desk, Cadence smoothed out her clothes and stood, "I've had an idea. I think we should go through Dr. Merton's medical bag."

"And what has led to this sudden urge?"

"It's the one place the EO has never searched properly. Think about it," she ticked the instances off on her fingers. "The morning the necklace went missing, the doctor went upstairs to get his bag so he could tend to your father. And when the EO searched the house after your father's death, Merton had his bag with him in the sitting room the whole time."

"Because he was looking after Desdemona, I remember."

"Well, I was thinking that maybe there's a reason he keeps the bag so close to him; maybe he's hiding something."

I smiled, blinking at her. "He's a doctor, love; they generally have to be ready in case of an emergency."

Cadence froze, mouth open. She stared at me for several seconds before continuing with a scowl. "Alright, I'll grant you that. But still, don't you think it'd be worth a look? Just in case? Just because no one else has?"

"Hey, you're the expert detective, not me. I'd never dream of squelching your investigative fervor."

She grinned a thank you, but stopped me as I started for the door, grabbing my arm. "So, you'll help me? It's not going to be easy to get the bag by itself. I'll need a distraction to make sure I don't get caught going through it."

I smirked, patting the back of her hand. "You make it sound

so difficult. I can guarantee you an uninterrupted half hour to go through the man's bag this very afternoon." Bringing her hand to my lips, I winked. "I am that good."

18

Chapter 18

For once in my life, I was to make good on my promises. Just after lunch, a small group of us retired out onto the veranda, basking in the sunshine. At a cough from me, Cadence excused herself inside, after which I asked Dr. Merton his thoughts on the current IPC medical school standards.

Henry balled his hands into fists, his glare digging into my forehead. We all knew how absorbed Merton could get on this single topic, having suffered through his lectures many times before. Once again, his reserve fell to the wayside as he ranted against the lax standards of the day and how absurdly easy it now was to obtain a degree in medicine as opposed to the enormous challenges he had surmounted as a student. It was some time before I could steal away to meet Cadence in the study. As the sun started to sink behind the horizon, I worried that she might have given up on me. But there was a light visible beneath the closed door and, casting around a wary eye, I eased open the door and slid inside.

Reclining on the large couch, Cadence had her feet propped up on top of the armrest, her head flat against the cushion at the opposite end. Her hands, curled into fists, lay resting on her chest. I leaned back onto the door until it clicked shut. Cadence didn't look up, closing her fists tighter.

"Well? Did you find anything?"

She opened her mouth, thought, and snapped it shut again, flicking her tongue over her lips. At last Cadence nodded. "I know who the murderer is...and I can't tell you."

I strode towards her, bracing myself against the back of the sofa as I leaned over her, face flush, my jaw clenched so tight it throbbed. "Cadence Turing, if you don't tell me, I'll–I'll...I'll go get the biggest magnet I can find and wipe you clean."

Rubbing her fists over her mouth, she wriggled across the couch until her head hit the arm rest. "It doesn't make any sense!" Cadence sat up, forcing me back, her lips firming into a line. "I have to know why. I can't tell you who until I've figured out why."

Straightening and screwing my eyes shut, I shoved her legs off the couch, dropping down into the seat beside her. Her feet landed on the floor with a thud, but the rest of Cadence stayed where it was, body twisted into an L-shape.

"I assume you found something in Merty's bag; can I at least know about that?"

Opening her hands, she revealed a glass vial in each. Without even a glance in my direction she tossed one into the air and landed it in my outstretched hand. The vial, small enough to fit in my palm, was filled, up to its hermetically sealed top, with a familiar red liquid.

"What the hell?" I rolled the tube across my hand, but inside the blood remained still. Squinting at the hand-written label, I forced the squiggles into focus until I could make out my father's initials and a string of numbers. "Why is this dated the night of the party?"

"The night your father was ill with a sudden bout of flu."

"You don't draw blood for the flu," I said, holding the vial up to the light.

Cadence pushed herself up onto her elbows. "I am so glad to hear you say that." Swinging her legs up onto my lap, she leaned forward, voice low. "This means that Dr. Merton had suspicions: suspicions that I've only had since your father's death."

"What suspicions?"

Folding herself even farther, Cadence sat up flush against me. "Don't you find it strange that your father should be taken violently ill a day before he's murdered?"

"Are you saying–?" A coldness like melting ice spread over my skin. I squeezed her ankle. "You think they tried to poison him; that the murderer succeeded the second time but failed the first."

"It's the most likely answer."

"What's in the other vial?"

"I'm not sure." She shook the tube, watching the purple liquid slosh from side to side. "He had three or four of these; they were the only vials not marked. I figured it was worth a closer look; he shouldn't miss it."

Nodding, I flexed my hand around the vial of blood, brow

furrowing. "Poisoned – but with what? And how? We all ate the same food at dinner."

Cadence sat up, resting her elbows on her knees. "There has to be something only Felix consumed."

Though the both of us must have been going over the night of the party in our minds, Cadence had several core processors worth of speed over my own organic memory banks and got to the answer first, standing with a jolt.

"Belinda's cider!"

We headed out to the kitchen without another word. Cadence pushed open the double doors, pausing on the threshold to ensure that no servants were around to hinder us. "Any idea what Belinda made the cider in?"

I moved past her into the room, gaze trailing over the dishes strewn about. "She usually uses this big, iron pot; it's old, the only one we have."

Opening and closing all the drawers we could find, we dug through sieves, pans, pots, and cutlery, all with no result. Cadence at last located the vessel in question shoved back on top of a cupboard. Climbing on to a chair, she dragged it down and handed it to me.

Placing it on the preparation counter, we looked inside with bated breath. Cadence, her tongue held between her teeth, ran her finger along the bottom edge. When she drew it back, it was covered in tiny, granulated crystals, which caught the light in ways nothing edible should.

She stepped to the cupboard behind us and picked up a spoon, scrapping the bottom of the pot and gathering up a good clump of the grit. I sat down, my head spinning.

"Aunt Be couldn't have poisoned the cider. It doesn't make any sense." Cadence grunted, focused on her new evidence. I slid farther down in the chair, my head bumping against the curved back. "There's no reason she'd want to kill dad. Besides, any of us might have had a cup of that stuff and been killed as well. Aunt Be is a lot of things, but reckless isn't one of them."

"I agree." Cadence cupped a hand underneath the spoon. "But to know for sure, I'll need a microscope, a computer with access to the vertex, and some time."

"To the shed, then."

I started forward, but Cadence pulled at my shoulder, stopping me. "No, it's alright; I'll go alone."

"I thought we were going to do this together, Cay!" I spread my arms out in front of me. "I need to know what's going on!"

"You will," smiling, she held my face in her hand, tapping her strange rhythm against my skin. "I promise. But I need to be sure, okay? For your sake, I need to be sure." She stepped around me and into the hall, leaving me behind without a glance.

Beating back feelings of deepening foreboding, I wandered through the house, hands buried in my pockets, so absorbed in my own thoughts that I didn't even hear Belinda call to me as I walked through the entryway.

"Chance? Chance, there you are!" She stood above me on the landing, throwing a black shawl around her that accentuated her vibrant yellow jewelry. "You've been quite invisible today; busy with work?"

"Something like that." I smiled, but it shrunk under the memory of what had just passed. Examining the middle-aged woman above me, I stepped up the first few stairs. "Aunt Be? Do you remember the night of the party, you made some of your special cider?"

Belinda drew back at the question, brows jutting upward as she moved to the top of the stairs. "Certainly I do, pet. It was as much of a flop as it always is." Scowling, she ran her hand over her hair, piled high on her head. "I can never get the cinnamon quite right..."

"Yes, well," I cleared my throat, looking away from her, "while you were making it, do you remember anyone hanging around? Watching you maybe?"

"No, no one. Most of the servants were still downstairs, waiting to clear up from dinner." Belinda started down the stairs. "You should have a talk with them, you know. I had to wash the pot out myself and everything; very lazy of them to leave it there."

"I'll be sure to mention something to them. So, no one tried to help you, or add anything to the cider?"

She let out a scoff, grinning and reaching out to me as she stepped down the last stair which separated us. "Help me with the cider – it's my recipe, love! No one knows what goes in it but me. Why do you ask?"

"Oh," I shook my head, taking her by the shoulders and kissing her cheek, "it's nothing, Aunt Be. Just a stupid idea I had. I haven't been thinking very clearly lately. This whole thing is so bizarre. Who would want to kill Dad? And why was he acting so strange? Did you know," I turned to her, almost managing a sincere smile, "that Desdemona saw him going to bed at eleven o'clock the night he died? When he was always such a night owl!"

Belinda shook her head, clicking her tongue against her teeth.

"He had been sick, dear." She wrapped her arm through mine, hugging it to herself as we walked down the stairs. "I saw him going up at that time myself. After my headache passed, I stopped off in the library to get a cube to read and your father was just leaving."

She stopped at the foot of the stairs, turning to look me full in the face. Her lips quivered as she caressed my cheeks. "You are so handsome, Chance. You get that from your father, you know."

I took one of her hands in my own, returning her smile. "Really? I always thought I looked more like mum."

Belinda pulled back, sputtering out laughter. "Oh, tosh! Verity was pretty in an old-fashioned sort of way, I suppose, but you," she poked her finger into my chest, "you look just like your father did when he was your age." Looking me up and down, she clapped her hands together and sighed. "No wonder your mother stole him away! Who could resist?"

I cocked my head to one side, eyes narrowing. "Stole?"

"Didn't your father ever tell you how he and your mother met?" I shook my head, and she threw her hands up into the air, lips pursing. "I'm the one who introduced them! We were dating at the time."

"You and Dad?" I was quick to snap my gaping mouth shut.

"Just casually, the way you do at university. I introduced him to Verity, and they just clicked right away; you could see it." Her gaze focused somewhere above my head. "It was all for the best, of course. Your father and I became too good of friends to be married."

Fiddling with her university ring, diamond shapes with nautili in the centers ringing the band, she spun it round her digit, voice quavering. "Now, they're both gone – my two best friends in the world."

I saw the tears in her eyes before she realized they were there and pulled her into my embrace, kissing her forehead. "Aunt Be, please; please don't cry." She snuffled into my chest, and I closed my eyes, so thankful that I had someone like her in my life. "It'll be alright; I know it."

She wrapped her arms around me, rubbing my back as she cried. "I love you so much, Chance." She pulled away and stared up at me, all joy gone from her face, her lips a taut line. "I'm not going to let anything happen to you."

"Aunt Be," I frowned, wrinkling my nose. "I'm the head of the household now, remember? You're supposed to let me take care of you."

The evening passed and Cadence remained unseen. The worry that had started festering grew from an idle concern at the back of my mind to a constant throb, never leaving me in peace. After dinner, Victoria attempted to engage me in conversation, squeezing and petting my thigh, but that night she wasn't just inconsequential and boring, but irritating.

Abandoned to my brooding, the rest of the night ticked away, until I gave up on my dove and trudged off to bed. I decided to read for a while, hopeful that a story cube would turn my mind away from dark mysteries for a time. Stealing into the library, I was startled to find Solomon still awake, the only person besides myself to still be so. We exchanged a few pleasantries, but seeing he was still hard at work, I tried not to bother him, wandering through the shelves and, on a whim, picking up the book copy of *The Wind in the Willows* that father used to read to me.

I closed the door to my rooms and walked to the bed, flipping through the book's thick pages. Tossing it onto my pillow, I had started to undress when I spied a small docu-chip sitting on my floor. I picked it up but was halted from examining it further by a knock at the door.

Cadence slipped in, not waiting for my assent to enter, and leaned back against the door, forcing it shut, hands trapped under her hips. She stared at me, tapping her fingers against the wood. "I need to talk to you."

I sighed, lowering myself onto the bed and untying my shoes. "Can't it wait until morning?"

"I don't think you'd want me to."

"Alright," I pulled my socks off, tossing them to the other side of the bed before standing. "Let me get changed, then we'll talk."

Cadence nodded. Turning my back to her, I unbuttoned my shirt, waiting for the door to open and close before undressing further.

The room remained silent. I cast a wary glance over my shoulder. Cadence, lounging against the door, her eyes glazed over, still watched me. I jerked my head towards the door. "I meant we'd talk in your room."

Her brow furrowed. "Okay?"

She made no move to leave. My mouth hung open, fingers frozen on the button of my cuff before I turned back to the task at hand with a sharp shake. Pulling my shirt off my shoulders, I smiled. "Is it customary on Whiston to watch people undressing?"

"I suppose so. I never really thought of it as a custom, though."

Walking to the bed and dropping my shirt on it, I faced my

companion with an amused grimace. Cadence sighed, pushing away from the door and crossing the room. She picked up my shirt with two fingers and moved it to one side, sitting. "I know what you look like under those clothes, basically. And you know what I look like under mine, essentially. So, what's the point in acting all uptight about it?"

I wanted to reply with something about human shame and dignity, but the whole concept was so alien to her that I didn't say anything at all, pulling my thin undershirt up over my head with a grunt.

Cadence scooted towards the top of the bed, nose wrinkling. "Seems like a bunch of fuss over nothing."

I tried not to smirk as I undid my belt. "That depends on whom you're looking at."

Her lips curled up into a small smile as she brushed hair out of her eyes. My movements slowed as I pulled my belt free of my trousers, my eyes trailing over her as they had on the AN-GRAV.

"So, does this mean that I can wander into your room and watch you undress?" Cadence offered no initial response to my query. She leaned back on the bed and my blood started pounding in my ears. "And you wouldn't scream or anything?"

"Well," Cadence's eyes met mine as she shifted her weight against the mattress, "you couldn't make me scream just by watching."

I could have had her right then and there. But like so many of the things I wanted, it was not to be. A loud crash from downstairs made us both jump, followed by heavy thuds and then a cry that reverberated through the silent house.

"Help! Somebody! Help!"

Cadence had already turned the doorknob before the first 'help' had finished sounding. I scooped my undershirt up off the floor and followed her. Belinda stood at the top of the landing, dressing gown clutched around her, and she rushed down the stairs ahead of us, our own foot falls close behind.

Recognizing the voice of panic, I called out "Solomon!" as we rounded the stairs. A shout of recognition sounded to our left and we scrambled towards the kitchen, a flurry of limbs. Two pairs of feet stuck out from the doorway and my heart stopped beating. When we reached the room, the sight that assailed us was unbearable.

Solomon leaned over the motionless body of his wife, her light blue nightgown torn as if from a struggle, her eyes closed. He pulled away when we entered; his face upturned, the tracks of his tears plain, but not as distinct as the angry red marks which scored Minerva's fragile neck.

Even before Solomon shouted, "Get the doctor!" the sound of running from down the hall reached us.

Henry, the first through the door, shoved me out of the way as he collapsed beside his mother. "Mum!" He held her face in his hands. "Mum!" Bending down, he put his ear at her lips. "She's not breathing!"

"Move, move!" Dr. Merton pushed his way into the room, forcing the two men away from Minerva. Frazzled, still in his sleeping clothes, his skin paler than his patient's, but his arms and cheeks were as red as her neck. He knelt onto the floor and began pulling things out of his medical bag, vials, bandages, and syringes spilling out until he found the small respirator.

Lifting Minerva's head off the ground, he slipped the plastic mask over her face, tugging it over her nose and mouth. That done, he put two fingers against her neck and waited. Frown deepening, he started pumping her chest with both hands. "What in god's name happened?"

"I don't know." Solomon's voice was hollow. Still on the floor, angled out of the way, he stared at his wife, face drawn in horror. "I was heading towards our rooms and I heard a noise. I came to see what it was–someone ran past me. Then I...is she going to be alright?"

The doctor was silent. He checked her pulse and his chin fell to his chest. Removing the mask, he nodded, replacing his tools in his bag. "I hope so; we won't know for sure until she wakes up. We need to get her to a hospital as soon as possible."

"I'll call an ambulance," Victoria offered. I hadn't even noticed her enter the room behind me, but I heard her as she left and begin dialing on the main phone.

My eyes met Cadence's; she pulled at her lips with her fingertips. She stepped out of the room and around the doorframe. I followed her, my heart sitting at the bottom of my stomach like a stale piece of bread.

Leaning against the wall outside, Cadence's eyes were downcast, her face looking sick in the dim light.

"Cadence, what the hell is going on in this house?"

"I..." She swallowed several times before shaking her head. "...I have no idea."

"But you said–!"

"I was wrong!" She pushed her hands back through her hair, shaking her head. "I must have been wrong."

19

Chapter 19

The ambulance arrived in minutes, and with it, the EO. Displaced from the kitchen, we settled into the sitting room to await instructions. Brisbois' stare was even grimmer than before, face unshaven and hair a disheveled mess. He began his customary rounds of questioning but approached the situation with a different tenor than before. The first few witnesses were in and out of the study in less than twenty minutes. He hadn't even gotten to Cadence or me before he strode into the sitting room, unclipping his restraints from his belt.

"Mr. Solomon Davers?"

Solomon stepped forward from beside the door where he had been hovering. Clearing his throat, Brisbois turned towards him with a firm nod. "Mr. Davers, I am arresting your physical and mental person under Article 9.86 of the Enforcement Act for the attempted murder of Mrs. Minerva Davers."

On their feet in an instant, everyone cried out; everyone except Solomon, who remained dumbstruck as Brisbois turned him around and activated the restraints onto his wrists.

"You have the right to remain silent," Brisbois continued as if he hadn't noticed the kerfuffle, although two EO officers stepped into the room behind him, attuned to brewing trouble, "but if you do not tell us something you later rely on in court, that evidence may be deemed inadmissible. You have the right to a lawyer of your choice for representation, from either the public or the private sector."

"Inspector! You—you can't be serious!"

Brisbois looked at me, brow furrowing as he frowned. "I am serious, very serious. Or does me putting this man in restraints and reading him his rights confuse you somehow?"

"Please," Solomon called over his shoulder as he was led out by the officers, "you're making a mistake!"

We all followed, rushing through the hallway like a waterfall through a narrow gorge, emptying out into the entryway in a cascade of sound. Henry pushed his way to the front of the group, protesting his father's innocence, only to have an EO officer block his path and shove him back.

"Solomon," I pulled Henry away, forcing him behind me and out of any further trouble. "I'll post whatever bail they ask for; don't say a thing!"

The poor man's walk to the front door was interrupted by the ambulance crew sweeping by with Minerva, suspended on top of a stretcher, her head bouncing from side to side. They knocked over one of the potted plants sitting by the door in their haste, but Cadence managed to right it, digging her hand into the base to keep it steady. Solomon was thrust out after the stretcher, begging to know how his wife fared, but to no avail.

I locked eyes with Brisbois, anger boiling up in me as I tightened my hand into a fist.

"Inspector, please," Cadence stepped in front of me, putting herself between the two of us. "I don't wish to question your authority on this matter; but Solomon has become a friend to me since I've arrived, and I know he's very dear to everyone here. How can you arrest him for this crime so quickly?"

At last Brisbois softened, his shoulders drooping and his glare disappearing, replaced by a tired, but not unsympathetic, frown. "I understand that this may be hard to accept," he glanced back to the group clustered behind Cadence and straightened, raising his voice to ensure that all could hear, "but it's the only possibility. The medics have informed me that the marks on Minerva's neck were caused by someone's bare hands. The strength required to crush someone's windpipe points to a male assailant."

"Mrs. Davers was visiting with Miss Eydis in her rooms just before the attack; she left to get them some drinks from the kitchen. Miss Tanith," Belinda winced at her name, turning away, "has told me that she was the first one on the landing after the cries for help and that no one came past her up the stairs. No one from the downstairs bedrooms could have made it back to their rooms without being seen by the others. It had to have been Solomon Davers."

I closed my eyes, hissing through clenched teeth, "But why? Why would he try and kill his wife and then call for help?"

"It's possible he saw what he'd done and was so filled with remorse that he tried to help her; I've seen it before. As for why he tried to kill her," Brisbois sighed, scratching the top of his head, "when I know, you'll know."

Pausing to ensure that no one wished to question him further, Brisbois gave a parting nod and exited the house, leaving the front door open in his wake.

"Henry." I took a deep breath and swallowed, forcing myself into some semblance of composure. "You should go with your mother. Go on, go," I cut him off before he could protest, waving him out. "I'll handle things here."

Nodding, Henry left at a jog, slamming the door shut behind him.

I turned to the others. Cadence stared down at herself, a clump of dirt stuck in her hand from when she had righted the potted plant. Desdemona hovered near Merton, running her hands over each other like scared mice, and Belinda stood to one side with Victoria, who patted the older woman on the back while she moaned, face in her hands.

"It's alright, Belinda, it's really alright." Victoria looked up at the ceiling, shaking her head, chest heaving under her skimpy negligee. "To think, we had a murderer in our midst all along. Minerva must have found out that Solomon killed Felix and he had to kill her to keep it quiet."

"Victoria, do you think about the things that come out of your mouth? Or do you just let them run free through your brain before inflicting them on the rest of us?"

Victoria's eyes went wide. Taking a step forward, her shoulders hunched, her lips curled up into an open-mouthed smirk. "I'm sorry; what did you just say to me?"

"I must have used words a bit too long for you: shut your trap,

Vicky." I jabbed my finger at her, voice rocketing up into a shout. "Solomon did not kill my father and he did not try to kill his wife! For god's sake, you've known him as long as I have, how can you even say something like that?"

I strode past Dr. Merton, heading for the phone on the far wall, drawing blood from the inside of my cheek with my teeth. Merton followed me with his wide, wet eyes. "What are you doing?"

"Calling my lawyer so I can post Solomon's bail."

Merton threw his hands into the air and took hold of my arm. "It hasn't even been set yet, Chance! It probably won't be until late this morning at the earliest. There's nothing any of us can do now." The doctor ran his hand through his sparse hair, looking at each of us in turn. "I suggest we all go to bed and try to get some rest. We need it."

While the other drifted towards their rooms like seaweed on the tide, Desdemona broke away and tiptoed over to me, tucking her white-blonde hair behind her ear. "Chance? Are you going to be alright?"

I rubbed my arms, forcing a sliver of a smile onto my face. "Yeah. I'll...I'll be fine. Thanks, Desdemona."

She nodded and darted away up the stairs, leaving Cadence and I alone.

Still staring at her hand, Cadence's breathing had ceased some time ago; a fact I hoped none of the others had noticed. I waited to see if she would move or speak or do anything useful and was about to give up when she sprung to attention, head snapping up as she marched past me. "You should try and get some sleep. I'll be in the library."

"What? Cadence? Cay!" My shout rang through the hall, echoing against the closing doors behind which Cadence disappeared.

Dragging myself up to my rooms, I soon found that any attempt to sleep would be fruitless. Lying awake smoking until dawn, I transplanted my restlessness from my bed to my father's study, where I passed the time by calling my lawyer every half hour or so to inquire whether Solomon's bail had been set.

Henry returned in these early hours, swaying on his feet, his eyes red from crying. To see the dear man in such pain was unbearable, but he insisted on sitting with me awhile, truculent and weary, until I bullied him into his room to try and sleep.

What the rest of the household did that day, I couldn't say. Committed to staying by the office phone so I could be ready to act the moment my solicitor called, I had both breakfast and lunch in the study, alone. I was informed just after midday that Solomon's bail had been set at 500,000 credits. The sum made me blanch, not because I was afraid to pay it, but because such a high bail attested to the authorities' confidence in Solomon's guilt.

It took some time to arrange for the money to be moved from my accounts since most of the family funds were still unavailable due to the circumstances of my father's death. But once the appropriate amount had been secured, I wired it to the authorities, who, in short order, sent me back a ticket of habeas corpus with which I could obtain Solomon's temporary release.

I gathered my things to make the trip out to the District 27 facilities at once. Exiting the study, I spied the library door ajar and crossed the foyer at a jog, eager to pick up my lady friend and be on our way, whether she liked it or not.

The drive to the EO Complex took place in silence. Cadence radiated displeasure, saying nothing, her breathing stilled. I tried to cheer her by telling her about my conversation with Belinda the previous night, but the tale seemed to depress her even further, pressing her down into her seat.

Our PT dropped us just outside the gates of the District 27 Government Service Center. We walked the rest of the way in, finding the appropriate division without incident. At no point were we allowed inside the buildings themselves, but stations outside each one offered an officer or clerk available to do business with the public. I slipped my notice of habeas corpus under the bullet proof window at one of these stations and was told to wait; the 'prisoner' would be outside after processing.

When Solomon shuffled through the doors, he was a changed man. His shoulders stooped, his eyes were glazed and listless. Rubbing at the stubble on his chin as if reveling in the unfamiliarity of it, the bedraggled state of his clothes spoke to the ordeal he had been through. His face brightened when he caught sight of us, a smile flashing onto both our faces.

"Solomon–"

"Have you seen Minerva? Is she alright?" His hazel eyes searched my own. "They won't tell me anything. I'm not even allowed in the hospital."

"I understand that she's still comatose," said Cadence matter-of-factly. "But they are hopeful she will recover."

I glared at her over my shoulder, her coolness grating, but I swallowed down the annoyance and tried to comfort the harried man in front of me, squeezing his shoulders. "We'll go check on her as soon as we get you home."

"Go check on her now." There was no arguing with the firmness in his voice as he stepped away, smoothing down his shirt as best as he could and adjusting a tie that wasn't there. "I can get myself back to the manor."

Dropping my hands to my sides, I sighed, looking at him askance. "Is there anything at all we can do?"

"Chance," Solomon's mouth opened and closed on its hinges as he turned, unable to meet my gaze. "You have to know that I would never do anything to hurt Minerva or your father. You know that don't you?"

"I know. And if the Inspector didn't have his head up his ass, he'd know it too." I reached back and wound my arm around Cadence's shoulders, pulling her to my side. "Cadence and I," I licked my lips and looked into her eyes, "we're trying to work this whole thing out. And I think we're almost there. I'm sure there must be some way we can prove you're innocent."

Cadence's brows pushed up under her bangs. Taking in a deep breath, she turned to Solomon, tapping against the back of the hand I had on her shoulder. "Sinc, we'll certainly try our best, Mr. Davers."

Solomon's gaze moved over her face. "Amazing. I wouldn't think you..." His eyes strayed to the hand she had over mine and he pulled himself up straight. "You're absolutely amazing."

Smiling, Cadence dropped her chin to her chest, squeezing my arm once before slipping out from under it. "I'll go call you a PT, Mr. Davers."

She walked towards the duty desk, Solomon turning to follow her progress. He slipped his hands into his pockets, shaking his head. "To think: she still cares about us; after everything we've done to her and her kind."

My heart jumped into my throat, cutting off my air and choking me.

Solomon glanced over at me. Mustering up a weak smile, he shrugged. "I've known about Cadence's true nature for quite some time, actually. The emotion tags she uses, her mannerisms; her tattoo is a derivative of the old Halcyon Enterprises trademark. I understand many of them have adopted such adornments over the years." He adjusted his glasses with one hand. "Artificial Intelligence is my field after all."

I stepped in front of him, blocking him from Cadence. "You're not going to–"

"No, no," Solomon raised his hand, frowning at my incomplete insinuation, "of course not. It's not my place to gossip about other people's biological make-up. I've always been fascinated by your family's history with the animanecrons, Chance. It's why I started working at Halcyon Enterprises in the first place; never dreamed I'd be lucky enough to meet one though." He leaned to see around me, nodding in Cadence's direction. "She is quite remarkable; and very fond of you, apparently."

"What do you mean, 'apparently'?"

Solomon jerked backwards, opening his mouth to speak. But his gaze fell over my shoulder, his mouth snapped shut, and I heard Cadence's familiar footfall behind me.

"Someone should be here to take you back to the manor shortly, Mr. Davers."

"Thank you." Solomon inclined his head to her before turning back to me, extending his hand. "And thank you, Chance. Please, call me as soon as you see her?"

"I will; I promise."

He nodded again before walking down to the PT bay at the other end of the complex, shoulders hunched, and head hung low. Somehow, I should have been able to spare him this; somehow what was happening was my fault.

I looked back to Cadence, waiting beside me, watching me with her cool inky eyes. Wrapping my arm around her shoulder, I pulled her to me, her warmth easing my mind.

20

Chapter 20

Armo Hospital sat just outside of Römer's 23rd district, close enough to the grasslands to be considered a retreat, but near enough to the city to be useful to the public. I hated hospitals; they gave me chills and they stunk with sterility, a chemical cleanness that lingered on the skin for hours.

Weaving our way through the labyrinthine corridors, Cadence and I stopped every so often at the information desks to verify that we were headed in the right direction. Minerva had been placed in the coma ward; a small collection of rooms as silent as a beach before a storm.

Depositing Cadence in one of the hard, plastic chairs in the waiting room, I gave myself a quick once over in a nearby window before walking up to the tiny, bullet-proof, plastic-encased nurses' station. Waiting for the attendant to turn her attention from the checkerboard of screens behind her to me, I spent several long minutes trying to figure out how the com system worked, in the end settling for tapping apologetically on the window and saying, 'Excuse me,' into any opening that might possibly carry sound.

"Yes?" The large woman inside the booth spun around in her chair. "Can I help you?"

"Yes, hello; we'd like to see Minerva Davers, please."

Nodding, she tapped away at an old keyboard under her desk. She stifled a yawn, but straightened after a moment, focusing on a screen which lived somewhere above my head. "I'm afraid that's impossible, sir; there's an EO ban against any visitors to Mrs. Davers."

"Oh, dear." My exclamation of distress failed to elicit any emotion from the nurse besides a vague glare of distrust. I backed away from the booth, bending over in a bow. "Well, thank you anyways."

Adding a certain reluctance to my step, I walked back to Cadence, formulating a plan. When I was a few feet away I whispered, "You need to cry."

Cadence's eyes darted around the room for some kind of contextual clue that would let her in on my meaning. "What?"

"I need you to start crying. Act like you're very upset."

She stared up at me, eyes widening. "I can't cry, Chance!"

"What?" I cast a glance over my shoulder. Sure enough, the nurse on duty was attempting to peer around me. We were without a doubt the most interesting thing that had happened to her all day, but the longer we spent arguing out of earshot the less interested she would become.

"I can't cry, not even a little, why would you even – I'm not built that way!" She gritted her teeth and squared her shoulders, staring into my abdomen as she worked herself into a panic. "Can you think of anything more stupid than a highly sophisticated and sensitive computer system that intentionally pipes salt water through itself? What would be the point in–?"

"Pretend!"

Glaring at the ceiling with enough malice to melt holes in it, she let loose with a deafening wail. The cry rolled up into her higher register, sounding like a diamond dragged down glass, and then wavered down into hearty, body-vibrating sobs.

Cadence buried her face in her hands and continued blubbering while I slid into the seat beside her, wrapping my arm around her. "Now, now! Oh, you dear child, I'm so sorry!" Dropping her head onto my shoulder, she let out a nerve-jangling shriek into my ear, which I was certain was one hundred percent intentional.

Her nurturing instincts taking over, the nurse stepped out of her bullet-proof box and bustled over to us, eyes shining with concern. "Is she alright?"

I patted the back of Cadence's head, attempting to extricate myself from her monkey-like grip. "Yes, yes, I'm–" she tugged me back down onto the seat and one of my pats turned into a sharp slap. Released, I stood before she could change her mind. "I'm sure she'll be fine. She and Mrs. Davers are very close, you see, and she's leaving for Paraesepe today – a death in the family. She doesn't think she'll ever be back, and, of course, Mrs. Davers may never wake up."

"How awful!" The nurse put a hand to her heart and cast a pitying glance down onto Cadence, who had lowered her wail to murmured cries and violent sniffling, hands covering her dry face.

"It's just such a shame that she can't...can't even say goodbye."

Cadence let loose another pained yell, the unexpectedness of which caused both the nurse and I to jump. Contorting in her seat, Cadence buried her face into the back of the chair. "She was like a mother to me! Oh, to have lost my real mother and my surrogate mother all in one day! I can't go on!"

"You poor, poor thing!" The nurse rushed over and hugged Cadence to her not inconsiderable bosom, suffocating her with tenderness. "I am so sorry, honey, so sorry!"

Cadence continued to whimper. The woman looked around the empty wing, biting her lower lip. Leaning back, she squeezed Cadence's shoulders. "If it really means that much to you, I could get you in to see Mrs. Davers for a few minutes."

"You could?" Cadence sat up, rubbing her face and eyes so hard they appeared red and blotchy. "Really?"

"Ye-es, but..." She looked around the waiting room and back to Cadence's sorrowful face. "Honestly, just for a moment."

Cadence smiled her awkward, shaky smile. "Thank you! Thank you so much, that would be wonderful."

"You stay here and I'll be right back, alright?" Beaming, the woman put a hand on my shoulder as she passed.

I sat next to Cadence, who had curled up into her seat, hugging her knees to her chin. "Anta, well thank you so very much for making me feel cheap and used."

"You're welcome; it's something I do for all the women in my life." I risked a glance at her and regretted it, her eyes pricking into me like needles of hate. "Well, how else were we going to get in?"

She didn't respond right away, stewing in her own unpleasant juices before answering with a pointed wave, "I thought, perhaps, that I could use the rapport I have developed with the Inspector to–"

"I've had quite enough of you two 'rapport-ing', thank you very much."

Cadence watched me, still scowling, but now in an unfocused sort of way. "You seem troubled by my connection with Inspector Brisbois. Why?"

"Because," fixing her with an aggravated stare, I chewed the inside of my cheek, "he obviously only wants to get to know you so he can sleep with you."

Lips pursed, she ran her fingers along her brow before nodding. "Yes...but you only wanted to get to know me so you could sleep with me too."

"It's different." Cadence opened her mouth and I raised a finger, shaking it at her. "And don't you dare ask me why because I haven't figured it out yet, but it is!" The vein in my neck throbbed. I took a deep breath. "For once, let's just do this my way, okay?"

Regaining her pout, Cadence dropped her feet to the floor as if they were made of lead. "Your way involves me duping well-meaning hospital staff. Your way, to use a common colloquialism, stinks."

My retort was interrupted by the return of the nurse, who led us back into the coma wing. Letting us into Minerva's room with some whispers about not touching any of the equipment or telling anyone about this, she patted Cadence's shoulder once more before disappearing back down the hall, the door sliding shut behind her.

I peered out the window in the door before turning back to Cadence. "It might stink, but it works, doesn't it?"

Ignoring me, Cadence leaned over Minerva, examining her body with cool scientific detachment while squeezing the unconscious woman's hand. Breathing into an oxygen mask, Minerva was a sickening sight: all pale, with tubes and wires sticking out of her arms and neck. Someone had delivered a bouquet of wilting yellow roses beside her bed; someone just as well-meaning had found an ugly yellow vase to put them in.

"What do you see?"

Cadence poured over Minerva for a few more minutes before giving her hand a final pat and sitting down in the chair beside her. "Based on the bruise on her head, I'd say her attacker tried to render her unconscious before strangling her. So, any thoughts about DNA under her fingernails are moot." She looked up, shaking her head. "I'm sorry, I see nothing here that would contradict the Inspector's findings."

"How is that possible? Solomon Davers didn't try to kill his wife and he didn't kill my father." Striding over to the bed, I willed myself to scrutinize Minerva's crumpled form.

"What is that?"

"What is what?" Cadence sounded tired, like she had that day on the train, but she leaned forward anyway, looking at the area of purplish skin on Minerva's neck I indicated, where there appeared to be a void in the bruise.

Cadence drooped back into her chair. "It's an impression on

the skin. Whoever strangled her was wearing a ring; something like a wedding ring, which Solomon Davers wears, so–"

"Cadence, humor me; really look at this. Does that look like a wedding ring?" She picked herself up from the chair and shuffled over to my side of the bed. I pressed the edge of the impression with my finger. "Can't you see that?"

With infinitesimal slowness, Cadence's brows curved up over her eyes. "Yes." She followed the path I traced. "Yes, I see it. What is that?"

"Some kind of pattern. Something..." I grabbed a pen and pad of paper off the bedside table. Closing my eyes, I let the pen move in the same pattern my finger had over Minerva's skin, "something...like this."

I opened my eyes. In front of me was a repeating chain of two hazy shapes, super-imposed over each other. The larger one, a diamond, held inside it a simple spiral, descending inwards on itself until termination.

I put a hand to my mouth. "Why do I feel like I've seen this before?"

Behind me, Cadence leaned in. Her eyes were wide and dark, and I knew she saw something there I didn't. "We need to get back to the manor. Now."

"What?" She was already moving for the door, heedless to my question, leaving me with little choice but to follow her. "Why?"

"I don't have time to explain." Flinging the door open, her stride turned into a jog. "This isn't over, not yet. We need to move quickly before there's another body to find." She looked back at me as we ran through the automatic double doors, the bright summer sun hitting her face, intensifying the glow of her smile. "I know who the murderer is."

Our PT shot out of the hospital bay like a rocket. I turned my eyes away from the glaring light of the setting Arrhidaean sun and watched the endless fields of orange grasses sway in the PT's wake like breaking ocean waves. In the seat next to me, Cadence sat upright, every muscle taut, her eyes scanning the landscape while she tapped her fingers against her lips.

I didn't bother asking her who the murderer was. She wouldn't have told me, but more than that, I wasn't sure I wanted to know. I wasn't ready to know. But ignorance would not be an option for long, so I enjoyed it while it lasted.

I wanted to pull Cadence close and bury my face in her hair, to breathe her in and forget everything that had happened since we met. But I didn't. Clearing my throat, I slid my hands into my trouser pockets, searching for my nix case, when my fingers brushed against the docu-chip I had found the night before.

I took it out with a murmur, drawing Cadence's attention. "I completely forgot. This fell out of a book I was reading last night; *The Wind and the Willows*." I passed it to her. "I thought it might be the will; maybe Dad stashed it there for some reason."

Examining the fingertip-sized disc, Cadence's lips twisted into a humorless smile. "Well, it may turn out to be nothing now. But I suppose it's still worth a read."

With complete disregard for my delicate mental state, she opened her mouth and slid the docu-chip against her upper palate. A soft click, which had to be the chip connecting with whatever drive she had installed there, and she removed her fingers from her mouth. Sitting back and tapping her hands on her thighs, she waited for the chip to load.

Her fingers stilled as her eyes moved back and forth, reading the document off her internal memory. Shoulders tensing, she blinked, taking a deep breath before starting again. She sat forward in her seat, hands seized around her knees, breath stilled as her eyes flickered at a phenomenal pace.

"Cadence?" I touched the back of her hand. Even hotter than usual, for a split-second I thought I felt her skin humming. "Cay? Cadence!" My shout jolted her back to the present and she swiveled around to look at me. "What is it, what does it say?"

She blinked a few more times before resuming her breathing, reaching into her mouth and removing the chip. Running her tongue along her lips, she wiped the corners of her mouth with her sleeve. "How far are we from the manor?"

"Probably thirty minutes or so."

"Can we go any faster?"

I began chewing the inside of my mouth. "He can only go as fast as the speed regulations allow, Cay; this isn't a flicker."

"I think Desdemona may be in danger. Real danger." Massaging her shoulder with one hand, Cadence shook her head. "I hope we can get back in time."

"In time for what?"

"To stop her murder."

21

Chapter 21

After her morbid pronouncement, Cadence and I spent the drive in tense silence. My gaze was drawn again and again to the clock that sat high in the divider between the driver and ourselves, while Cadence's focus remained on the setting sun. Was she being theatrical? How great could the danger be? Another murder seemed unthinkable. My questions were answered when we pulled up in front of the manor. Cadence opened the door to the PT before we'd stopped, her foot brushing over the gravel until she hurled herself out. Following her as quick as I could, I tossed some credit chips in through the PT window as I ran after her.

Cadence burst through the front door, shouldering the plank of wood away and almost off its hinges, and taking the main stairs two at a time. "Desdemona! Desdemona!"

Solomon rushed out of the library, a pad tucked under his arm. "What's going on?"

Cadence turned back at the top of the stairs as I pounced on him. "Solomon, where's Desdemona?"

He stepped back, face creased with worry. "She went out to the gazebo a little while ago – why, what's wrong?"

Cadence bounded down the stairs, making such a racket that Victoria stuck her head out from her bedroom, scowling. Taking the corner at the bottom of the stairs at speed, Cadence hung on to the banister, swinging herself around the corner and heading down the hall.

Leaving Solomon gaping in my wake, I rounded the corner after her and, unable to catch sight of her, kept moving into the dining room. The doors to the veranda hung open, the breeze of a coming storm making them creak. The smell of soft grasses and rain was in the air, weighing heavy on me as I ran outside.

Reaching the sea of bushes that surrounded the gazebo on either side, I slowed, sweeping the dim terrain for any sign of Cadence or Desdemona. I jogged farther up the path and, before I knew what had happened, I was pulled down into the undergrowth. Filled with adrenaline, I struggled against my unseen attacker and was about to cry out when Cadence's voice slithered into my ear.

"Quiet!"

I ceased fighting and tried to catch my breath. Cadence released me, and after a moment, I made out her form in the dying light, crouching behind a piece of topiary and staring at the darkened structure in front of us.

"Cadence, what–"

Silencing me again with a sharp 'shush,' she motioned for me to stay where I was. Low and silent, she crept through the bushes towards the gazebo. I waited, every muscle screaming in impatience.

From the gazebo, there was a loud crash. Then, another. And then, worst of all, a high-pitched scream. Cadence's voice rang out like a siren, violent and desperate:

"Chance, stop her!"

A person rushed towards me out of the black. I tackled them to the ground without a second thought. A hand scratched at my eyes, a knee planted itself in my liver, but I held on until I had subdued them. Pulling back, I peered at the body beneath me, squinting as I tried to make out a face. A shaft of light cut across us and the stranger became family in an instant.

"Aunt Be?"

"What the hell is going on?" Solomon hurried towards us with Henry, Victoria, and Dr. Merton close behind, the flashlight in his hand jittering over the dark ground. He swung the beam of light up to the gazebo, catching the staggering figures of Cadence and Desdemona.

Cadence eased Desdemona down the stairs, one arm slung around her waist, the other holding the banister. Limping, Desdemona clutched her throat, where deep red marks were already visible. "She–" Desdemona struggled through a coughing fit, drawing in oxygen in a gasp, "–tried to strangle me!"

Belinda struggled against me, writhing in the grass. "Ridiculous!"

Sitting back, I let her get up, staring at her, slack jawed. Brushing herself off, Belinda threw a hand out at the injured woman. "You can't believe her, Chance! She's a thief and a junkie; your father told me so." She glared at the younger woman, grinning. "He was never going to marry her."

Desdemona wrested out of Cadence's grip and hobbled forward, shouting as loud as she could. "Yes, he was! He was! Felix knew everything and he didn't care; he loved me!"

"You stupid little bitch!" Belinda rushed at her, hands outstretched. I scrambled to my feet to restrain her while Cadence did the same with Desdemona. "He loved me! He always loved me! We were going to be together!" I shoved her back and she stumbled away, dark hair a tangle, eyes wild. "You were just in the way, just like Verity!"

Her words struck me like fists. "What?" I pulled her to me, my fingers digging into her arms. "Belinda, what are you talking about?"

She pushed me away with a scoff, rolling her eyes. "Oh, Chance! Why do you think your father married your mother in the first place? You think he loved her?" Sarcasm dripped off her words like poison. "You weren't old enough to know it, but your father and mother hated each other. It was the money he wanted, not her. And then she didn't even have the decency to give him that. He couldn't let everything his family had worked for be ruined!"

"You're the beautiful serpent."

Belinda jumped, swinging around with her hands clenched. "What did you call me?"

Cadence tightened her grip around Desdemona's shoulders. "That's what Felix used to call you. I've read the love letters."

"But—but—"

"You missed one docu-chip when you destroyed the others." Cadence shook her head and looked away. "You and Felix had been having an affair for years. Why deny it now?"

"What?" Solomon stepped forward, the lines of his face exaggerated by the deepening shadows. "Belinda! How could you? You and Verity were friends – best friends!"

Still staring at Cadence, Belinda ran her hands down her face, barking out a laugh. "Friends? She was the golden girl; she got everything I ever wanted. How could I be friends with someone like that?"

When she turned back, it was if she saw me standing there for the first time. Her eyes widening, she stretched her hands out towards me. "I loved your father more than anything in the world, Chance. I always did, from that first moment we met in school. And when he asked me to help him with your mother; how could I say no? He...he promised he'd marry me; after..." She sucked in a shuddering breath, caressing my cheek. "I've tried to be a mother to you, Chance; I've tried to make it up to you."

I felt the ground shift under my feet and stumbled backwards, only to find that it was me and not the terrain that had grown unsteady. Looking into Belinda's eyes, eyes I had known all my life, I asked the question I didn't want answered. "Aunt Be.... are you saying that you...that you and Dad...killed my mother?"

She turned away, hands covering her mouth, and nodded.

The whole world went silent. Even my heartbeat stilled. Then, there was a peal of thunder, far away, but deafening.

"I think we should go inside." Keeping her gaze focused on the ground, Cadence stepped down from the gazebo, helping Desde-mona. "Mr. Davers?"

Solomon grabbed Belinda by the shoulders, his mouth a grim line. "I'll call Inspector Brisbois."

Henry took Desdemona from Cadence with a nod and the rest of the group trailed inside without us. I fought against the urge to collapse onto the lawn. I didn't think I would ever get back up again if I did.

A soft rustle and Cadence was at my side, tugging my arm but avoiding my eyes. "Chance, come on. Come inside."

"Did you know about this?"

Releasing me, she brought her hands close to her chest, com-pressing each finger in turn. Her words tripped out in strangled jerks. "I suspected it might be a possibility, yes."

"And you didn't tell me?"

"I tried. I tried, but–" Her head shot up and her brow wrin-kled, gaze moving over my features as she lifted her shoulders, spinning her hands over each other. "I didn't want to–to...upset you unduly."

I bit down on the inside of my mouth, closing my eyes. "You didn't want to ruin the dramatic effect, you mean."

Cadence winced as if my words were a lash against her skin. "Chance, I'm sorry, I–"

I sliced my hand through the air. My head ached and my stomach churned. "I have had enough of your literary fantasy, Cadence. This isn't a book; this is my life. This is my family, damn it. You can't just come here and...and..." I looked up into her eyes, glowing bright in the dark, and the fire left me. Turning away, I began the long walk back to the house alone. "You know what? Forget it. You couldn't understand anyway."

Chapter 22

We shuffled into the sitting room to await the EO for what I hoped was the last time. Belinda sat by the door in a stiff-backed chair, Solomon keeping watch close by. Sinking into the couch on the other side of the piano, Victoria sat beside me, much to my chagrin, and began playing with my hair.

Henry took up a comforting station behind me, but when Cadence entered, she gestured for him to come over and, without a moment's hesitation, he did. She whispered something in his ear and his face went pale. After a moment, I heard his light tread hurrying up the stairs.

The doorbell rang with a funereal tone. Straightening in our seats, we listened as the front door opened and a troop of EO officers bustled inside. A handful of them passed by the sitting room and we heard several more taking up stations in the entryway. At last, Inspector Brisbois made his grand entrance, sweeping into the room with his restraints in hand.

"Miss Belinda Tanith, I am arresting your physical and mental person under Article 9.86 of the Enforcement Act for the attempted murder of Miss Desdemona Eydis. Under this article–"

"And the murder of Verity Hale."

Brisbois blinked several times, closing his mouth with a snap. He peered around Belinda to where Cadence had stretched herself over a chaise. "What?"

"It's quite true," said Solomon, stepping forward. "She confessed."

"She did, Inspector, we all heard her." Merton went to pat Desdemona's shoulder, but seemed to think better of it, turning to face Brisbois instead. "Apparently, she and Felix killed Verity together."

Brisbois stared down at Belinda with a less than professional gape. She stood, rolling her shoulders back as she shrugged. "I was in love."

Her flippancy refocused him. Clicking open the restraints, he leaned down to slip them over her hands and wrists. "Miss Belinda Tanith, I am arresting your physical and mental person under Article 9.86 of the Enforcement Act for the attempted murder of Miss Desdemona Eydis and under Article 9.01 for the murder of Mrs. Verity Hale. Under these articles–"

"And the attempted murder of Minerva Davers." Cadence unwound a loose thread from the pillow she had wedged beneath her shoulders. "And the attempted murder of Felix Hale; that should be in there too." Brisbois gave a strangled exclamation, drawing her attention at last. "What?"

"Have you gone utterly mad?"

"My neural map is uncorrupted, I assure you." Cadence sat up to make room for Henry, who had returned from upstairs at last. "You said, Inspector, that the strength needed to strangle some-one bare-handed pointed to a male assailant; but Belinda here is in impressive physical shape. I am also sure that you noticed the bruises on Minerva Davers' neck, and the void therein."

"Yes, the attacker was wearing a ring. Which, of course, Solomon Davers wears."

"You see, but you do not observe, Inspector Brisbois." I was sure Cadence intended to pause for dramatic effect, but she was forced to hurry on by Brisbois' sullen glare. "I don't blame you, I didn't either at first, but Chance did." She gestured to me, smiling.

"There's a pattern in that bruise. A pattern that looks," Cadence dug through the pockets of her pants and produced the crumpled piece of paper I had drawn on earlier, passing it to Brisbois, "like this. It's a university crest, commonly found on class rings." She tapped the paper once more. "Chance's mother wore a ring like this once – and she wasn't alone."

Cadence's gaze fell to Belinda's hand. The inspector straightened. "Miss Tanith, may I please see your ring?" He slipped it off her finger without waiting for her consent, comparing the band to the pattern on the paper. The sharp widening of his eyes was all the confirmation any of us needed.

"But I don't understand!" Solomon, who had stepped away from Belinda when the EO arrived, now moved back towards her, staring. "What possible reason could she have for wanting to kill Minerva?"

"I can't think of one," said Cadence. "But could someone describe Desdemona for me, please?"

Victoria sighed, dropping her hands into her lap. "She has long white blonde hair. She's thin; sickly thin, frankly. A little over one and a half meters tall–"

"She looks like mum," Henry cut in, "especially in the dark."

Nodding, Cadence spun on her heel and began pacing. "Just before Minerva was strangled, she was with Desdemona in her rooms. It was late, the lights in the hallway were off, and Minerva walked out of Desdemona's room and went downstairs. Then, she was attacked." She stopped in front of Belinda, meeting her wild stare. "You made a mistake; you thought it was Desdemona's throat you were crushing."

Belinda collapsed into her chair, groaning. "How was I supposed to know they'd been talking?"

"And the attempted murder of Felix Hale, Miss Turing?"

"I don't think there's much 'attempt' about it, he is dead." Victoria slid down in her seat, yawning.

Cadence's hip jutted to one side as she rested her weight on one leg. "Did everyone really think that Felix just happened to catch flu the night before he was murdered?"

Happy to see everyone adopting an open-mouthed gape, I allowed myself a derisive snort. Cadence almost smiled, but smothered it, perhaps remembering my words by the gazebo and thinking better of taking pleasure in the proceedings. She stepped into the middle of the room, hands outstretched. "Is anyone familiar with orpiment?"

"It's a kind of crystal," said Henry, scooting to the edge of his seat.

"Correct. Do you know what one of the main components of orpiment is?" She waited with the patient air of a schoolteacher. No one answered. "Arsenic. Of course, you can't just grind it up in someone's glass or anything like that. It takes a lot of skill to extract arsenic from orpiment, not to mention the proper tools. But the shed outside is stocked with all manner of scientific equipment, including all you'd need to extract chemicals from stone. And for a geologist, that wouldn't be difficult at all, would it?"

"Even if I am aware of the procedure," Belinda stood and stepped forward as if already on the witness stand, "you can't prove that I had any orpiment, let alone that I made arsenic from it. There isn't a single orpiment crystal near this house; where would I have gotten my hands on some?"

"You brought it with you. I've been looking at it since the night we met."

Belinda tried to back away, but there was nowhere to go, the wall butting into her back as Cadence slipped her hand under the strand of yellow stones around her neck. "This is orpiment. And I would be willing to bet that there are some stones missing. Stones you used to cook up a nearly lethal dose of arsenic."

Allowing the necklace to fall against Belinda's skin, Cadence leaned back, jabbing a thumb towards the door. "There's a pot in the kitchen – quite a big one. Belinda used it the night of the party to make her famous cider." Cadence dropped her hands to her sides, tapping against her thighs. "She made the cider, she cleaned the pot, but she didn't do a very good job. There's residue in the bottom: apple juice, alcohol, and small traces of arsenic."

I lifted my hand. "How could she be sure that none of us would drink it?"

"She couldn't. But she knew that you all weren't fond of the brew; it was a fairly safe assumption that only Felix would imbibe."

The thought of what might have happened if Solomon, or Desdemona, or Henry had tried a cup made me shudder. I dropped my head into my hands. "But...if Belinda tried to poison Dad once, why not just poison him again with a larger dose? Why bash his head in?"

"Oh, she didn't." Cadence sat back down next to Henry. "Dr. Merton did."

Everyone gasped, but no one made as much fuss as Merton, his hands clenched into fists at his side, shaking with righteous indignation as he shouted, "Miss Turing, how dare you! How dare you make such a horrible accusation?"

Unmoved by his outburst, Cadence brushed a hair off Henry's shoulder. "Felix Hale was poisoned, and no one suspected a thing." She turned to him, hands wafting down into her lap. "Except you."

Henry, his gaze fixed upon Merton, reached inside his jacket pocket and removed the vial Cadence had discovered earlier, dropping it into her hand. She held it up for all to see. "I found this in Dr. Merton's effects."

Merton strode forward, back arched like a frightened cat. "You had absolutely no right to go through my things!"

Cadence winced, pulling the vial to her chest. "I know, and I felt slightly guilty about it, but it was in the pursuit of justice. For those of you who can't read the label–" she met the doctor's angry stare with cool defiance, "–and I do thank you for labeling it, Doctor– it says, F.H. and the date of the party."

Brisbois plucked the vial away from Cadence, tapping his foot as he turned his attention to Merton. "Care to explain this, Doctor?"

Dr. Merton pushed his glasses up the bridge of his nose, stuttering. "Dr–drawing blood is a perfectly normal medical procedure–"

"For the flu? Since when?"

Merton held up his hands. "Alright! Alright, I'll admit I was...concerned about Mr. Hale's symptoms. I took a blood sample and was going to test it later, but then he was killed. It hardly seemed to matter after that."

"Naturally you were concerned. It's not as if you hadn't seen those symptoms in this house before."

Merton's jaw quivered as he stared at the floor. "I don't know what you're talking about."

Cadence blinked up at him. "Verity Hale, of course."

23

Chapter 23

"Are you honestly suggesting that I had a hand in murdering not one, but two people? Both of whom were my friends and my patients?"

"No. I'm suggesting that you covered up the murder of Verity Hale to save your own reputation and killed the man who had been blackmailing you for twenty years."

Staggering back, Merton jerked his hand up to his chest. Cadence stood, walking around him as if he wasn't there. "I read the coroner's report on Verity's death. It detailed her illness quite extensively: vomiting, muscle contractions, fever, confusion – all the symptoms of arsenic poisoning." Slipping her hand into her shirt pocket, she took out the docu-disk I had given her earlier, holding it so close to her face that her eyes crossed. "Then there's this."

Cadence strode out of the room. In a sudden dash that would

have been comical under other circumstances, we all rushed to follow her, dogging her steps down the hall and into the library.

She turned on the computer at the small desk nestled in the far corner of the room, the large screen flickering to life and bathing us in its unnatural glow. Slipping the chip into the drive, she clicked out her thanks. In an instant, a window opened, containing several pages of a document. Even as I collapsed into the nearest armchair, the others gathering around, I couldn't look away.

"Felix's will! My god!" Staring up at it, Solomon's jaw hung slack. "How did you find it?"

"I didn't." Cadence walked over to me and perched on the arm of my chair. "Chance did – again. He's much sharper than you all give him credit for." I pulled my gaze away from the screen, but Cadence was on too much of a roll to notice my wide-eyed stare, turning to the inspector instead. "It was stuck inside one of the books. Mr. Davers had the right idea, looking for the will in here; except he was thinking about it as if it had been lost, rather than hidden."

"Hidden?" said Henry, stepping back from the desk.

Cadence shrugged. "How else could it have ended up inside a book?"

"Why not just destroy it?"

"Oh, I don't think the murderer hid it. I think Felix did."

Brisbois lifted his brow in a question.

"Felix was working on an important document late at night and hadn't told anyone but Solomon, correct? So, it can be assumed that what he was writing was very sensitive. If he was interrupted while working on something he wished to complete in secret, the most natural place to conceal it would be some-where close by," Cadence got to her feet, gesturing to the shelves around us, "somewhere inconspicuous and hard to find with the naked eye," she walked to a shelf and drew her hand down a row of books, stopping at the gap where my tome had been and look-ing at me before continuing, "and meaningful enough that he wouldn't forget where he put it."

I dropped my head into my hands, the jaunty animal cast of *The Wind in the Willows* dancing through my mind. To know that the book had meant as much to my father as it had to me; the lump in my throat grew larger and I thought I would choke on it. I couldn't breathe until Cadence brushed her hand across my shoulders, her fingers warm through my clothes. My throat re-laxed, at least a little, and I swallowed, squeezing her hand as she drew away.

"Felix told Solomon he was working on a new will – one that would enable him to enter into his marriage with Desdemona as a 'new man'." Flipping the document up across the screen, pages of legalese flew by. The screen stuttered as the computer jumped from one document to the next and Cadence stopped on a letter, unaddressed but written in my father's voice. Cadence stepped back and allowed his words to speak for themselves.

My father had been desperate to save the company. He and Belinda poisoned my mother slowly, although he delivered the final dose to Verity. In his haste, Merton had seen him, forcing my father to use what he knew about the shoddy doctor to blackmail him into silence. He understood now that he had made a mistake for which he could never forgive himself, but he hoped, with all his soul, that one day we could do it for him.

"This is insane," Merton turned his back to the screen, dragging his hands down his face. "Felix was delusional! If I'd known anything like that was going on, I would have gone straight to the EO."

"I'm sure you meant to. But you were a young doctor, at the beginning of your career; you couldn't have people finding out about your personal problems."

Merton ripped his eyes away from the floor, fixing them on Cadence. She met his gaze and walked towards the young woman collapsed on the sofa. "Desdemona, I'm sorry to have to ask you this, but please: how did you end your drogan addiction?"

Jumping at the question, Desdemona drew her arms tight against her quavering form. "I..." It was a moment or two before she was composed enough to speak. "I...went to a...rehab clinic. In Cayeux."

"Alone?"

"N–no..." Tears began dribbling down her cheeks and she didn't bother to wipe them away. She shook her head with all the petulance of a small child, sucking on her bottom lip as she tried not to sob aloud. "I...I went with my boyfriend – Douglas Morton."

Victoria piped up beside me. "Morton?"

Cadence rolled her eyes. "He couldn't very well keep a name that was tied to a criminal record. A slight change was all it took to leave that life behind him forever. Or so he thought."

All eyes turned to the doctor, whose normal twitches had intensified to a near constant quiver as he gripped the insides of his elbows, venom boiling in his eyes. "How–how did you know?"

"Chance overheard you and Desdemona. You called her Dezzi; hardly a name you'd use for someone you'd just met." Cadence brushed a lock of hair away from Desdemona's face. "Besides, I saw the needle marks on your arms when you came to help Minerva. And the vial of drogan in your bag cinched it."

Henry removed a second vial from his pocket and handed it to Brisbois while Cadence shook her head at Merton, jaw clenching. "A young doctor with a drug habit. Felix found out, of course. He was sharp. He knew how to read people."

"He...he blackmailed me." Collapsing back into the wall, Merton looked from face to face, finding nothing but distrustful glares. "He was going to ruin me!"

"So, you've kept quiet all these years. Tending to the Hale family, living in fear that at any moment, Felix would change his mind about keeping your little secret. And after that, who would believe anything you said? A filthy addict?"

Merton jerked back from the words as if they stung, screwing his eyes shut against this barrage of the truth.

"Then Desdemona reappeared. Not on your arm, but his. She had gotten clean and stayed clean. She made her choice; it wasn't the drugs, and it wasn't you." Sighing, Cadence drew her hand through her tangled hair. "It must have felt like a miracle when you realized what Belinda had tried to do. That's why you took the blood: to blackmail her into silence while you killed the man she loved."

For a moment, Merton looked subhuman, lurching forward with hungry eyes, his back hunched. "That man took everything from me; my whole life, I was a slave: seeing to his every need, caring for his friends and family without making a cent, without receiving so much as a kind word." He dropped his hands to his sides, shaking his head. "But I didn't kill him. And you can't prove that I did."

Cadence whirled around to face Brisbois, crossing her arms over her chest. "The first thing that made me doubt Chance's guilt, Inspector, was the placement of the body. You've assumed from the beginning that Felix was killed in his room and because of this, his son must be the killer, because he was the only one with access."

Smiling, Brisbois shoved his hands into his pockets, warming to Cadence's amateur detecting. "Mr. Hale was killed in his room. The murder weapon was found there, and the door was locked from the inside."

"Would you agree, though, that it is possible that someone could have entered Felix's room, locked his door from the inside, unlocked the connecting door to Chance's room, and then placed the key under the body? And then, after exiting through Chance's door, use Chance's own key to lock the door behind them?"

Waving his hand through the air, Brisbois nodded. Cadence grinned. "Chance had difficulty finding his key that morning. It was on the floor, even though he was sure he left it on the bedside table, as he usually does. So, what was it doing down there?"

Henry snapped his fingers. "Someone slipped it in under the door after they locked it!"

Brisbois scowled, shaking his head. "Why go to all that trouble?"

"To frame Chance. Murder is a life sentence on this planet; that'd be reason enough to give the Enforcement Office a gift-wrapped killer. Keep them from looking too closely."

"May I remind you, Miss Turing, that three people saw Mr. Hale entering his room and locking the door? Alone?"

"One of those three is currently in custody. Belinda, did you really see Felix going into his room that night?"

Belinda fixed Merton with a cold stare, her lips twitching up into a sneer. "No, I didn't."

"Another witness is now looking more like your prime suspect and would therefore have ample reason to lie. Then of course," Cadence looked over her shoulder with a soft smile, "there's Desdemona."

Whimpering at the sound of her name, Desdemona wiped the tears from her face. "Um, yes? Yes, I saw Felix."

"Desdemona, could you repeat exactly what you said to me earlier? About what Felix looked like when he went into his room?"

"I just thought that he looked tired," she said, shrugging. "I assumed he was still feeling ill, the way he was leaning to one side and dragging his feet."

"Dragging his feet?"

Desdemona dropped her hands to her lap, digging her teeth into her bottom lip. "Well, there was a shuffling sound...when Felix went in." She turned to me with a mournful smile. "He doesn't usually shuffle, does he, Chance? Felix is a stomper."

Jaw tensing, Brisbois dragged his hand down his face. "Miss Eydis, why didn't you tell me this before?"

Desdemona's eyes welled-up with tears once more. "I di–didn't think it was important. Everyone knew he'd been ill."

"I'm sorry," Solomon raised his hand, "I don't quite follow."

"Someone was carrying Felix; someone smaller in stature. They had their arm around the body," Cadence wrested Brisbois to her side and flung her arm around his waist, ignoring his surprised sputtering, "leaned it against them like this," she tilted so the inspector's full weight was against her torso and shoulders, "and dragged it in."

She released the man without another glance. "The weight must have been enormous, enough to make anyone shuffle."

"So," said Brisbois, fixing his suit with a grimace, "if he wasn't killed in his room, where did it happen?"

"Right out there. Or to be more accurate..." Cadence marched out of the library and past the EO officers who had gathered outside, our little group trailing behind her. Stopping in front of the main doors, she pointed to where her feet had come to rest. "...right here."

The inspector looked at the floor, saying nothing. Folding her hands in front of her hips, Cadence shrugged. "If you don't believe me, check the FASCs."

Crouching down, Brisbois popped open the FASC service door, pulling back his sleeve and reaching inside. Face contorting, he licked his lips and swallowed. There was a click of a FASC being lifted off its rail and he withdrew it, wincing. The brushes of the FASC were covered with dry blood and torn pieces of flaking skin. Victoria choked down a retch. Henry had the foresight to shield Desdemona's face in his shoulder, so we avoided another of her fainting spells.

"Poor little things," Cadence gazed at the gore encrusted FASC with fondness. "All they know is that when something hits the mat, they're supposed to clean it. They didn't realize it was Felix's face."

Calling over an EO officer from the front door, Brisbois instructed him to get the FASC under evidence quarantine as soon as possible. Once the officer had gone, Brisbois took a moment to clean his hand with a worn handkerchief and, unless I was mistaken, get his gag reflex under control. Henry broke the silence, brow furrowing.

"Hold on – how did he get upstairs with the body? Felix must have weighed over 200 pounds. If someone tried dragging him up the stairs, one of us would have heard or seen something."

Patting him on the shoulder, Cadence headed down the long hallway on the right. We followed her past the kitchen to the hallway's dead-end, where she depressed the small brown button once more and revealed the dusty dumbwaiter.

Solomon examined the space from a distance, his hand on his glasses. "What makes you think they used this?"

"Besides it being logical?" Cadence lifted a finger. "Henry, could you climb inside there, please?"

Dutiful as always, Henry attempted to crawl into the small space. Grunting and hissing, he tried to force his tall frame into the stunted box, but in the end, he gave up, prying himself free. "I can't fit; not unless I shrunk."

"Or broke a few bones." Cadence rolled back on her heels, hands clasped behind her. "It's why Felix's arms and legs were broken post-mortem; to make him fit in there. I also have this," she produced the shred of my father's jacket from her pocket and handed it to Brisbois. "I'm sure your men would've found it if they'd been looking properly." Beaming, she inclined her head towards me, missing Brisbois' glare. "Chance found it in the wheel of his breakfast cart."

"I imagine it was Belinda who cleaned up the blood while Merton posed the body upstairs." We wandered back into the entryway, following Cadence as if she was the leader of a demented brass band. "Henry said it was very hot in his room that night. His rooms butt up against the kitchen wall, which houses the incinerator. Someone put it through its paces, but it seems to have trouble with cloth. I found more rags inside of it."

"Miss Turing."

"Yes, Inspector?"

Brisbois tilted his head towards her ear, voice a low, but still audible, murmur. "This is all...amazing, actually, but you still haven't given me anything to prove that Dr. Merton killed Felix Hale. I need something more concrete."

Turning towards Henry again, who was staring off into the distance with a befuddled look on his face, Cadence cleared her throat. He came to attention, going through his pockets and depositing yet another item into her hands. Smiling her thanks, she turned back to Brisbois. "Will this do?"

Sitting in the palm of her hand was a pair of glasses almost identical to those worn by Dr. Merton. Except these were cracked, splattered with a dried brown substance that had to be blood.

"Do you remember when you had Dr. Merton sign for the release of the body? He had trouble reading the tablet." Cadence pushed her prize towards Brisbois. "It's because these are his glasses; he's wearing a spare pair, about two or three years old, I should think. Have you ever tried to beat a man to death while wearing glasses? They would go flying." She pointed to one of the potted bushes which stood by the door. "I found them there; in the plant."

A flurry of movement made me jump, but it was too late to react in any meaningful way. Merton had his arm flung around my shoulders, pulling me against him, and the sharp stab of a needle plunging into my carotid artery took my breath away.

"Everyone – stay back!"

24

Chapter 24

Desdemona screamed and Brisbois pulled his taser gun, his finger sitting next to the trigger as he struggled to find a clear shot. The EO officers by the door likewise drew their weapons, inching forward from either side.

As they attempted to outflank him, Merton tugged me this way and that. "Stay back, I said! I'll put so much drogan in him, he'll be dead before he hits the floor!"

Henry strained against Cadence's hand, held flat against his chest, while she curled her free hand into a fist at her side. "You won't do that."

Barking a laugh over my shoulder, Merton continued shuffling back to the door. "And why not?"

"Because you'll be dead before you can push that button."

I didn't dare to do more than tug at the arm around my shoulders, the needle stinging with every shift of my body, its pen-like housing digging into my skin. For a split-second Merton's arm was gone and I heard him fumbling the front door open, his other hand staying steady on the plunger. A breeze blew past me, and his arm returned, crushing my windpipe.

"Dezzi! I did this for you – for us!" Shouting, his spit slickened my cheek. "I love you; I've always loved you. That man, you didn't know what he was really like! This whole family is soulless: hollow, heartless machines. I – I didn't kill Felix, I shut him down." I jerked as the needle moved deeper inside me. "And I'll do the same to him if you don't let me go."

Brisbois lowered his taser, eyes fixed on Merton. "Back off." The other EO officers glanced at one another, their guns still up. Brisbois turned to them with a bark. "Back off!"

My neck throbbed and every time Merton pulled me backwards my heart raced, sure that the jarring motion had squeezed some drogan from the needle. We stumbled down the stairs to the nearest Enforcement Office PT. Merton wrenched the passenger side door open with his free hand and, leading me in after him, slid over the seats until he was behind the wheel.

Switching hands so he could operate the controls, he jammed his finger against the ignition button. The vehicle hummed to life and he shoved at the needle. "Close the door!"

Leaning over, I pulled it shut, trapping myself inside. The PT gave a lurch and we started forward, gathering speed. Sitting on the edge of my seat, my hands splayed over the dashboard, I licked my lips, trying to keep my voice from shaking. "Dr. Merton...please–"

"Shut up!" I flinched as the needle tore at my skin. "I've spent most of my life listening to Hales gibber on and I'm not going to do it now; keep your mouth shut!"

I gave a curt nod, hissing as pain radiated down my shoulder. We both looked up and, at the same moment, we saw Cadence run straight into the path of the PT.

If she had put more distance between herself and the car, Merton might have had time to swerve, or at least time to run her down. But the shock of seeing a body so close so suddenly, made him flail, one hand ripping the needle from my neck, the other turning the car into a hard-left bank.

My stomach lurched as the PT began to flip, the whole world tilting like an amusement park ride. But before the top of the vehicle crunched into the ground, before the endless skid across gravel and dirt began, the back end of the car clipped something solid.

Curled up in the roof, my every muscle ached as I came back to consciousness. Dr. Merton lay a few inches away, moaning, cuts all over his face from his broken spectacles.

The windows hadn't shattered, but they were damaged enough that a few swift kicks dislodged the one beside me. Pulling myself out, I crawled away from the wreck on my belly, the gravel biting into my skin. Once I was clear of the PT, I pushed myself up onto my hands and knees, shaking.

The trees, several feet away, swam before my eyes. Lifting my head, I blinked away the drops of rain that had started to fall. The earthy smell of burning plastic filled my nostrils and, at last, the trees shifted back into focus as did the prone figure sprawled in front of them.

"Ca–Cadence?"

Face down on the ground, her arms were spread in front of her, legs pulled up against her torso; even from a distance I saw the wide gash which ran up her shoulder.

She wasn't moving.

"Cadence!" Scrambling to my feet, I heard nothing but ringing as I stumbled towards her too still frame, panic and terror pumping blood through me so hard I feared my heart would burst. I fell to my knees beside her and, careful of her most obvious wound, I turned her over.

There was a rough scrape across her cheek and several more on her arms and hands; still, she didn't move. I lifted her head into my lap, ignoring the rush of EO officers that moved around us. "Cadence, can you hear me? Cadence! Please, Cay – please!"

"Stop. Shouting." Her face twisted into a wince. "I'm not deaf."

Pulling her up into my arms with more roughness than may have been wise, I held her head to my chest as an unexpected peal of laughter erupted from me. Finding wetness at the edges of my eyes, I buried my face in her hair, wiping the would-be tears away before someone else could see them. "You are a very, very stupid woman, do you know that?"

"I couldn't let him hurt you, Chance." She struggled to sit up, holding me for the briefest of moments. "Are you still angry with me?"

"Yes. No. Shut up." I showered kisses across her forehead, massaging her arms and shoulders as if I were afraid she would fall to pieces without warning.

My ministrations provoked a loud hiss from her, and I pulled away, wincing. I had forgotten about the gash in her shoulder, and it seemed Cadence had too. She straightened, prodding around the edges of the cut. Bringing her hand in front of her, she stared at the red stains on her fingers.

"I..." Cadence looked at me, at her bloodied hand, and back again, mouth hanging open. "I...hurt myself."

"Yes." I shook myself, the full implications of her wound sinking in. Gathering her up in my arms, I got us on our feet, glancing at the milling EO officers with newfound concern. "Yes, right – we better get that looked to before someone–"

"Chance!" Henry rushed towards us, pushing EO officers out of the way. "Chance, are you alright?"

I nodded, swaying back a step, but was unable to avoid Henry's heartfelt embrace. He wrapped his arms around us both, squeezing us like ripe fruit and shaking with relief. Pulling back, the sensation of something slick on his hand soon captured his focus.

"Blood!" He twisted Cadence toward him before I could intervene. "Cadence, you're–" The sight of her injury silenced him like a gag. A clear plastic panel was visible through the gash, a collection of thin tubes and cables behind it, with strange fluids flashing through them.

Staring at her shoulder, hypnotized like a toad caught in a snake's gaze, Henry lifted his bloody finger, pointing at the cut as he stuttered, "You– you– you're–"

Fear of discovery making me much less tactful than I would have been otherwise, I yanked Cadence away, stepping so close to Henry that the tips of my shoes touched his. "Yes, I know, it's all very shocking, but she's just the same Cadence as ever, and we both adore her, so if you'd rather she not be deported, give me your jacket before anyone else sees, please."

Swallowing, Henry nodded, but he remained frozen in place until I hissed his name. Jumping into action, he pivoted around to the other side of Cadence, helping me shield her from view as he slipped off his coat and placed it over her shoulders.

I took my first deep breath, more at ease now that my guest remained under wraps. The moment of peace was short-lived, however, as an enraged Victoria appeared before us, railing and red-faced.

"You idiot! You stupid, blithering idiot, you could have gotten him killed!" Victoria clutched at me, tearing me from Cadence's side and looking up at me with wide, suspicious eyes. "Chance, darling! Are you hurt?"

I peeled her off me, grimacing. "No, Victoria, I'm fine. In fact, I'm finally fine enough to tell you that you are the most frigid, self-serving bitch I've ever met, and if I never see you again it will be too soon."

With a self-righteous gasp, Victoria writhed free from my grip. "Chance! What are you saying?"

Groaning, I hung my head, pushing my hand through my hair. "Oh, don't pretend that I've broken your heart. Please? I'm too tired."

"But...Chance!" Her eyes flickered from my face, to Henry's, who struggled in vain not to laugh, and then rested on Cadence. Victoria's jaw clenched. "Chance, stop it. Stop it this instant! We're going to get married!"

"I can think of at least ten inanimate objects I'd want to marry rather than you."

The slap stung, but after receiving similar treatment from Cadence, Victoria's strike felt like a sharp gust of wind. Narrowing her eyes into pinpricks of green, she stomped her foot, every bit the spoiled brat throwing a fit. "You– you bastard! I can't believe – screw you!"

"You already have."

Victoria gave a strangled cry and, after slapping me again, marched back to the house in an absolute fury, telling anyone who would listen that she had never been subjected to such treatment in all her life and EO or no EO she would be packing to leave that very minute.

Turning to watch her go, Henry bared his teeth in a face-splitting grin. "Bye, Victoria." He looked back at me, slipping his hands into his pockets. "I love you."

"You've wanted me to do that for some time, haven't you?"

"Since we were three."

25

Chapter 25

"Chance – Cadence! Thank god you're both alright!" Solomon strode towards us, breaking away from the group of EO Officers who were leading Belinda out the front door. He patted me on the back, helping me forward. "Let's get you inside."

I was happy to comply; the front drive had become a circus of EO officers and their PTs, everyone rushing in different directions and shouting into their radios. The horrors of the day didn't need to be compounded by watching Belinda and Dr. Merton forced into PTs, cursing all the while.

Our trip inside was interrupted by a passing EO medic who insisted on running some preventative diagnostics. I rested on the front steps while his equipment whirred, Cadence and Henry waiting by my side. Solomon excused himself to the study to make some calls before the media got hold of the story.

My med scans revealed nothing out of the ordinary besides

an elevated heart rate and some scrapes and bruises. Cadence refused medical attention with great politeness, much to the medic's concern. Struggling to stand on my shaky legs, I spied Inspector Brisbois walking towards us from the lawn and I groaned aloud.

Cadence noticed him as well, gaze fixed on his approach even as she nodded to Henry. "Now might be a good time, Henry." She smiled, her eyes narrowing. "Maximum confusion."

Humming his assent, Henry patted my shoulder, grinning. "Be right back."

As Henry retreated inside, Brisbois walked up to us, slouched, his hands slung in his pockets, as if we were mingling at some low-key party. He bowed to Cadence. "Very cleverly done, Miss Turing."

Cadence clasped her hands in front of her, masking her wince with a smile. If she had had paws, she would have been licking them. "Thank you, Inspector! That's kind of you to say."

Tilting his head to one side, Brisbois leaned in, his hand at his chin. "It does occur to me, however, that during your investigation, you seem to have broken a few laws."

Cadence mimicked his posture, nodding with a serious frown. "Only some very, very minor ones, Inspector."

Rocking back on his heels, he smothered a smile. "It also occurs to me that you have overlooked one tiny detail."

"Have I?"

"The Negrescu Necklace." Brisbois spread his hands palm up in front of him, shrugging. "Tell me, in your amateur opinion, who made off with that?"

"I don't think anyone made off with it at all, Inspector." Shaking her head, her long black locks bouncing around her face, Cadence smiled.

Brisbois opened his mouth to respond when a hesitant EO officer approached him from the house, clutching something in his hands.

"Um, Inspector Brisbois, sir?"

"Yes, Daniels, what is it?"

"We, uh, found this sir," shifting from foot to foot, Daniels stretched out his hand, "hanging on the banister, sir."

The Negrescu's blue jewels gleamed in his gloved hand, its white chain clinking as Daniels passed it to Brisbois, who was staring bug-eyed and slack jawed. Coming back to himself with a shake, his grimace hardened into a suspicious scowl.

My girl was, as always, unfazed, looking at the necklace with a raised brow. "Perhaps someone just misplaced it."

Gazing heavenward, Brisbois jangled the necklace, biting the tip of his tongue. "Ye-es... perhaps they did." He shoved the necklace at me, and I took it without comment, just as surprised as he was to see the damned thing but determined not to show it. "Are you going to be staying on Arrhidaeus much longer, Miss Turing?"

"Yes, she is." I cleared my throat, stepping closer to her. "She'll be getting an apartment in Römer soon, I shouldn't wonder."

"Hmm." Brisbois forced a hollow, thin-lipped smile. "It might be best then if, in future, you left investigations to the Enforcement Office, Miss Turing." He threw his hand into the air, taking a step back. "Just a thought. I better get back to headquarters. I have a report to file and I'm almost certain that no one will believe me." He shook his head, shouldering past me. "Not even a little."

We made our way inside and I waited until the front door clicked shut behind us before rounding on Cadence, shaking the Negrescu at her. "How the devil did this end up back here? And on the banister of all places!"

"Henry can explain it to you." She patted my shoulder. "I need to fix myself."

Walking past Henry, loitering at the bottom of the staircase, she gave him a smile and nod. He returned the gesture with a wide grin, arousing my suspicions even more.

I drifted towards the staircase, my hands in my pockets. "Do you need any help, love?"

"No, thank you. I'm just going to put a skin patch on it for now." Pausing in mid-step, Cadence tilted her head to one side, massaging her wounded shoulder. "Although I may ask you to oil me later..."

She continued up without another word, oblivious to the inane grin her suggestion had inspired. Henry leaned into me, his hand on my shoulder. "I don't think that means what you think it means, Chance."

"Shh," I waved him away, eyes fixed on the closing door to my rooms. "Let me have my fantasies."

The sound of the latch snapping shut released me from my lustful thoughts and I focused again on the puzzle at hand, turning to Henry with a furrowed brow. "What did Cadence mean, 'you can explain it to me'?"

"Explain what?"

"How the necklace miraculously reappeared on the banister."

Laughing, Henry slid his arm around my shoulders, walking us through the entryway. He glanced left and right before leaning close and whispering, "Because that's where I hung it."

"Wh–what? Henry!" I pulled back from him.

"Cadence had me retrieve it before her big reveal." His placid face was colored by the slight upward curves at the corners of his mouth. "Are you really that surprised?"

"Well! I–I...yes!"

"I took it the night of the party, when everyone was tending to your father."

"But–" I swallowed, wetting my dry mouth. "Where on Arrhidaeus did you hide it when the EO searched the house?"

Henry ran his hand over his chin, one eye closing as he winced. "I put it in a knot hole in the cherry tree outside my window."

A laugh burst free from me as I rubbed the back of my neck, almost smiling. "How did Cadence work that one out I wonder?"

"I think we both told her," said Henry, casting a glance behind him towards the upstairs landing. "The night of the party, we talked about how we used to put secret messages and things in trees. She must have seen the tree outside my window and made a lucky guess. And I wasn't exactly discreet about how much I wanted it. Not that I was going to keep it for myself!" He whipped around to face me, eyes wide. "I was just going to send it in to a museum somewhere; an anonymous donation, something like that."

"Believe me, if Cadence hadn't figured that part out, she would have turned you in on the spot."

Henry smiled and sighed. "When I came inside, I hung the

necklace on the banister. I knew the EO would find it when they were milling around."

"Well." It was all I could think of to say, drained as I was. I shook my head, squeezing the necklace into my palm before thrusting it at him. "Well, if it really means that much to you, Henry, take it."

He stared at my outstretched hand. "What?"

"Take it, I don't want it, and god knows you're probably right. It belongs in a museum, where it can't do anyone any more harm."

Holding his breath, Henry took the necklace from me, letting it drape itself around his knuckles. "You don't really think the necklace had anything to do with this, do you?"

Shrugging, I meandered away towards the sitting room where I hoped to get my hands on a large drink. "I'd rather not take any chances."

As if seeking a kindred spirit, my attention turned to Desdemona as soon as I entered. She stared out the window, sitting on the far side of the room, one arm pulled over her stomach and her thumb lodged between her teeth.

I sat beside her on the couch. If she noticed me, she didn't show it, continuing to stare out the window as if in a trance.

"Are you alright?"

"Me? Yes. Yes, I'll be fine." Lowering her frail hand from her quivering lips, she turned and looked at me with empty eyes. "Belinda really hated me, didn't she?"

I thought of a hundred comforting lies, but my mouth ran off on a subroutine of its own. "Yes. Yes, she did."

Desdemona hazarded a weak, toothless smile. "Chance...I

know you never really warmed to me. But," placing her hands over mine, she met my gaze with sudden earnestness, "I honestly did love your father."

"I know." Looking across the hall and into the library, I thought of the will Dad wrote the night he died. "For what it's worth, I think it's pretty clear he loved you too."

Desdemona squeezed my hands before moving her own back to her mouth, chewing on her fingers. I fidgeted. "What will you do now?"

She collapsed back into the couch, rubbing her arms. "I don't know. Go back to the employment agency, I guess. Try again."

The tiredness in her voice broke my heart. It was the same weariness I felt, but magnified by the loss of not just family, but everything else that mattered too. I still had people in my life to support me; Desdemona was alone.

"Listen; you don't have to go through all that if you don't want to." Running my hand through my tousled hair, I tried to sound as casual as possible. "They always need typists at the office. I'm sure we can arrange for you to go back to your old job, or something like it."

Desdemona woke a little at that, her small mouth falling open. "You'd do that for me?"

I mustered up a smile, shrugging. "Of course." With a hesitant jerk, I put my hand on her shoulder. "After all, you're practically part of the family."

Through all the haggardness I spotted a hint of color returning to her cheeks. "I think I'd like that. Thank you, Chance."

"Naturally, you're welcome to stay here as long as you'd like, until–"

Desdemona stood, shaking her head and smoothing out her skirt. "That's alright; I know a place where I can stay."

I nodded, trying not to look relieved. "I can arrange a PT for you, if you like."

"Yes, thank you." Desdemona took a step towards the door but stopped, pulling away from it like a mouse from a hole. "If you think...do you suppose it's alright to go now?"

While looking around the room I had once considered part of my home, the empty pit in my stomach, expanding ever since the whole ordeal began, now swallowed me whole.

"Yes - it's all over."

26

‹❦›

Chapter 26

The next handful of days passed in a blur of affidavits and statements, meetings with the district attorney, and more. I made several trips into Römer to see my father's lawyers; despite my insistence, they were reluctant to allow Desdemona any income from the estate. But, in the end, I succeeded not just in setting up a small stipend for her, but in securing her an apartment and a position with the company as well. There was also a memorial service for my father to arrange, as well as the large task of introducing me to the staff and acquainting me with the way Halcyon Enterprises, my company, ran.

In the middle of all this, Minerva awoke, starting her recovery by harassing all the male nurses in the facility – a promising sign of her returning health. Dad's funeral came and went; an unruly blur, with so many strangers and vague acquaintances in attendance that I got lost in the sea of condolences.

Solomon and Henry, who had been staying at the manor to help with all the arrangements, soon headed home to welcome Minerva back from the hospital. Busy clearing up a few final things with Solomon in my father's study, I didn't look up when Cadence poked her head in around the door.

"Oh, hello, Mr. Davers." She gave a small wave. "Sorry to interrupt, but my PT is here, and I wanted to say goodbye."

"What?" I shot up from behind the desk. "Goodbye? What are you talking about?"

"Well, I've located a suitable apartment for myself in Römer, and have acquired a trade license so I can begin to accrue my own income, so I–"

I strode towards her, hands outstretched, gaping at her. "When– when did you do all this?"

"Over the last few days."

"I could have helped you!"

Cadence clasped her hands together. "You were busy with other things, and you've already done so much for me. I couldn't ask for more help. I managed." She leaned to one side to see around me, nodding to Solomon. "It was very nice to have met you, Mr. Davers."

"The pleasure was mine, my dear." Solomon rose halfway from his seat, smiling. "I do hope we'll hear from you soon."

Waving in answer, Cadence patted my shoulder and exited, all within a matter of seconds. My mind refused to work, remaining blank even as the gears whirred at a deafening pace. At last, something clicked, and I rushed out after her. "Wait a minute, wait a minute!"

Cadence turned with a confused grimace, which deepened

into something like alarm when she saw me running towards her, arms waving in the air.

"Just hold on!" I reached her a few feet away from the front doors, my breathing labored as I clasped her shoulders. "I don't–? Why do you–? Couldn't we–?"

All the questions were answered in my mind as soon as they came shooting off my tongue. I dropped my hands from her. Of course, she couldn't stay. I had never intended her to. And why would she want to? Drawing my hand down my face, I attempted to regain some composure. "Do you have a mobile or something?"

"Not yet. But I may in future."

I threw my hands into the air, bringing them down against my legs with a smack. "Well, how am I supposed to keep in touch with you then?"

Cadence began tapping on the back of her hand, the same trill of beats that had become so familiar to me. "Are you sure you want to keep in touch?"

"Of cou–" Dropping my gaze from her face, I slid my hand into my pocket, pride preventing me from agreeing too fast to such a question. "Well, yes, I– I may want to look you up at some point. Or the Inspector might – for the case, you know."

Cadence looked away, the tip of her tongue poking out from between her teeth. "I've acquired a stall in the Entertainment Market. Shouldn't be too hard to find." She glanced at me from beneath her brow with a shaky smile. "I'll be around if you need me."

She placed both hands on my shoulders, her fingers still tapping, the heat of her through my clothes as delicious as ever. Leaning forward, she brushed her lips against my cheek.

"Goodbye, Chance."

The distinctive hum of a PT from outside was the only sound aside from my shallow breathing. Cadence stepped away and, without another word, turned on her heel, scooped up her bag, and left.

I stared at the closed portal at a loss. Cadence wasn't coming back. The black hole in my chest began to suck at me again, the drowning sensation interrupted by a polite cough.

I glanced behind me. Leaning around the study door, holding onto the frame with one hand, Solomon flashed me a quick smile, jabbing his thumb over his shoulder. "Chance, if it's alright with you, I think I'll head home now."

The down-to-earth nature of his request brought me back to reality quicker than a slap in the face. I strode over to him, rubbing my cheek red. "Sure, sure! Of course, yeah." I gestured to the desk. "Would you like me to call you a PT?"

Stepping back from the door, Solomon waved. "No, no need. It's such a lovely day, I think I'll walk." The study door, the one which led outside, stood open, the room filled with sunshine for the first time I could remember. Solomon walked through it, giving a last salute in my direction. "I'll see you at work, I'm sure."

I tried not to let that thought terrify me, and in distracting myself from it, I remembered something else.

"Solomon, before you go–"

He stopped just over the threshold, pivoting on the ball of one foot like a dancer.

"Cadence, she...she had this odd little habit of tapping her fingers. She seemed to do it all the time: on tables, herself, even on me, occasionally. Does that–I mean is that some sort of animanecron...thing? Would you know?"

Solomon dropped his other foot to the ground, eyes widening. Clearing his throat, he crossed his arms over his chest. "Well, Chance, you...you have to understand that in many ways, animanecrons are much more physical, much more conscious of the bodies they inhabit, than humans. Affection and love are more physical for them than for us, in many ways. They developed this, this amazing lexicon of body language to indicate various types and levels of... social attachment. You see?"

I stared at him and waggled my head 'no.' He sighed, massaging his temple. "Her tapping is actually strings of binary code repeated in sequence. It doesn't translate very well into Common Tongue, but it's her way of expressing her feelings for you. Her...affection."

"Oh." My eyes darted around the room for several seconds before I remembered Solomon was still there. "Uh, oh. Well, that's...yes. Thank you, Solomon."

He nodded, smiling in a way that made the sudden prickling of hair all over my body feel somehow indecent. Alone, I collapsed into the armchair nearest the door, letting the cool breeze soothe my feverish skin. I wanted to have a nix, but didn't; I wanted to take the coldest shower in existence, but I didn't do that either. Amid the sweet smell of Arrhidaean grasses blowing through the open door, and the distant chirping of birds in the ash grove, all I could do was think about her. I knew I would for the rest of my life.

About the Author

Robin Jeffrey was born in Cheyenne, Wyoming to a psychologist and a librarian, giving her a love of literature and a consuming interest in the inner workings of people's minds, which have served her well as she pursues a career in creative writing. She holds a BA in English from the University of Washington and a MS in Library Science from the University of Kentucky. She has been published in various journals across the country as well as on websites like The Mary Sue and Introvert, Dear. She currently resides in Bremerton, Washington. More of her work can be found on her website, RobinJeffreyAuthor.com.

Robin would like to extend her sincerest thanks to everyone who made this book possible, from her editor and sister Megan Jeffrey, to all her beta readers, to her husband Philip Allen, and to everyone who ever encouraged her to sit down and put words on paper. Without those supportive voices, she never would have made it this far. Thank you.